BLAZING
OBSESSION

BLAZING
OBSESSION

DAI HENLEY

Copyright © 2014 Dai Henley

The moral right of the author has been asserted.

Apart from any fair dealing for the purposes of research or private study, or criticism or review, as permitted under the Copyright, Designs and Patents Act 1988, this publication may only be reproduced, stored or transmitted, in any form or by any means, with the prior permission in writing of the publishers, or in the case of reprographic reproduction in accordance with the terms of licences issued by the Copyright Licensing Agency. Enquiries concerning reproduction outside those terms should be sent to the publishers.

Matador
9 Priory Business Park
Kibworth Beauchamp
Leicestershire LE8 0RX, UK
Tel: (+44) 116 279 2299
Fax: (+44) 116 279 2277
Email: books@troubador.co.uk
Web: www.troubador.co.uk/matador

ISBN 978 1784620 516

British Library Cataloguing in Publication Data.
A catalogue record for this book is available from the British Library.

Typeset in Aldine by Troubador Publishing Ltd
Printed and bound by CPI Group (UK) Ltd, Croydon, CR0 4YY

Matador is an imprint of Troubador Publishing Ltd

daihenley@gmail.com
www.facebook.com/BlazingObsession
www.twitter.com/DaiHenley

PROLOGUE

August 3rd 1998

It was midday. Pat, my PA, looking puzzled, put her head around my office door and said, "James, these two police officers would like an urgent word with you. I'll make sure you're not disturbed."

Minutes earlier, looking across my Canary Wharf BMW showroom from the office window, I'd noticed the police officers talking to Judy, my receptionist.

Nothing unusual, I thought. Probably enquiring about another stolen car or checking out false number plates. BMWs were high on the list for such crimes.

After the preliminary introductions, Sergeant Hawkins and Constable Lee sat around the coffee table, both looking as if they'd rather be anywhere else but my office. They'd removed their caps and laid them in their laps ceremoniously.

The sergeant's body language bore the demeanour of a veteran; his lined, lugubrious face epitomising 'been there and done it all'. Constable Lee appeared altogether different – young, bright and eager, more like a teenager who hadn't yet started shaving.

"What's this about?" I said.

Sergeant Hawkins did most of the talking.

"I need to ask you some questions, Mr Hamilton."

"Sure, go ahead."

"Do you have a family?"

"Yes. My wife, Lynne, stepson Georgie and my two-year-old daughter, Emily."

"Do you own a cottage in Lymington?"

"Yes. Why do you want to know?" A sense of unease passed over me. Sergeant Hawkins ignored my question.

"And where are your family now?"

"They're down at the cottage. I had an important business meeting here this morning. I'm about to leave to join them."

Sucking in a deep breath, he said, "I'm sorry to have to inform you, Hampshire Police have confirmed there's been a serious fire in the early hours of this morning at your cottage. You should brace yourself for some tragic news."

He exchanged a glance with his colleague. My heart started thumping.

He took another deep breath. "There are three bodies inside, a female and two children, one male the other female. I'm sorry to have to inform you they all perished. They'll need to be formally identified, but we have reason to believe they are your wife and children."

I shook my head. "No, no, it can't possibly be true! I'm seeing them later today. You must have the wrong cottage or something." Again, the police officers didn't reply but maintained their serious expressions.

From that point on, everything they said became a blur. I'd arranged a sailing lesson for Georgie the next morning, before meeting up for lunch with Lynne and Emily at the Royal Lymington Yacht Club. So it couldn't be true.

I found it hard to explain to friends later the precise conversation I'd had with the police officers. I felt detached from it. Like watching a TV drama with someone else playing my part.

I only recalled snatches of the conversation that followed: *'explosion', 'suspected gas leak', 'unexplained incident, possibly a crime scene', '3am', 'firefighters did all they could to rescue them'.*

Sergeant Hawkins continued. "Is there anyone else we should inform? Your wife's parents, for example?"

"Look, I'm telling you this can't be true, officer. You *must* be mistaken."

"I'm afraid not, Mr Hamilton. We've checked and double-checked. Believe me, I wish it wasn't true."

He asked about Lynne's parents for a second time. I stared out of my office window in a trance, trying to grasp the enormity of what he'd said.

"I'm sorry, Mr Hamilton. I need to know who else –"

Sergeant Hawkins had trouble keeping the emotion out of his voice. "Who else we should inform."

The realisation of what had happened seeped into me. I dropped my head to my hands.

"No… No …"

"Mr Hamilton …"

I looked up at the sergeant. "Sorry… yes. Her mother. We'll… we'll have to tell her mother, Margaret… Margaret Cove. She lives alone in Limehouse Basin, a mile from here." I gave them her address. "She'll be beside herself."

"Would you like us to break the news to her?"

"Yes. I'd really appreciate that."

They suggested a family liaison officer could be arranged for me. I feebly declined. Said I'd be ok.

I wasn't.

Once the police officers had left, many questions shuttled back and forth in my mind: why did this happen when I'd stayed here in London? Could I have done something to save them if I'd been there? Did they suffer? Oh, my God, I hoped not.

Pat entered my office. I think the police officers had asked her to keep an eye on me.

She'd been with me since I started my business. Fifteen years older than me, she became a widow four years ago. She knew me better than anyone else on the planet. Apart from Lynne, of course.

"Are you OK, James?"

"Pat, I can't believe what they said. As Lynne and the kids were sleeping in the cottage last night, an almighty explosion ripped the place apart. Probably a gas leak, they said, but they'd called it an 'unexplained incident, possibly a crime scene'. Pat, they're dead!"

"What?" Pat put her hands to her mouth and collapsed in the chair opposite my desk. "Are they sure? This can't be true!" She started crying.

I knelt next to her and put my arm around her in a bizarre role-reversal. I fought back my own tears.

"What are you going to do?" Pat said, as we detached ourselves.

"I don't know. I want to go down to Lymington… now. But the police strongly advised against it. Apparently, there's nothing I can do."

"Oh James!"

"They said, because the Hampshire Fire Service and police are still investigating the cause, they won't allow me anywhere near the cottage. Said I'll be in the way."

"Probably best if you don't go then."

"I suppose you're right. It's better if I spend the time with Lynne's mother. Oh, God! She'll be in a terrible state. I'd better let Alisha know what's happening too."

Alisha, Lynne's best friend, had known her since they were five years old at infants' school.

"If there's anything I can do, please let me know." Pat dabbed her eyes with a tissue and breathed in deeply, trying to pull herself together.

"Thanks, Pat."

I left enough time for the police to have broken the news before driving to Margaret's house. Alisha had already arrived. Margaret had been so upset that one of the police officers suggested she shouldn't be alone. They called Alisha at work. She appeared there in an instant. Then the police officers left, saying they'd call back with any further information.

Margaret, slumped in a sofa, her eyes already red-rimmed, held a moist tissue in her hand. I sat next to her and hugged her. She whimpered like a beaten puppy, noisily sniffing back her tears. "James… James… please tell me… it isn't true …" Her body couldn't stop shaking.

Sometimes, all three of us tearfully hugged each other tightly.

I knew I had to be strong, stiff upper lip and all that, but eventually, I got caught up in the communal crying too.

Alisha worked as a sales rep for a pharmaceutical company. She'd broken some rules, I'm sure, and brought Valium tablets with her. She handed one to Margaret with a glass of water.

"Here, take this. It'll help."

It had the desired effect and later, we sat in stunned silence over endless cups of tea, deep in our own thoughts, not knowing what to say to each other.

When we did speak, we each repeated our disbelief.

I thought about jumping in my car and speeding down to Lymington regardless – I wanted to see with my own eyes what had happened. Only then would I believe it. But I felt an obligation to stay and comfort Margaret and Alisha.

We desperately hoped the phone would ring at any minute and be told it was a dreadful mistake.

★

Later in the afternoon, Margaret's phone did spring into life. She was in no state to answer, so I picked it up.

"I need to update you on what's happening, Mr Hamilton." Sergeant Hawkins' voice had recovered the unemotional, factual tone he'd adopted when we first met. Part of his training, I suspected.

"The Hampshire Fire Service and the local police need more time to identify the cause of the fire before we can release preliminary details. This'll take three or four days, I'm afraid."

He paused before continuing, "Thought I'd better warn you, the media have caught up with the story. Don't be surprised if they contact you. I'd advise you not to say anything yet. We'll release a statement to them when we have more facts. For now, we're still treating this as an unexplained incident."

"What does that mean, exactly?" I said.

"Just that. We won't rule out *anything* at this stage of the investigation."

I didn't know what to say.

"Oh, I've got some more details best discussed in person. When can I see you?" I explained I was still with Lynne's mother and he thought it a good idea to come to her home.

He arrived within half an hour, accompanied by a uniformed female officer, PC Kate Williamson, a stocky thirty-something-year-old, with cropped blonde hair framing a round, sympathetic face. The sergeant came straight to the point once inside the house.

"During the investigation, I'm afraid the bodies will have to remain *in situ*. It's possible this will turn out to be a crime scene so we don't want to destroy any evidence. When we've completed our investigation we'll take your family to Southampton General Hospital."

"What do you mean… a crime scene?"

"I've told you, nothing's ruled out at this stage of the investigation, Mr Hamilton. It's normal procedure."

Nothing felt normal to me anymore.

"The coroner's been informed. In view of the circumstances, he'll want to carry out a post-mortem and hold an inquest. We'll have more details then about the precise cause of death."

In the background, I heard anguished sobbing and muffled sounds from Margaret. Alisha continued to hug her and PC Williamson offered Margaret some fresh tissues.

Sergeant Hawkins continued. "There's very little left of the cottage I'm afraid. Most of the thatch has collapsed or been destroyed. Only the walls are standing. Did you keep anything of value there, any personal items?"

I shook my head. "Er… no, we bought most of the contents with the cottage, so there is – sorry – was, nothing personal or valuable there."

"Good. So there's not much point in you visiting the site, unless of course you specifically want to."

"Well, I *do* want to. I feel I should be there… with them."

The sergeant shook his head. "I don't think it's a good idea. There's nothing you can do. From the information I've received, you'd be upsetting yourself unduly."

"What about my family? When can I go and see them?"

"I think not for four or five days. The pathologist is confident he can formally identify the bodies from the dental records of your wife and stepson and from DNA traces for your daughter. So we won't need formal identification."

My chest tightened with every statement he made.

Sergeant Hawkins said, "There's one more thing you need to know. The pathologist will carry out the post-mortem soon. The inquest will take place soon after. It'll be adjourned to a future date to take into account the results of the investigation." He paused.

"At least this will allow the coroner to release the bodies. Then you can make the funeral arrangements."

Margaret uttered another guttural sob.

Sergeant Hawkins stood and said, "I'll leave PC Williamson here to provide support for you. She's a trained family liaison officer. She'll act as your main conduit with the police and is available to you, 24/7. If you have any issues, just let her know."

"OK," I said, grateful that Margaret would have someone to support her when Alisha and I left.

*

I blanked out the days following the fire. I don't know what I did. I could barely remember speaking to anyone. Or whether I slept or ate any meals.

I did remember reading letters of condolence. I couldn't stop visualising the gruesome discovery of the bodies by the firefighters and police officers.

Or hearing their anguished screams as they tried to escape the flames.

I recalled similar emotions when my parents died in a car crash nearly twenty years before. I was twenty-two. I'd not dealt with it particularly well then, either. But this grief bit into me more viciously.

I made a point of not watching the TV news or buying a

newspaper. Several reporters had tried to contact me, but I declined to talk to them, taking the advice from the police, who kept them informed with regular statements.

The next day, I met Alisha at Margaret's house and told her, "I feel so guilty. I can't help it. Why did this happen when I wasn't with them? It's incredibly unfair."

"Don't beat yourself up, James. Sometimes these things happen."

"If a gas leak did cause the explosion, shouldn't I have sorted it out earlier?"

"But we don't know the exact cause yet, do we?"

She hugged me tightly as I choked back my tears.

★

Two days later, I received a call from the local police station in Blackheath saying a senior investigating officer and a detective constable wanted to visit me urgently. They appeared on my doorstep at our house a mile away shortly after the call.

Tall and skinny with a lean, mean, pocked face, DI Flood looked roughly the same age as me. The sergeant, a younger man, aged thirtyish with dark skin and brown staring eyes, wore a crumpled dark-grey suit at least one size too small for him.

The DI spoke first. "I'm sorry for your loss, Mr Hamilton. We're part of the Hampshire Police Major Crime Team based in Southampton. We've concluded our initial investigation. I don't want you to broadcast this yet but we've now strong reason to believe the fire at your cottage was not caused by a gas explosion."

"What did cause it then?"

"We believe someone started it deliberately."

"What? That's ridiculous! Why would anybody want to do that?"

"That's what we're trying to find out. Sniffer dogs confirmed the presence of petrol, which had been poured through the front door letterbox and set on fire. The flames travelled quickly up the adjacent stairs. The occupants would have stood no chance."

"That's impossible! Who'd want to destroy my family? And why?"

"These are the questions we want to ask you, Mr Hamilton. First, can you explain where you were on the evening of the fire?"

Expecting a more sympathetic approach, this question, thrust at me like a dagger, unnerved me. The detective sergeant poised his biro over his notebook expectantly.

"Well… at home."

"Can anybody vouch for that fact?"

"No… no… not really. I worked late, picked up a Chinese takeaway on the way home. Called my wife to make sure they'd got to the cottage safely and then went to bed about 10.30."

"And why didn't you go down to the cottage with them?"

"I had an important business meeting early the next morning. As I told your uniformed guys, I was about to leave for Lymington when they came to my office and broke the news."

"I see. Do you normally go down separately?"

"Well, actually, no. This is the first time it's happened. Usually I drive down with my family on a Thursday evening and we drive back together on Sunday."

"So this is the first time your family slept at the cottage without you being present?"

His accusative tone caused blood to rush to my head.

"What are you implying?"

He remained silent and stared at me.

I snapped, "Don't be bloody ridiculous!"

"Mr Hamilton, we're ruling nothing out at this stage. We're treating this as a possible murder case. Would you mind if we carried out a search of your home? You can agree voluntarily or I could get a warrant."

I thought if I'd said I was anything less than being happy to have them search my home, they'd handcuff me and take me in for further questioning.

I stood up, threw my arms in the air and said, "Fine, go ahead."

"We'd like to take away any computers belonging to you and

your wife. Our technical team will look at them; see if they can find out any info to help us discover the perpetrator."

"Take whatever you like. What else are you doing to find the person who did this?"

"We've got several scenes of crime officers down at Lymington looking for DNA evidence or any other clues."

"And how long will it take?"

"It's a major priority. We also have DCs from the Major Crime Team interviewing possible witnesses. If there's any more news I can release to you, I'll let you know as soon as I can."

As they both got up to commence their search, he turned to me and said, "There's just one more question I'd like to ask you. Is there anybody you know who'd be motivated enough to carry out this arson attack?"

I didn't need to think too deeply.

There could only be one candidate… but he was in jail.

PART ONE

CHAPTER ONE

I first met Lynne in September 1995. She worked as a sales manager in a Mercedes dealership I'd bought to add to my burgeoning group of prestige car dealerships, including BMW, Jaguar and Porsche. With turnover now approaching £200 million, I felt that at last I'd joined the big boys' table.

Bill Rogers, the general manager we'd inherited, introduced us.

As we shook hands, her smoky-blue eyes locked onto mine. I couldn't bring myself to look away first. A tremor passed through my body.

Meticulously applied make-up enhanced her exquisite chiselled features. A smile I'd defy anyone to resist returning and an immaculate blonde bob completed her allure.

She wasn't wearing a wedding ring.

"Since we found out about the takeover, I've looked forward to meeting you. I have loads of ideas. Can I go through them now?"

The intensity of the energy transmitting itself across the desk left me reeling. Some of the ideas were great, too. We spent over an hour discussing them.

I spent the rest of the day talking to the other managers. From previous acquisitions, I'd learned the importance of getting to know them well early on and discussing how we operated. Some managers wouldn't cope so we'd replace them. But I prided myself on always doing it compassionately and with a generous payoff.

However, my first impressions of the other managers were good. One in particular impressed me.

John Hartley, manager of the leasing department, didn't lack confidence or charm.

"Such a pleasure to meet you. Heard a lot of good things about your company," he said, squeezing my hand tightly as his tanned faced broke into a smile, revealing a perfect set of teeth.

Aged forty-five, he stood over six-foot tall, powerfully built with a mop of silver-grey hair, which he occasionally swept back with a manicured hand. He oozed charisma.

"You know, I'm really excited about joining your group. There's so much more I could achieve with the right backing."

The deep timbre of his voice exuded a belief in himself I'd not encountered before. He could have worked on TV voice-overs or read the BBC news.

I'd been looking for someone to expand our leasing division across the rest of the group of dealerships. Within the week, I'd appointed him to head up this operation reporting to Peter, my business partner, with a wide-ranging brief to develop this side of our business. We set him challenging targets.

"Can't wait to get started," he'd said, smiling broadly. "I'm looking forward to smashing these targets. I usually do." A combination of *that* voice and *that* smile led me to believe he would.

Before leaving the dealership, I spoke to Bill Rogers again.

"Tell me more about Lynne. She appears too good to be true."

Leaning back in his red leather chair, he said, "Ah, Lynne. I thought you'd be impressed. Most people are. Unusual to have a woman heading up a sales team in the car trade, isn't it?"

"It's a first for me. Tell me more about her background?"

"Well, I have to say she's doing a great job here, despite her personal problems. She went through a messy divorce a couple of years ago."

"Really?"

"The guy she married turned out to be a complete shit; used to knock her about a bit. Been shagging anything in sight, too. Once she found out, she finally divorced him. The problem is he's never accepted the marriage is over."

"Why? What's he been doing?"

"Oh, you know, keeps harassing her, roughing her up, making her life hell. I think it's still an issue."

I couldn't understand why a stunningly beautiful woman would put up with such a prick.

She'd told me she was thirty-two, had an eight-year-old son and lived a few minutes away from me in Limehouse. I could possibly see her apartment block from my penthouse close to West India Quay at Canary Wharf.

Her interests and hobbies included jogging and going to the gym, something we had in common, although I hadn't done much of either for months due to working on the acquisition. My trousers now fitted far too snugly around my waist. I promised myself I'd do something about it.

Next day, suitably motivated, I decided to join the gym close by at Westferry Circus. I spent at least an hour there most evenings for a fortnight working hard to get back in shape.

I don't believe in fate; my father always taught me to take responsibility for my own destiny, something I practised throughout my life.

But one evening at the gym, I spotted Lynne on a running machine. My heart lurched – I felt like a teenager again.

Her sleek, effortless running style glided over the treadmill. It wouldn't have surprised me to see her on the front page of the marketing leaflets the gym used.

A couple of guys glancing in her direction whispered something to each other, obviously discussing what they'd like to do to her. I felt like punching their heads in.

Fortunately, a treadmill became vacant next to hers. I pretended not to notice her as I set it up, hoping she'd see me first. She didn't. She watched the TV screen showing the latest news.

She almost lost her stride when I said, "It's Lynne, isn't it?"

She did a double take before realising who I was.

Slowing down the treadmill, she said, "Hi. What a surprise. How long have you been a member?"

"Just joined. Haven't done much lately. Been too busy building my 'empire'." I used the two fingers on both hands to indicate quote marks and smiled.

I added, "Can we have a chat later?"

"Sure. See you in the cafe in about an hour."

She pressed the speed button on the treadmill. I nodded, delighted I'd reached base camp.

She entered the cafe wearing her trademark, stunning smile.

As I moved the chair back for her to sit, I breathed in the fresh, clean, soapy smell of someone who's just showered, which I always found slightly erotic.

I asked how she got on with Bill, her boss.

"Oh, Bill's great. Without him, I don't think I could have managed to run the sales department. He's been like a father to me. Not that I'd know *exactly* what a father should be like."

"What do you mean?"

She took a long sip from her glass.

"Oh, it's too long a story. Maybe I'll tell you one day."

I wanted to learn more, but it didn't seem the right time to pursue it. I changed the subject.

"How's your little boy?"

"Georgie? He's great! We've recently moved to a flat in Limehouse. He's quite excited."

"It's just you and Georgie living there then, is it?"

"Yes. My mum lives close by. Looks after Georgie after school when I'm at work. Actually, I can't stay long. Mum's minding him now. I always like to be home before Georgie goes to bed."

Looking at her watch, she said, "I'm late already."

She stood and slung her gym bag over her shoulder.

"Well… can we have a chat next week… after working-out?"

As she reached the door, she turned, smiled, shrugged her shoulders and said, "Sure." Little flirt, I thought.

★

We met every Tuesday night after our workouts for the next three weeks. In between laughing at my mildly funny jokes, we shared our life stories.

She wanted to know how I spent most of my time.

"Me? I spend every waking hour building up my business. It's become an obsession, I suppose."

"And what about your home life?"

"Doesn't exist at the moment. Since my divorce three years ago, I've kept my head down. Concentrated on the business."

"How long were you married?"

"Five years."

"So, are you enjoying single life?"

"It's OK."

"You must have plenty of girlfriends, good-looking guy like you?" She gave me *that* smile again.

"Oh, yes… hundreds! I've had my moments, but to tell the truth, I've never understood women. Doing business deals are much easier… and less complicated in my experience." She pulled a face in disbelief.

I wanted to hear more about her background. "OK, it's your turn now."

She placed her coffee cup on the table and took a breath.

"Well… my mum and dad divorced when I was three. He's never been in touch."

She sighed. "My mum remarried, but my stepfather wasn't much better. He treated us both badly and disappeared off the scene when I turned eight."

"Oh, that's not good," I said. I'd already told her my parents loved each other deeply and I was their golden boy. I remember my childhood with great affection.

"In any case, I got married, but divorced two-and-a-half years ago. And, as you know I've got Georgie." Her face lit up again at the mention of his name.

"I expect your mum's proud of him?"

"Are you kidding? He's Grandma's only topic of conversation and the centre of her universe. She's worse than I am. She thinks he'll be running the country when he's old enough."

Stirring her coffee absent-mindedly, she continued.

"There's only one problem. There's no man in his life. Mum says he needs a role model. His father's a complete waste of space."

"Why? What's the problem?"

At last, I thought.

But her face distorted to a deep frown again. "To be honest, he's causing us a few problems. I'd rather not talk about it."

"That's OK."

Having parked the ex-husband issue, we chatted away again like old friends – it felt intoxicating and flirtatious. We discovered we had a great deal in common: cars, movies, good food, golf and travelling. She even knew something about my football team, Arsenal.

A couple of times, we completed each other's sentences, resulting in Lynne having a fit of the giggles.

How I loved that sound.

*

Pat had cajoled me into holding a party for my fortieth birthday. I'd have been happy to let it drift by; I didn't want to be reminded of middle age just yet. She'd invited all the general managers of the dealerships and my golfing buddies from my address book.

"Is there anyone *special* you'd like to invite?" I knew Pat implied I might have a secret lover. She'd always been trying to set me up with a long-term partner after my marriage broke up. I'd loved to have told her about Lynne, but let it pass. It was far too early.

Pat arranged a dinner at *Bertorelli's* in the West End, my favourite restaurant, for over a hundred guests.

Two days before my party bash, she said, "Bad news, I'm afraid. Bill Rogers can't make it. His mother's had a stroke. He's spending time with her in a care home in Brighton."

"Shame, I like Bill."

"This means there's no one going to be there from your latest acquisition. Can you think of anyone else who could take their place?"

"Actually, there is someone, the sales manager." I couldn't stop the words tumbling from my mouth.

"Good. What's his name?"

"*His* name is Lynne Burrows." I waited for her reaction.

"Oh, Lynne. OK, I'll invite her and her husband. Give me the details."

"It'll be just Lynne. She's divorced."

"Oh. Interesting," she said with a twinkle in her eye. "Well, I can easily adjust the table plan. I'll send her an invite."

My nerve-ends tingled with the thought of Lynne sharing my fortieth birthday with my friends.

It proved to be a life-changing event.

On the big day, Pat pointedly said, "Now don't forget, I don't want you there before 7.30pm. There's nothing for you to do but turn up."

"God, you sound like my mother. I'm now approaching forty, you know, in case you hadn't noticed. I promise I'll be there at 7.35pm precisely."

Pat had arranged a taxi to take me to the restaurant and as I entered the private function room on the first floor, she thrust a glass of bubbly in my hand and showed me the table plan. She'd placed Lynne next to me. "Is that OK with you?" she said. "I can quickly change it if you're unhappy."

"Are you mischief-making again, Pat?" I feigned an annoyed expression. "Actually, it's perfect."

I caught sight of Lynne talking animatedly to one of the dealership managers, a glass of bubbly in one hand. She looked stunning in a scarlet strapless dress. I found it difficult to stare anywhere else.

We savoured exceptional Italian cuisine washed down with a full-bodied Tuscan *Brunello di Montalcino*. The chattering sound level ramped up several notches. Lynne and I were no exception. There wasn't a moment's hesitation in our conversation and a lot of laughter as we flirted outrageously. Several guests glanced in our direction and smiled.

After dinner, Tom Riley, my long-time golfing partner, made a witty speech and presented me with a limited edition print of a 1953 Jaguar XF120 at Le Mans. I knew just the place for it in my apartment.

Despite good-natured heckling, I responded, thanking the guests for sharing my birthday. Then the lights dimmed and a huge cake with forty candles arrived on the table, accompanied by a chorus of *Happy Birthday*. Everybody clapped and cheered as I pretended to run out of breath blowing them out.

As I sat down, Lynne said, "Well, that went down well. I didn't know I was sitting next to *Mr Popular!*"

"I didn't know myself until now."

The music started and I introduced her to Pat before I mingled with the other guests.

The DJ played great disco hits of the '80s and within a matter of minutes the dance floor heaved with a mass of bodies frantically gyrating under a dramatic light show.

Towards the end of the evening, the DJ played slower schmaltzy records. I sought out Lynne and said, "Fancy a dance?"

"Well, as it's your birthday and you're the boss, I don't suppose I can refuse, can I?"

Holding her in my arms with our cheeks brushing together, I couldn't have been happier. And I didn't care who knew it.

During the last record of the evening, a dreamy number, I

kissed her neck. It felt the most natural thing to do. She didn't flinch.

I'd knocked back the best part of a bottle of wine, which led me to feel confident enough to suggest she came back to my place. Previously when I got into these situations, I chickened out – my fear of rejection kicked in. But this felt right.

Similarly intoxicated, she agreed.

Around one o'clock, most of the guests had left. We put on our coats and merged into London's still-hectic, crisp November evening.

I hailed a taxi and, in the darkness of the cab, the only illumination coming from the neon lights of the city, I squeezed Lynne's hand and got a squeeze back. I couldn't resist attempting another kiss. Lynne pushed me away, looking in the driver's mirror to see if he noticed.

"Later! Be patient," she giggled. I returned to hand squeezing, willing the cab to jump the red lights.

As the lift zoomed up to the twenty-third floor of my apartment block, I couldn't contain myself any longer. I threw myself at her and kissed her passionately on the lips. We didn't release our clinch until the doors opened.

As we entered the penthouse, I flicked on the light switch. I'd bought the apartment a couple of years previously and asked an interior designer friend to advise me on decor. I spared no expense. A fabulous blend of contemporary-style interiors, magnificent lighting and colour schemes made coming home after a hard day's work a pleasure. The stunning night views over the Thames and Canary Wharf added to the effect.

Lynne spun around taking it in. "Wow!" she said. "What a place! Like something out of *Ideal Home*."

I caught her arm on the second spin and dragged her towards me, our lips colliding. Finally letting her go, I said, "Never mind the architecture. How about a night-cap?"

"Think I'd better have a coffee. I'm starting to slur my words. Do you have any decaf?"

"Sure. Make yourself comfortable." I waved at the oatmeal leather settee as I went into the kitchen. "Be two minutes."

As I topped up the percolator from the tap, she followed me into the kitchen and wrapped her arms around my midriff. I felt her head against my back.

Putting the percolator down on the kitchen worktop, I turned, and taking her face in both my hands, I kissed her fully on the lips again.

It was time...

★

"Would you like that coffee, now?" I'd already showered and thrown on a pair of boxer shorts and had a mug in each hand. Lynne laid half-asleep in my bed, partially covered by a sheet, a shapely leg dangling over the side.

"That'd be great." She sat up, blinking, pulling the sheet around her body in embarrassment, holding it close with one hand. Given the intimacy we'd enjoyed all night it seemed incongruous. With her other hand, she attempted to sort out her dishevelled hair before reaching for the coffee mug.

"I didn't think you'd be seeing me like this. I must look a wreck!"

"Well, you're the best wreck I've seen... at least this morning."

I slid next to her in bed. We both cupped our hands around our coffee mugs.

"What time is it?" she said.

"Around 10.30. Do you have to go?"

"No. It's my ex's turn to have Georgie this weekend. He'll bring him home about 4.30."

"Good. What did you think about last night?"

"That's hardly etiquette, is it? Are you looking for marks out of ten?" A grin split her face.

"No! That's *not* what I meant. Did you enjoy the party?"

"Oh, yes, I haven't had such a good time in years. What a fantastic night! You've got great friends and I got on so well with Pat. We spoke for ages. Thinks a lot of you."

I put my empty coffee mug down on the bedside table and said, "Fancy scrambled eggs and toast? It's my signature dish."

"Love some."

I nodded in the direction of the bathroom and said, "By the time you've showered and re-floated the wreck, it'll be ready." She threw a pillow at me and giggled.

"I scored you a 'ten', but make that an 'eight' now."

Fifteen minutes later, she wandered into the kitchen shoeless, wearing my navy-blue dressing gown, which swamped her body, the sleeves hanging loosely over her hands. She'd re-applied her make-up and in the weak November sunlight filtering into the room, her face glowed.

After we'd breakfasted and dressed, we shared a slightly awkward silence. I sensed neither of us wanted to leave each other's company.

"Fancy a walk down the riverside?" I said.

"Sure. Fresh air would be great."

As we strolled along, she put her arm through mine. I couldn't believe we'd only met six weeks earlier – it felt so natural.

We shared a late lunch in the *Fine Line* pub on the riverside at Fisherman's Walk.

As she toyed with the pasta on her plate she said, "What was life like with your ex?"

"Good... at first. But I realise now I caused the break-up. I worked all hours; I became obsessed with building my business. I thought I was doing the correct thing, you know, being the breadwinner and all that. I didn't give our relationship the priority it deserved. Silly of me, really."

"Well you can hardly blame her for being upset, can you?"

"Oh, no, I don't blame her. Since the break-up, I've often asked myself whether I loved her enough. Does that make sense?"

"Yes, it does."

"I always think if you love someone deeply, you'd move heaven and earth to please them."

I glanced at my watch and remembered about Lynne's ex returning Georgie.

"Would you like me to take you home? It's four o'clock."

"That would *not* be a good idea. Nick would be furious if he knew I'd seen another man."

"What? I don't understand. He's your *ex*-husband. Does he expect you to live like a nun?"

"Listen, my life's complicated. To be honest, he's making my life hell." She replaced a stray hair back behind her ear.

"Still causing problems?"

"Afraid so. I know it's right he should be able to spend time with his son. But he's not a good influence on Georgie. Nick pumps him for any information he can find about what I'm doing, where I'm going and who I'm seeing." She looked defeated.

"He turns up all times of the night, slags me off and threatens me if I ever see another guy. I had to get a restraining order. But it's only a piece of paper. It's not police protection. He ignores it most of the time. It's pathetic!"

For the first time since we'd met, her eyes glistened. The self-confidence she'd displayed last night at the party and at my pad evaporated.

She reached inside her bag for a tissue. I leaned across and hugged her shoulder.

"If he knew about me spending the night with you, I don't know what he'd do."

She drew a deep breath and, as she exhaled, said, "Sorry to get like this. I really enjoyed myself last night, you know. I'd forgotten how wonderful it is to be cared for and appreciated."

"How did you get hooked up with Nick?"

"A question I often ask myself. I suppose he was the first guy who ever paid any attention to me. I thought the way he treated me was normal. And when Georgie came along, I felt trapped. Didn't want to do anything to upset our family."

"But you divorced him."

"I had to. It got so bad. His rants got worse, became more physical. I didn't want Georgie to see that. I surprised myself, having the strength to do it."

"Sounds like you're not much better off now."

"No, but at least I'm not having to put up with him every day of the week. And Georgie's not seeing us fight all the time."

"That's true."

I looked at my watch again and said, "Let me sort out a cab for you."

I turned to her and said, "Are you going to the gym on Tuesday? I'd love to see again."

"Are you sure?"

"Yes, of course."

"Thanks for a lovely time."

Standing outside the pub, waiting to hail a cab, we kissed

and hugged continuously. I hoped it would never arrive but it did. From the kerb side, I watched the taxi until it disappeared out of sight. The image of her woeful facial expression framed by the taxi's rear window remained in my head for a long time.

She'd be seeing Nick within the hour.

CHAPTER TWO

November – December 1995

On the following Tuesday night, after working out, we met up in the gym's cafe.

As we sipped our Diet Cokes, a token of our fitness regimes, I said, "Everyone says how lovely you looked on Saturday night, how nice you are and what a great couple we'd make. Did you get any comments?"

"Oh, one or two, like, 'I suppose you'll be up for promotion soon'. And, of course, the other managers told Bill about it. He's seen it all before. Thing is, all they know for sure is we sat down, had dinner and danced together. Big deal! I told them to get a life."

I smiled and said, "Listen, Lynne… this may sound soppy, I know it's only been a matter of weeks but…I think we're meant for each other. I dunno, it just feels right. I want to see more of you. In fact, don't laugh, but I think I'm a little bit in love with you."

She didn't laugh, but feigned surprise, although I suspect she'd already guessed how I felt.

"James, I… I don't know what to say. I feel the same way… really I do. But there are too many problems."

Using her fingers to emphasise each point, she said, "One,

I have Georgie to think about. I don't know how he'd react. He loves his dad. Two, Nick'd go berserk if he knew there was another man in Georgie's life and three, the rumours and innuendo in the office can't be good for either of us, but especially for you." She reached for her glass, took a sip and sat back in her chair.

I stared into her extraordinary eyes and said, "I don't have all the answers right now. But if you're happy to keep seeing me, I'll come up with something."

"Oh, I don't know."

"Well, for starters, I'd love to meet Georgie. See how we get on."

"It's a big step. Georgie's bound to tell Nick, then there'll be trouble, believe me. He's a thug. I wouldn't wish that on you."

I couldn't believe she allowed herself to be controlled in this way. I said, as sympathetically as I could, "Are you going to spend the rest of your life in dread of Nick? You and Georgie deserve better." I leant forward and reached for her hand.

Pausing for a moment she said, "I know you're right, but it's difficult. Actually, I'd love you to meet my best friend, Alisha. We're very close."

I smiled. "Sure. Is she going to run the rule over me?"

"Let's say I'd trust Alisha with my life."

★

The following week, we chatted away at our usual seats in the cafe after working out in the gym. Pouring a Diet Coke into a glass, she said, "I had a long chat with Alisha last night. She thinks you're mad."

"Perhaps I am."

"But she agreed with you. I shouldn't let Nick dominate my life. She thinks you're too good to be true. She feels you *could* be my knight in shining armour, but wants to know if you've got any chinks. Can you make dinner, Thursday night?"

"Yes, of course."

"What about the *Grapes* Pub in Limehouse Basin? About 7.30?"

"That's fine. What's Alisha like?"

"Oh, we've known each other forever. We're more than just great friends. She's more like the sister I never had, even though she's black and I'm white. I attended both her weddings and commiserated with both her divorces."

"Did she have any kids?"

"Fortunately, no."

"What does she think about your ex?"

"Nick's always been jealous of our friendship. There's no love lost between them."

"What does she feel about men, now?"

"Not a lot. She's had some awful experiences. Best not to get her started on the subject."

"I'll avoid it, don't worry."

She flashed a mocking smile. Wagging her finger under my nose, she said, "You'll have to do a lot to impress her, be warned!"

I felt like a schoolboy again.

★

They turned up at the bar just as I'd ordered a pint. Alisha, her short, black, lustrous hair framing a pretty, dark-skinned face with dark brown eyes, was an inch or two shorter than Lynne with a similar curvy figure.

She made a point of looking me up and down as if I was something the cat had brought in. Taking off her coat, she nodded at my pint glass.

"Taking on Dutch courage, are we?"

"Alisha, give him a break! Poor man's obviously nervous. You know what they're like." Lynne winked at me, trying to lighten the mood.

Over dinner, I learnt that Alisha Alleyne worked as a sales rep for a pharmaceutical company based in the West End. Born to druggy parents in Trinidad, they'd divorced when she was five. Her grandparents thought she'd have a better life living in England. She had an aunt who'd married a wealthy white businessman living in Swiss Cottage and they'd brought her up.

When we got to the coffees, Lynne excused herself to visit the loo. Alisha leant towards me and said, "You know, Lynne's a special person. She's been a wonderful friend to me. Especially when I was going through my divorces. Despite her own problems, she was always there for me. I don't want to see her hurt anymore. She *deserves* a better life."

"Look Alisha, I love her. I want to be with her all the time. I don't care what it takes. "

"You've no idea what you're taking on. You'll have gathered by now her ex is a complete arsehole." The waitress almost spilled the coffee as she topped up our cups.

"What does Georgie think about him?"

"Oh, he idolises him. Nick spoils him rotten. Makes it difficult for Lynne."

"There must be a way of getting it sorted."

Before she could answer, Lynne appeared at the table, looking anxious and flushed.

"You'll never believe who I bumped into in the bar on the way back from the loo?" she said, catching her breath.

"Oh, don't tell me!" Alisha said. "Not Nick?" Lynne nodded.

"He's drinking with a guy I've not seen before. I couldn't avoid him. He asked who I was with in the restaurant."

Alisha said, "What did you say?"

"I didn't want him to cause a scene. I panicked. I said I was with you, Alisha… and your new boyfriend." She closed her eyes tightly shut as if expecting a blow to the head.

"What!" Alisha exploded.

"Well, suppose he came in to check on me? You know what he's like." Lynne trembled.

Standing up, I said, "Look, this is bizarre. He needs to know you're seeing me. What's the worst that can happen? He won't try anything on in a public place. It's time someone let him know his days of dominating you are over. I'm going to have a chat."

Lynne said, "I don't think that's wise."

Ignoring her, I made a move towards the door then realised I wouldn't recognise him. I didn't want to pick on the wrong guy. "Alisha, come with me. You can point him out."

"Sure. This'll be interesting," she said, with a mischievous gleam in her eye as she turned to Lynne, who had both her hands up covering her mouth.

He appeared older than his thirty-five years and shorter than I imagined. Good-looking, in a rugged kind of way, he had hooded eyebrows and a square jaw. He wore a black leather jacket and blue jeans reminiscent of the Jets gang members in *West Side Story*.

He stood at the bar smoking and talking to an overweight bald man with a neck the size of a night club bouncer – only the communication ear-piece was missing.

"Sorry to interrupt, but can I have a word?" Adrenaline coursed through my body. I felt light-headed.

"Who wants a word?" Nick said, glaring first at me, then at Alisha. "Oh, Alisha's new boyfriend, I assume." He slurred his words and sneered as he stubbed out his cigarette in the ashtray on the counter. I noticed a tattoo in the shape of a snake encircling his wrist as he did so.

"Er… not exactly. I think there's been a misunderstanding. I'm seeing *Lynne,* not Alisha."

A ten-second silence followed whilst he gazed down at the ground and took in what I'd said.

"And who the fuck are you, then?"

"My name's James and I've been seeing Lynne for a few weeks. I just thought as a matter of courtesy, you should know."

"*As a matter of courtesy,*" he mimicked my words. "I don't do courtesy."

His words and the way he spat them out put me on my guard. I guessed correctly. He looked away and then turned back, his clenched right fist swinging towards my face in a wide arc – fortunately too wide, giving me time to react before contact could be made.

Moving my head back out of the way as the punch grazed my chin, I grabbed his wrist and elbow with both my hands and using his momentum, I swung his arm up behind his back sharply. He yelped in pain. Now woefully off-balance, I kicked his feet from underneath him forcing him to the floor, pressing my knee on his back, squashing his face hard against the polished floorboards.

I felt the veins in my neck pumping blood.

I wondered what 'Baldy' might do whilst my hands were full, but the landlord, sensing trouble, stepped in to restrain him. Lynne, who'd followed us into the bar, stood behind Alisha and pressed her face into Alisha's shoulder, not bearing to look.

"I want you all out of here. Now!" the landlord barked. I let go of Nick and he and 'Baldy' slunk off towards the door. Nick stared at me, eyes bulging and yelled, "You'll be sorry you did that, you tosser!"

We waited for a few moments, giving them a chance to get away before the three of us put on our coats and went to *The Frigate*, another pub across the road.

After I'd bought brandies to settle our nerves, we retreated to a quiet corner.

"Well, how exciting!" Alisha said.

Lynne, still shaken, said, "I can't believe two grown men were fighting over me. It's so embarrassing. I don't know what Nick'll do now. He won't have liked me seeing him humiliated."

Alisha said, "Well, as far as I'm concerned it's about time he got sorted out. He's alright bullying and threatening women, but the first time he's had to deal with a real man, he screws up."

Turning to me, she said, "Where did you learn to look after yourself like that? I'm impressed."

Not something which came easily to her, I thought.

"I went on a Martial Arts class for a few months when I was young. My dad thought it would be good for me."

Lynne said, "You know he won't leave you alone now, don't you? He'll be like a wounded animal." The brandy had settled her nerves a little.

"We'll have to handle it, Lynne, won't we? He's got to realise he can't go on like this. I think we've had enough excitement for one night, don't you? I'll rustle up a cab to get you both safely home. If he troubles you again, Lynne, you must let me know. OK?" She nodded weakly.

★

Over the next few days, the 'Nick' problem took up every one of my waking moments before I came up with an idea. I decided to meet him again once he'd cooled down and tell him my relationship with Lynne would have no effect on him seeing Georgie whenever he wanted to.

But given the circumstances of our first encounter, I felt I needed a back up plan in case he still didn't accept me being on the scene. I hoped I could use something in his past.

I called Tom Riley, my golf partner, who worked for a firm of lawyers specialising in criminal matters.

"Good of you to spend some time calling your old mate. Bet you couldn't drag yourself away from... er... what was her name? Lynne?"

"Yes. Actually, you could make yourself useful for once. I need a criminal check on someone. Can you help?"

"Sure. I've got my contacts. Give me the details." I told him all I knew about Nick Burrows and he promised to get back to me as soon as possible.

Two days later he called me. "Did you know there's a court order restraining him from harassing a certain Lynne Burrows?"

"Yes, I know. It's not working. Anything else?"

"Yeah, he's got a criminal record; charged with affray in a pub three years ago and fined. There's a suspicion of drug dealing but the police don't have enough evidence to pin anything on him. I assume his ex is the same lovely Lynne who works for you?"

"Yes, he's still giving her a rough time. I'm hoping to find out something I could use to get him to back off."

"If you're serious about this I can put you in touch with a

contact of mine. He's got a personal surveillance business. It's a bit cloak and dagger, and bloody expensive, but he always delivers. We don't ask too many questions. A round-the-clock watch for a couple of weeks might throw up something."

"Thanks, Tom. You're a pal."

He gave me the number, which I called immediately and set up a meeting in my office on the first available day we were both free.

★

Roger Pendleton wasn't what I imagined. I had in mind someone wearing a dirty grey crumpled mackintosh, a trilby and several days' growth of beard.

Instead, a fit-looking fifty-year-old, over six feet tall with a military bearing sat opposite me in my office. He looked more like a hospital registrar with a smart navy suit, sober striped tie and polished shoes.

"I love these BMWs," he said, wistfully staring out of my office into the showroom.

We engaged in small talk about the cars he'd owned. That's what I loved about my business. Everyone had a view about cars, the ones they loved and the ones they hated.

He produced a brochure which included an impressive CV. He used to be a senior officer in the Special Investigation Branch. His speciality was technical surveillance. He'd also reached the rank of Detective Inspector in the Metropolitan Police and spent a year on secondment working with the LAPD in Los Angeles, advising them on security matters. He said people usually referred to him as RP. It fitted.

He made notes as I explained that I wanted to get Burrows to stop harassing Lynne. I pointed out that what he'd hate most was losing contact with his son, Georgie. I passed on the information Tom had given me.

He studied his notes intently. "I'll try to find out what the police concerns are. I'll get a photo sent to me, too. I suggest we keep him under our noses for the next couple of weeks. See what that brings."

"Sounds OK." After negotiating the costs – Tom was correct, they weren't cheap – we agreed a date for the follow-up meeting. I felt optimistic and excited about what he might discover.

I'm always happiest when I have an action plan.

*

I called Lynne the day after the confrontation with Nick, keen to assess her state of mind.

"How are you?"

"Oh, I'm fine. Still can't believe you were fighting over me. Alisha says it's one of the best things to have happened to me for ages – 'bit of a turning point', she said, Nick getting his come-uppance. She's so impressed by how you handled the situation. Actually, so am I."

"And what about Nick? Has he spoken to you?"

"Yes. He came to collect Georgie this morning for his weekend visit. He's hugely embarrassed by what happened. I don't think I've ever seen him like that. Mind you, he called you a 'tosser' again and threatened to sort you out if you ever took his place in Georgie's affections."

"You know I'd never do that. Nick'll always be his dad. That won't change. Anyway, I've had an idea. I've decided to meet up with him soon, man to man, let him know what I think. I'm sure I can convince him I'm not a threat."

"Are you sure it's wise? I don't think you know who you're dealing with."

"It's the only way, Lynne."

"The only reason he'll see you is to beat you up. He's so hot-headed."

"Well, give me his number. At least let me try."

Reluctantly she gave it to me and said, "Are you sure you still want to be involved with us after all this?"

"Of course I do."

She must have been convinced because she invited me to Christmas Day lunch in three weeks' time. She wanted me to meet Georgie and her mother, Margaret.

I felt a huge surge of relief. After witnessing the brawl, I thought she'd never want to see me again.

★

Two weeks later, Pat buzzed me in my office. "Roger Pendleton's here to see you. Shall I bring him through?"

We shook hands and he made himself comfortable at my desk. Pat brought in a pot of coffee.

RP said, "I've got something interesting to show you. Do you have a videocassette player? Meant to ask when I called."

"Of course," I said, as I walked over to the corner of my office, and slid back a polished beech panel revealing the equipment. He passed me a video tape. I switched on the TV, placed the tape in the player and clicked 'Play' on the remote.

RP said, "I know the pictures aren't great but let me talk you through what we've found. One of my guys videoed this scene outside a nightclub in the West End last week."

A dark, murky rain-splattered picture partially relieved by

bright streetlights and neon signs flickered onto the screen. The first shots, taken from a distance, zoomed in every few seconds highlighting two men wearing dark jackets and trousers talking earnestly to each other whilst frequently looking over their shoulders.

"Keep watching. In a second, you'll see Burrows and the other man exchanging a packet. We've got a good shot of that. There… did you see it?"

"No. It's so dark."

"Give me the remote and I'll replay it and freeze it at the best shot." I passed it over.

"There! That's it. Can you confirm one of the men is Nick Burrows? You need to be sure."

"Well, I've only met him once, but it *was* memorable." I peered into the screen, my eyes narrowing, trying to focus on the shadowy figure. "Yes, that's definitely him. But he could be handing over a Christmas present for all we know."

"You're right, of course. That's why we followed Burrows' associate. We wanted to get a better picture of him on camera too. Then I planned to use my contacts to identify him. If he had a criminal record, especially in drug dealing, we'd be getting somewhere."

"Well?"

"I can't tell you how I got the info, but yes, he has done time for dealing in ecstasy tablets and other Class A drugs. His name's Frankie Richards. He's been a minor crook and ne'er do well ever since wearing long trousers. We're not sure where he is in the gang's pecking order, but it's highly probable his source is Burrows."

I let out a low whistle.

RP continued, "I think this *may* be enough to put the

frighteners on Burrows if you have to. Show him a copy of the stills from the tape and he'll know you're onto him."

"Look, all I want is to get him to back off. I don't want him put away. I think he should still be able to see his son. When the boy's older he can make up his own mind."

Stroking his chin, RP said, "Well, when you meet him, point out just the *suspicion* of drug dealing in addition to his harassment charges would force the courts to reconsider his continuing contact with the kid. That's the key to getting what you want, I'd say."

Nodding, I said, "OK, I like the idea. Let's see if it works. How soon can you get the stills to me?"

"Oh, in the next couple of days. I'll bring them to your office. Would you feel happier if I came with you to see Burrows?" Feeling I could handle the meeting myself, I declined his offer.

Good to know he'd help if things turned nasty though.

★

By the third week of December, the Christmas shopping craziness reached its climax. London's lights blazed in the West End and Canary Wharf, Christmas tree lights twinkled in hundreds of offices and their windows sparkled with fluorescent Santa Claus figures and cotton-wool snowflakes.

I'd never understood the amount of stressful effort the whole country made at this time of the year; buying presents for loved ones who didn't want or need them and stocking up provisions which could support a three-month siege. And for just two days' gorging.

My parents' death in a car crash happened on 12th of December twenty years ago.

I'd wanted to cancel Christmas ever since.

But this time, I looked forward to Christmas lunch with Lynne's family.

On the big day, I took two bouquets, one each for Lynne and her mother. They gushed like schoolgirls as I handed them over. I could see where Lynne got her good looks. Margaret would win any Glamorous Grandmother competition. Her skin glowed and her blonde hair, although fading into shades of grey, framed similar chiselled features.

Fussing around me like a small terrier, she made sure the food and wine was perfect. She reminded me of my mother.

Following a sumptuous roast turkey with all the trimmings, we enjoyed pulling crackers and laughing at the corny jokes.

Georgie and I worked on assembling a *Lego* racing car I'd bought him as a present. Lynne had tipped me off that it would be well received. It proved a good way to get to know him. He was bright and chatty and smiled a lot. We got on well.

Thoughts of Nick were put on the backburner, at least for this special day.

★

I knew getting a meeting with Nick wouldn't be easy. And I could only guess what he'd do when I told him I knew about his drug dealing. I planned to meet him in a public place for obvious reasons. I wasn't up to being ambushed by him and possibly 'Baldy'.

RP brought over the best stills from the video tape on the morning of New Year's Eve. I called Nick later that day.

I didn't want to give too much away on the phone. I always preferred face-to-face situations. I gave a lot of thought about where to meet him. I chose the Pavilion Tea House in Greenwich Park, by the Royal Observatory, which dominates the skyline high above the park. It would be particularly busy over the New Year's holiday.

"It's James Hamilton." I waited for a response. Eventually it came.

"What d' ya want?" His monotone voice appeared disinterested.

"I'd like to meet up to discuss our situation… like grown-ups."

"We've met, haven't we?"

"We have, but we didn't achieve much did we? I only want to chat with you."

"About what? I don't need anything from you. Just keep away from Lynne and Georgie. We're going to be together again soon."

"Er… I don't think so. Look, I don't want to say too much on the phone but I've got some information which will interest you."

"What information?"

"I'll tell you in person."

After a short silence, he hung up on me.

I hadn't expected this. He left me little choice but to play my ace card. I didn't feel especially good about it.

I left it for an hour and rang him back. I got his message service.

"I know all about your business relationship with Frankie Richards. Unless you meet me tomorrow, I'll pass over the information I have to the local police and remind them of your restraining order and your record of harassment. It's up to you."

I left him the address of the Pavilion Tea House and suggested we meet at 11am, New Year's Day.

"If you don't show, fine. Just think about your ongoing relationship with Georgie."

★

The new year, 1996, dawned mild and sunny. I got to the Pavilion Tea House so early it hadn't yet opened.

I'd spent New Year's Eve quietly at Lynne's apartment, watching TV with her and Georgie. I'd hardly drunk anything. A throbbing hangover would be the last thing I wanted to endure in the meeting, assuming Nick turned up. I left Lynne's apartment shortly after midnight. I told her about meeting Nick the next day.

"I bet he doesn't even turn up. If he does, good luck, you'll need it."

I walked around the park for an hour rehearsing my approach. Several joggers and cyclists were already into the first hours of their New Year resolutions. Mine was clear. I wanted to be with Lynne and Georgie without being hassled by Nick.

The cafe opened at 10.30 and as the first customer, I chose a seat at ground level close by the entrance. I had a good outside view through the floor to ceiling windows. By 11, the cafe was half-full. Every time someone entered, I looked up expectantly. I didn't know what to do if he didn't show. I had a vague idea of contacting RP to ask him what should be my next move.

Around 11.15, as I thought about making the call, Nick appeared at the entrance, a scowl creasing his face. Holding the door open before entering, he scanned the tables before spotting me. He flicked a still-lit cigarette end out into the courtyard, ambled over and flopped into the seat opposite. I offered a handshake, which he declined.

"You said you had some information for me." He thrust his hands into his pockets, leaned back in his chair and crossed his legs.

"Don't you want a cup of coffee or something?" I said.

"No. Not with you."

"Please yourself. You know Lynne and I are in a serious relationship. We hope to be living together soon. I appreciate you wanting to continue seeing Georgie – that's fine. But I don't want you hassling Lynne… or me. You've got to realise it's over between you and her."

"Who the bloody hell do you think you are? You can't tell me what to do or how to live my life. I'll do what I want."

"Fine. Then I'll take my information to the local police station. Which means you'll possibly not be allowed to see Georgie. That's why I can tell you what to do."

Taking his hands out of his pockets and clasping them together on top of the table, he leaned forward and said, "I don't believe you've got anything on me. You're bluffing."

Slowly and deliberately, I laid the three most incriminating stills from the video tape on the table.

"Here, you can have these with my compliments."

He picked them up one by one and stared at them intently. I studied his reaction. Surprise and disbelief.

Compounding his discomfort, I added, "These stills are from a video tape of your meeting with Frankie Richards. I've got a file on him too. He's got an interesting past, hasn't he? I think the police would want to know why you're in contact with a convicted drug dealer outside a night club."

A lengthy silence followed whilst Nick kept shuffling the photos and staring at them continually, not believing what he saw or heard.

Finally, he looked at me and said, "You bastard!"

"I'd be more of a bastard if I went straight to the cops without giving you a chance to maintain contact with Georgie, wouldn't I? Look, I didn't want to resort to this but you've forced me to. Why can't you stop harassing Lynne? I'd be happy for you to see Georgie as often as you wanted."

He spat out the words, "You tosser! I've told you. I'm going to get back with them."

"Not a chance. It's never going to happen. Anyway, that's my proposition. I think I've been very fair."

He stared out of the window before standing up. Turning back to me, he said, "I'll see," as he walked towards the door leaving the photos on the table.

I ordered another coffee and reflected on the conversation. It had gone as well as I could have hoped. I reasoned he'd never say, "OK, you win" so his, "I'll see" I considered a result.

★

Meeting Lynne later at her apartment, I told her about the meeting.

"What? He actually turned up?"

I explained that, because of our chat, I believed he wouldn't harass her anymore. I implied I'd made an emotional appeal to him; for Georgie's sake, he ought to let us get on with our lives. She remained unconvinced.

I decided not to tell her about Nick's sideline. Not yet, anyway. She'd have been mortified to think Georgie could be exposed to knowing about his father dealing in drugs.

"He's a devious so and so. I can't believe Nick would agree to anything proposed by you. I'm utterly amazed."

"I can be quite persuasive, you know."

Squeezing her hand, I said, "Let's carry on as we are for a few months... see how things pan out with you, Georgie and me? Oh, and you must let me know how Nick behaves. It's important to tell me if he's still bad news. OK?"

"I don't appear to have much say in the matter, do I? You're so persistent!" She smiled and leant towards me, nuzzling her face into my neck.

It felt good.

CHAPTER THREE

February – April 1996

Every time we met, now three or four times a week, I asked Lynne whether she'd had any trouble whenever Nick contacted them or when he collected Georgie every other weekend.

"I can't believe it. He's not as aggressive as he used to be about who I'm seeing. He still makes sarcastic comments about my family and friends, but I can handle that."

"Good. Pleased to hear it."

We often chatted about the business.

I told her the dealerships were firing on all cylinders. "They're flying, breaking sales records all over the place. I'm particularly pleased with John Hartley. You remember him? We promoted him from your company to group leasing manager. He's got off to a great start – pulled in loads of business."

She looked at me quizzically. "Really? Personally, I think he's just a jumped-up salesman with the gift of the gab."

Her hostile tone took me by surprise. I put it down to professional jealousy.

*

A few days later, Lynne and I celebrated Valentine's Day with dinner at *Bertorelli's*, the scene of our first serious encounter at my fortieth birthday party in November. She looked especially beautiful – her faultless, translucent skin glowing in the soft lights of the restaurant.

I'd already sent her a bunch of red roses and a card declaring my undying love for her. Her card to me extolled the same gushing sentiments.

We discussed our future on the basis that, so far, Nick appeared to be behaving himself. We felt nicely relaxed after sharing a bottle of *Lanson* champagne.

Lynne, smiling sheepishly, said, "I'm not sure how you're going to take this, but I won't be drinking alcohol much more after tonight."

"Oh, why not?" I said. She stared at me, continued smiling, saying nothing. Suddenly I realised what she meant. "You don't mean –"

"I'm pregnant!"

"You're what?"

"I'm having *your* baby!" Her smile widened, wider than I'd ever seen. Although we'd taken some precautions in our first few passionate encounters, I remembered we hadn't been as diligent as we should have been.

My emotions overtook my brain's capacity to absorb the ramifications of adding to my new 'family'. Lynne's delight was obvious. If this is what she wanted, then I wanted it too.

Grabbing my hand under the table, she said, "I know it's unplanned but I'm really pleased. Do you *want* to be a dad?"

"Of course I do. It's just… er… so unexpected. You've had time to get to grips with it. Yes… yes… I'm delighted. Of course, I want to be a dad. Wow!"

Still overwhelmed, I said, "Well, another bottle of *Lanson's* called for I think… especially as it'll be a few months before you can drink again. Tell me more. When's our baby due?"

"Not until August. We've plenty of time to get organised."

"Who else knows?"

"Well, Mum, obviously. She's as excited as me. And Alisha. She's equally chuffed. Oh, I also told Georgie. Of course, he doesn't understand everything, but he seems excited about having a little brother or sister. I haven't mentioned it to anyone at work yet. I thought we could leave that until later."

Feeling slightly miffed, I said, "It appears everyone knew before me."

"I'm sorry. I couldn't contain myself. Actually, I only told them tonight, just before you picked me up."

I felt better, but didn't have good vibes about Nick's attitude if Georgie told him the news, as I'm sure he would. But tonight wasn't the night to share my thoughts. She knew I'd be ecstatic once I'd had time to think about it.

After my divorce from Annie, I never thought I'd be a dad. We'd discussed it when we were together and decided to have children later in life. We never got that far.

In the months following, I found myself looking at children's clothes and toys in department stores, wrestling with the question; did I want a boy or a girl? I was caught up in the exhilaration of having someone with my genes roaming the planet long after I'd departed.

★

On a dull Monday in early February, Peter, my business partner, and I were reviewing the first three months of our new group leasing business with John Hartley. The figures were already spectacular.

"As you can see, we've exceeded the last quarter's sales targets by some margin." Hartley's smooth, cultured, BBC voice dominated the room. "You'll have to get a Securicor van to deliver my bonuses!" The margin between self-confidence and cockiness was paper-thin.

The only blot on his copybook had been a row he'd had a month earlier with a newly appointed female member of his admin team. She'd come to Peter's office in tears. Said Hartley had 'lost it', called her a 'useless tart'.

Peter and I challenged him about it. He waved his hand in the air and said dismissively, "Oh, she screwed up some paperwork, that's all. I can't have anyone on the team who won't pull their weight."

"Well, it's not acceptable. She's only just started. And she's a kid, basically. You'll need to show a bit more patience, John."

"I'm sorry. I want the department to be the best, that's all. Should I apologise to her?"

"I think you should."

"It won't happen again, I promise you."

★

Back in my office after the meeting, my phone burst into life. It was 3.30pm.

"James! Thank God you're there!" Lynne sounded breathless and agitated. She spoke quickly.

"I'm worried about Georgie. Nick asked if he could have him stay an extra night over the weekend. Said he'd take him directly to school on Monday morning. It seemed churlish not to agree." I heard her sniffle.

"He never arrived. The school called my office, but I've been in meetings all day and stupidly, I didn't check my messages until just now."

"Calm down! I can hardly hear what you're saying."

She took another deep breath.

"Sorry. Mum only found out about it when she went to pick him up from school. He never arrived. I've been calling Nick ever since. There's no reply. I can't think what's happened." She started crying.

"OK. Try not to worry. I'll go round to Nick's flat straight away. Give me the address. I'll call you as soon as I get there. Where are you?"

"I'm just leaving the showroom to go to my flat."

"Is your mum there?"

"Yes."

"Good. I'll see you soon." I stood, kicked my desk, turned and then kicked my wastepaper bin hard. It careered across the floor, bouncing against the wall, scattering papers in all directions.

*

Nick lived in a ground floor flat in a scruffy street in Poplar, a mile from Lynne. The front door had seen better days and the closely drawn curtains in the window had faded to the colour of dirty sand.

I rang the doorbell several times, and getting no reply, I looked up at the upper floors hoping to see signs of life. I rang the bell of the flat above, labelled, *A. Nazir*.

"Yes?" The intercom crackled.

"I'm trying to contact Mr Nick Burrows. Do you know if he's around? It's urgent."

"Well, no. He's not." He spoke with a cultured, singsong, Indian accent. "I saw him with his son yesterday morning, leaving the flat. He carried a suitcase and the boy had a large rucksack on his back."

"Did he tell you where they were headed?"

"No, he didn't. I'm his landlord and he owes me rent. I shouted after them. They ignored me. If you see him, please remind him he's a month overdue." The intercom shut off abruptly before I had time to question him further.

Heading to Lynne's flat in pouring rain, the wipers worked hard as the streetlights refracted the oncoming traffic's headlights. My brain raced to work out my next move.

Margaret opened the door. With anxiety scrawled over her face, she said, "Thank God you've arrived. Lynne's beside herself."

I told them both what happened at Nick's flat. "We'll have to go to the police," I said. "And they may ask if Georgie has a passport, as a matter of routine."

I'd recently seen a TV programme about abduction and for some reason, this fact stuck in my brain. I hoped I wasn't over-reacting. It was the landlord's mention of suitcases and rucksacks that bugged me.

Lynne exclaimed, "What! You think Nick's taken him abroad? You can't be serious?"

"No, of course I don't. It's one of the things the police'll want to know. Does he have his own passport? Is it here?"

Slumping back down into a chair, she said, "Not long before Nick and I separated, we went to Disneyworld in Orlando, Florida. About three years ago. Georgie was five or six. It was a vain attempt at saving our marriage. We added Georgie to Nick's passport. I assume he's still on it."

As she stared firstly at her mother and then at me, her eyes, already slightly red-rimmed, trickled with tears, realising the implication of what she'd said.

"Let's go to the police. Now. Come on. Oh, and bring a photo of Georgie with you."

Sobbing profusely, she wailed, "I... I... can't believe it.

What's made Nick do this? He'd been acting more sensibly lately."

Putting my arm around her, I squeezed hard. "I'm sure there's an explanation. We don't know the full story. I'll get your coat."

★

We drove to the nearest police station in West India Dock Road in Limehouse, a few minutes away. Neither of us spoke as the swishing tyres and wipers interfered with our thoughts, which we kept to ourselves. Lynne got through almost a box of tissues as she dabbed her eyes constantly.

After outlining our predicament to a polite and understanding ruddy-faced duty sergeant, he showed us through to a private interview room and told us a senior detective who had experience of abduction would be along shortly.

"I'm Detective Sergeant Evans. I'll be your Investigating Officer. And this is Detective Constable Liz Ashburton."

You could pass DS Evans in the street without noticing him. Average height, average weight, neat haircut, dull clothes, aged around thirty-five with a strong Welsh accent.

DC Ashburton, in her mid-twenties, blonde, green-eyed, around five feet five inches and heavily built, wore a constant, steely, no-nonsense expression.

Noticing Lynne's distress, she offered her a glass of water. After Lynne had taken a sip, DS Evans said, "OK? Sergeant Williams has outlined your concerns to me, but can you start from the beginning?"

I explained my relationship with Lynne and that, although I wasn't the child's father, I'd visited Georgie's last known whereabouts.

Lynne tearfully told the officer about her difficult relationship with Nick and the background to the contact and the restraining orders, following the physical abuse she'd suffered.

"He's such an arsehole! This is typical of him. He only thinks about himself. Doesn't give a shit about anyone else."

I'd never heard her go off like this before. I expected more of a response from the detectives but I guessed they'd seen many cases of abused women in the past.

After an hour of questioning, note taking and working through a checklist of documents running to two pages, the DC took them to be uploaded into a computer.

DS Evans leant back in his chair and said, "Since Mr Burrows hasn't formally asked to take the boy away, this looks like a clear case of abduction, which is a criminal offence. And we can't yet rule out the possibility that your son's been taken overseas." He ran his tongue around the inside of his mouth each time he made a point, a habit I'd noticed earlier.

Lynne let out a gasp.

"And the fact it's been now, what ..." glancing at his watch, "around ten hours since he wasn't taken to school, as arranged, and almost thirty hours since the last sighting of him, is of concern."

My impatience with the process kicked in. I resisted blurting out, *"Of concern* hardly covers the magnitude of the problem, does it?"

"The eyewitness account about your ex-husband and the boy being seen with a suitcase and rucksack is a big issue. We'll need to get officers onto that immediately. I'll go to Burrow's apartment block and take a statement from the landlord and from anyone else who may have seen them."

Lynne interrupted. "Why are you so sure they've gone abroad?"

"Well, I'm not a hundred percent sure, but you told me about your trip to umm …?" He looked at DC Ashburton, who'd returned to the room. "Orlando," she said.

"Ah, yes, Orlando, Florida. To visit Disneyworld. Sounds like it could be the likely bait for the boy to agree to go with his father."

"What are you going to do about it?" I said sharply, mindful of time rattling by.

The DS ignored my exasperation. "We'll contact the National Ports Office and request an all ports warning. Mind you, if they've already left the country it's a waste of time. I'll get officers to check the passenger lists on flights out of the London airports to Orlando starting on Saturday. If that draws a blank we'll widen our search."

Lynne sobbed again.

"We'll also file a Missing Person Report on the Police National Computer. Every police station in the UK will have photos, descriptions and the last-known whereabouts of your ex-husband and the boy."

Turning over a page of his notebook and scanning it, he said, "Oh, and with the eyewitness evidence we have and the time that's elapsed since the last sighting we'll be able to get a search warrant for your ex-husband's flat. I'd be keen to see if there's any evidence suggesting what his plans are. I'll conduct the search first thing tomorrow."

"Is there anything we should be doing?" I said, keen to show Lynne I, too, desperately wanted to get this resolved.

"You could think about anywhere else they might have gone. And, of course, if you hear anything, please call me."

"What are the chances of getting Georgie back quickly?" I asked.

Before answering, he did that thing with his tongue again.

"Honestly, it's hard to say. But tracing someone these days is a whole lot easier. Everyone leaves an electronic footprint. We'll get cooperation from the credit card companies and mobile phone operators, if he has one, to locate them. Finding them may not be that difficult, but this is not the main problem."

"What is, then?"

"If they've gone abroad, it's going through the red tape and the courts that takes the time. Once we know for sure, I suggest you get hold of a family solicitor experienced in these aspects as soon as possible. DC Ashburton can give you a list to choose from."

Sitting back, forcing the front legs of his chair off the ground and placing his hands behind his head, he said, "I don't think there's much more we can achieve tonight." He stood and offered his hand to each of us. "We'll do all we possibly can to get your boy back safely, Ms Burrows."

Lynne broke down again, crying uncontrollably. I tried pulling her close to me to comfort her as we stood to leave, but she brushed me off.

As we walked to the car, holding our coats above our heads to protect us from the rain, I said I'd stay at her place so if any news came in overnight I'd be on hand. She nodded.

As soon as we arrived, she disappeared to the bedroom without saying a word. Later I found her curled in the foetal position, fully clothed, her eyes shut. Her erratic and shallow breathing betrayed her concern. I lay on my back on a sofa bed in the sitting room, my mind racing, thinking about anything else that I could do to get Georgie back home.

I concluded it must have been the combination of my

blackmail attempt and Lynne's pregnancy which drove Nick to abduct Georgie. On both counts, I pleaded guilty.

It concerned me, too, that I hadn't told the police or, more importantly, Lynne about employing a private investigator to spy on Nick and using the information to get him to back off hassling her. I decided to tell them both the next morning.

I woke to the sound of a coffee grinder whirring in the kitchen. By the time I got there, I saw Lynne, wearing a blue dressing gown and a towel tied in a turban around the top of her head sitting on a breakfast stool, clutching a coffee mug. She barely acknowledged me. I poured myself a cup.

I asked, "Do you want me to fix toast and scrambled eggs with your coffee?"

She shook her head. "Coffee's fine."

"Lynne, you've got to eat something. It'll only take a few minutes. "

She glared at me and said, "Do you think me being pregnant made Nick do this? Or maybe *you'd* said something to upset him?"

It wasn't quite an accusation, but was implied in the tone of her voice.

"I don't think so. Maybe it's just the pregnancy. To be honest, telling Georgie first wasn't a good idea. I'm certain he'd have told Nick. You should have let me tell him, or you could have told him yourself."

"Oh, so you think it's *my* fault do you?" Some of the anger she'd displayed last night at the police station returned in her voice.

I topped up her coffee and said, "No, of course not. You know Nick's unpredictable. He needs careful handling. You said Georgie was excited about having a brother or sister and if he told Nick, that would have got right up his nose."

"None of this would have happened if I hadn't met you." Her voice shot up an octave or two.

"What's that supposed to mean?"

She yelled, "You, a big shot businessman, you thought you could handle Nick. You totally underestimated him. He's capable of anything. Because of you he's taken my son to… God knows where!"

"Look, I know you're a bit stressed but —"

"A bit stressed! Of course, I'm a bit bloody stressed. My son's been taken away from me… I may never see him again!"

Sobbing, she banged the coffee mug down hard on the granite worktop and stormed out of the kitchen, slamming the door behind her.

I'd lost my appetite. I sipped my coffee whilst staring out of the apartment window down towards Limehouse Basin. Last night's rain had given way to a bright, sunny spring Tuesday morning. From this vantage point, the slowly moving traffic and the even slower moving barges and ferries on the river appeared normal and ordered – such a difference from the drama unfolding before me.

I called Pat and explained that Lynne and I wouldn't be in for the rest of the week. I told her I had to deal with a family problem.

Lynne came back into the kitchen. She'd dressed and applied make-up to her cheerless face.

She said, "Now what do we do?" I ignored the contempt in her voice.

"I think it's best if you stay at home today in case Nick or Georgie make contact. I'll go down to the police station and chivvy them up. I'll call you later.

"Oh, I'm going to tell them something which may help. Sit down for a minute. Let me explain."

I left nothing out, finishing with, "I didn't *want* to blackmail him. I tried hard to reason with him. If he'd agreed, I'd never have had to show him the photos. You know what he's like. He wouldn't compromise. I had no option."

She glared at me with increasing antagonism.

Eyes blazing, she said, "You lied to me. You said he'd backed off because you'd persuaded him to. Now my son's been taken away by a drug dealer. Thanks a lot!"

She stormed out of the kitchen again before I could say anything. I desperately wanted to hold her tight, tell her how much she meant to me.

I followed her. I pleaded, "I'm sorry! I'm sorry! You know I'll do anything to get Georgie back. Anything. I'll call you later." The door slammed shut in my face mid-sentence.

CHAPTER FOUR

April 1996

Later that morning, I went back to the police station and asked to speak to DS Evans.

I told him about my meetings with Roger Pendleton and Nick. When I finished, he said, "What did Burrows say when he left you?"

"He just said, 'I'll see.' After that, he seemed to respond. He's not harassed Lynne since. I thought I'd cracked the problem."

"So you thought you'd *cracked the problem*? By taking the law into your own hands?" His Welsh accent heightened the sarcasm in his voice.

"Leave the video tape with me. It'll help us get the search warrants we need to search Burrows' flat."

"Have you made any progress?"

"I suggest you come back this evening with Ms Burrows, say about six. I'll update you both then."

He opened the door for me to go and said, "I'll think about what we do about your blackmail attempt."

"Look, all I wanted was for him to obey the court order not to harass Lynne. It's not a big ask, is it?"

★

"We've made headway in this case. I assume you've heard nothing your end?" DS Evans appeared bullish when Lynne and I turned up at the police station that evening. She'd hardly said a word to me on the way there.

"No," I replied, "nothing."

"Well, it's good news and bad news. The bad news is I can confirm they've left the country."

Lynne let out a loud, "Oh no!" and slumped further down in her chair and covered her face with her hands.

"The good news is that we know where they went. There are only four flights a day to Orlando out of Gatwick, so it easily checked out. We've confirmation they left on a British Airways flight at 11.20am on Sunday."

DS Evans was coming down with a cold and he blew his nose noisily as Lynne started crying. I tried consoling her by trying to clutch her hand. She immediately withdrew it.

He continued, "You'll be pleased to know we got the warrants we applied for. We've searched Burrows' flat and impounded a PC, and as we speak, our computer geeks are going through the hard drive."

"How long will that take?"

"Hard to say, but I can already tell you an unsuccessful attempt had been made to wipe out the memory. That may be significant. We'll have more information tomorrow afternoon." He wiped his nose again and replaced his handkerchief carefully in his pocket.

"It would help if we knew which credit cards Burrows uses. Do you have any idea, Ms Burrows?"

Lynne, who'd appeared to have taken a vow of silence, stared down at the floor and shook her head.

"OK. We'll, we'll start with the most common ones and work our way through. There may be clues from the data stored on the PC once the techies have hacked into it; otherwise, it's a hell of a workload. Could take days." He appeared resigned to this being the case.

★

I'd arranged an urgent meeting with a solicitor specialising in abduction cases and the next morning, after persuading Lynne to come with me, we were sitting opposite him in his office in Albemarle Street in Mayfair.

On the way, Lynne maintained her icy silence. I tried unsuccessfully to make conversation, but gave up.

William Groves, an urbane, bespectacled, fatherly figure confirmed that child abduction, even to a friendly country like the US, was a minefield of regulation and red tape. He told us that even if the procedures were followed meticulously, it could take the court at least three months to get a hearing and that could only happen after Georgie had been found.

"A few of the cases I've been involved in are horribly complicated. And only a minority of the three hundred UK child abductions cases a year are sorted out amicably and swiftly. A high number of cases remain unresolved many years later."

Lynne stood, realising her hopes for a speedy reunion with Georgie had disappeared.

"That's it! I've lost him. I've lost my little boy. I'll never see him again. I know it!" She swept towards the door and flung it open so wide it rocked on its hinges.

I mouthed an apology to the startled Mr Groves before following Lynne out of the office and onto the street, where I struggled to calm her, breathlessly assuring her the situation wasn't as bad as she thought.

★

I called RP. I told him about the abduction and the meeting with police and that I'd admitted to them our plan to sort out Nick. I wanted to meet up later that day. He'd have an opinion, without doubt.

His office on the second floor of a Regency building in St James's Street, off Piccadilly, resembled a colonial home in Singapore rather than an office in Mayfair. A thick flowery oriental carpet covered the wooden floorboards. Bamboo shutters at the windows, two huge ceiling fans and walls, each painted red, yellow and ochre covered with black and white photos of big game hunters displaying their trophy kill, completed the illusion.

I couldn't take my eyes off a magnificent tiger's head with snarling teeth adorning the wall behind RP's huge, oval, mahogany desk. A large brown, leather, button-backed chesterfield and two matching chairs surrounded a low coffee table.

I expected a dusky handmaiden wearing a sari to dispense the tea, but instead, an attractive thirty-something blonde secretary wearing a short skirt and high heels did the honours.

Taking in the exotic surroundings, I said, "Wow! How do you get any work done here?"

RP, as immaculately dressed as ever, grinned and said, "Are you referring to the decor or to Lucy?"

"I think both."

"They're not too shabby, are they? Anyway, let's get down to business, shall we?"

As RP poured the tea, he said, "Since you told me about the abduction, I've come up with an idea to get Georgie back home as soon as possible *and* sort out Nick. It'll cost a few pennies, but I don't think that's a problem is it?"

"Roger, I don't care what it costs. If this isn't dealt with soon, I'm going to lose Lynne… *and* my new addition. What have you got in mind?"

RP leant forward, his earlier frivolity replaced by a more serious tone. "Nick and the boy must be found quickly. I'm not sure the police are best placed to do this. Once they get the credit card usage data, they'll know where he is, but they'll always be a few days out of date. Then we've got to rely on the Met getting the maximum co-operation from their US colleagues to follow up swiftly. I'm not convinced they will."

"So?"

"Even if they do find them, you've then got to go through the courts. You told me that's at least three months' delay at best, right?" I nodded.

"So it seems to me the quickest route is to get Nick to return with the boy *voluntarily*."

"Roger, you must be joking. Why would Nick do that?"

"Hear me out. Lynne'll do *anything* to get Georgie back, true? Why can't she go to Florida with you? I can get the credit card info too. I'll update *you* and you can track him down. Once you've located Burrows she can meet up with him. Tell him if he returns with Georgie, she'll give him another chance at saving their relationship – become lovebirds – possibly even set up home together again."

"You can't be serious?"

"I know she's expecting your child, so it won't be easy to convince Burrows this is a good idea. But, he's obviously obsessed with her and of course he'll have Georgie all to himself. He *may* go for it."

"What about the abduction and possible drug-dealing issues? Surely the police won't let them go?"

He answered without hesitation. "I admit this is the

weakest part of the plan. Lynne will have to sound totally convincing when she says she's persuaded the police to drop any charges providing Nick returns with Georgie on a voluntary basis immediately. They probably won't, but she's got to persuade him there's a chance. She needs to put in an Oscar-winning performance."

I considered the implications of what RP had said.

The obvious thought sprang into my head. "What happens when they arrive back in the UK? How does Lynne extricate herself from the position she's engineered? I can't believe she'd really want to set up home again with that sick bastard – well, at least I hope not."

Pouring more tea, RP said, "Well this is the good bit. When they land, we'll tip off the police or do it through Crimestoppers, which is better – it's anonymous. The police will immediately arrest Burrows and charge him with the abduction. They'd possibly need more evidence for charging him with drug dealing. But given the fact he's tried to abduct the boy once, he most likely won't be granted bail."

"How long will he get?"

"Hard to say. Based on what we know, maybe three, four years if it's proven that he planned to keep Georgie in the States long-term. You can add on a couple more years if the drug dealing is proved."

He opened his desk drawer and, reaching inside, he pulled out a white foolscap piece of paper and wrote in bold strokes with his Mont Blanc pen.

"What I think we need to do is this. Point one: assuming Burrows uses a credit card, the police can get a warrant to get the information from the provider if they suspect criminal activity. I can get the same information as the police. Don't ask how.

"Point two: I'll keep you updated with the data so you can track him. The information will always be two or three days out of date, so it won't be easy but at least you're on the ground in the same State. Means a bit of legwork for you."

Scribbling down the next item, he said, "Remember, no one's more motivated than us, which is more than can be said for the Orlando Police Department or any other PD for that matter. To them it's just another job. Believe me, they've got their hands full with their current crime rates."

When he finished scribbling, he said, "Point three: once you've found him, you'll need to arrange a reunion with Lynne and she can turn on the charm. Convince him to return voluntarily."

"How can I do that? He'll kill me if he spots me in Florida." As I spoke, I had a brainwave. "I wonder if Alisha would come with us? She could set up the meeting. She'd be a great support for Lynne, too."

"Makes sense. You're starting to think like a detective now."

"What happens if he doesn't want to play ball?"

"Well, it's still a result, isn't it? I know we still have to go through the courts to get the boy back to the UK. But we'd have located him and we can keep the pressure on the legal eagles to get the case heard quickly. From what your family lawyer said, it'll mean just three months' delay after we've found them. And its likely Lynne can be with her son every day until the US court allows them to return."

I'd been telling myself for the last two days that I'd do *anything* to get Georgie back.

Now I'd have to prove it.

"Roger, this is way out of my league. Let me discuss this with Lynne and Alisha."

"Sure. Oh, before you go, let me show you our inner

sanctum. I don't show this to all my clients but I thought you'd appreciate it. It's recently been fitted out with the latest gizmos."

He took me through a side door to a room resembling Mission Control in Houston – split-screen monitors, computers flashing red, green and blue lights and recording equipment, which made my latest Bang and Olufsen hifi system look antique.

Five or six young men and women, dressed mainly in jeans and T-shirts, earnestly scanned the monitors or tapped at keyboards.

"This is the way things are going. You have to be one step ahead of the bad guys these days."

*

I arranged to meet up with Alisha and Lynne later that evening, but first, I visited DS Evans.

In the same interview room, he briefed me on progress and told me they'd had a breakthrough. He explained they'd discovered credit card details on Nick's PC, which although incomplete, pointed to one of the major providers. The police had a team working closely with them, but had no information yet.

I had mixed feelings about this. The police appeared to be making progress, but if they got to Nick first, we'd be caught up in an extradition process which didn't have a good track record as far as getting swift results were concerned.

"The breakthrough I referred to is that, following a search of Burrows' dustbin at the rear of his flat, we found a set of kitchen scales with a smidgen of a white substance on them and it wasn't baking powder. It's been analysed by the lab and their report confirms traces of cocaine." He ran his tongue around his teeth for the hundredth time before continuing.

"Of course, anyone could have placed these scales in his bin, but together with the video tape evidence you brought in, there probably is a case to answer. You don't use scales unless you're breaking down drugs into marketable packets."

I felt we were getting somewhere at last.

I said, "What's the position on getting Burrows extradited from the US now we can add the possibility of drug dealing to the abduction case?"

"A lot better. But it's not a nailed-on certainty. We've got to convince our friends across the pond there's enough evidence to justify, what they call, 'probable cause'. And I'm sure you've discovered that extradition isn't straightforward. And we've still got to find him."

*

The meeting at my place with Lynne and Alisha didn't start well. Over an Indian takeaway I put forward RP's proposal.

Lynne spoke first. "So, this is your new *plan,* is it?" I ignored the sarcasm. I'd gone through it as patiently and as calmly as I could. She questioned every aspect. When I got to the part about her having to suggest to Nick that they try to re-kindle their relationship, she lost it.

"You want me to do what? Are you crazy? Have you any idea how ludicrous this whole idea is?"

Alisha, who'd been quietly thoughtful throughout said, "I'm sorry to say it, Lynne, but I think the plan's OK. Definitely worth a try."

Whatever Alisha or I said, Lynne continued being sceptical, negative and unconvinced. After an hour, I lost my patience.

Throwing down my pen on the coffee table, I said, "OK. So how else do you want to proceed? Do nothing? Let events take their course? Everything we've heard so far points to a long, drawn-out court case involving thousands of pounds in legal costs. And that can only start *after* Georgie's been found. I think our plan has a better chance of success… don't you?"

Lynne gazed into the far distance, ignoring us both.

We spent another two hours going over and over the same ground, sometimes shouting, sometimes with prolonged silences, before she finally screeched, "OK! OK! My head's spinning. God, I've never known *anyone* as persistent as you!"

She let out a long sigh, looked at both of us and said, "I suppose I've got nothing to lose. All right. Arrange the flights. I'm not happy with any of this, James. And what will the police say when they find out I've left the country?"

"I don't see how they can stop you. You're trying to find your son. I think as long as you're in contact if they want more information it's not a problem. I'll tell them if you like."

Alisha said, "Well, I'm up for it. Lynne, you can't let Nick get away with this. When's it going to end with him?"

Lynne stroked her developing bump. "I'd better talk to the doctor about flying. I think I'm OK, but I need to check."

Reaching for her hand, I gazed into her eyes and said, "I'm *sure* this is the correct thing to do. I know you're going through hell now and what you've got to do won't be easy. But, if the plan works, Georgie will be home with us before you know it."

CHAPTER FIVE

March – April 1996

Lynne's doctor gave her the go-ahead to fly. He said she could travel between three and seven months into the pregnancy. At just over five months, this surely allowed plenty of time to get Georgie home.

Once I knew, I got Pat to sort out our first-class tickets for the flight to Orlando early the next day.

We landed mid-afternoon, Eastern Standard Time, and stayed in the Hyatt Regency Hotel within the airport terminal for the first couple of nights. Georgie had now been missing for four days. The plan we discussed endlessly on the flight included a visit to Disneyworld, showing pictures of Georgie to the front-line staff at the entrance to the most popular attractions.

Lynne thought the idea a complete waste of time.

"What's the point of that? Thousands of people visit there every day. No one's going to recognise him."

Although secretly, I agreed with her, I said, "I know. But at least we're doing *something,* aren't we? Better than moping around at home. It's only until RP can get us more info from Nick's credit card."

We spent the evening rehearsing what Lynne would say to Nick once we found him. "I don't know if I can do this," she said on more than one occasion. Alisha and I spent hours convincing her she could. We even role-played the meeting. I played Nick, with Alisha advising Lynne what to say. Although surreal, it kept us focussed on the plan.

Having Alisha in the team proved to be a good idea.

She said, "Think what it means, Lynne. If you pull this off. Not only will you have Georgie back, you'll get that scum-bag of an ex-husband of yours put away for a while."

We didn't have to go to Disneyworld. RP called early the next morning to say Nick had used his credit card at Orlando Airport to rent a car on the evening they landed. The amount paid suggested a month's hire.

He'd used the card again at a motel in Kissimee the following day and later at Disneyworld. The next day, he bought fuel from a petrol station on the outskirts of Miami, 250 miles south of Orlando.

"This is good isn't it?" I said.

"Well, yes, but by the time the credit card companies process the charges and my contact gets me the info, we're always going to be at least two days behind Burrows. We've got to hope he stays in one place for a while. But at least we're on his tail."

"Why do you think he's headed for Miami?"

"Could be because two million people live there and it's renowned for high levels of drug dealing. Maybe he thinks he can make a living there under the radar."

He said he'd call again as soon as he had more information.

*

We checked out of the hotel immediately, hired a Ford Explorer and headed down the Florida Turnpike taking us directly into Miami. We couldn't do anything more until we heard from RP.

DS Evans phoned me later that morning as we were booking into a small hotel in South Beach, Miami. I'd already told him about our plan to travel to Florida.

He appeared surprisingly sympathetic. He'd witnessed many abductions like ours and not many had a happy ending, he'd said. He actually wished us luck.

He told me the police had continued to carry out their own surveillance on Frankie Richards, Nick's drug dealing partner, as a result of the video tape I'd left with the detective.

An undercover cop had caught Richards in possession of cocaine and caught him in the act of supplying two grams to a spotty-faced youth under one of the bridges spanning the Thames footpath near Greenwich Pier. Richards had already served time for a previous offence. He therefore faced a serious amount of time in custody.

He didn't take much persuading to 'grass-up' Nick as his supplier in return for a more lenient sentence.

"The case against Burrows has built to the point where a prosecution now appears likely," DS Evans said.

Another break proved even more significant. RP called an hour later to say that one of Nick's credit card charges paid for a one-star motel, Shona's, along the busy Tamiami Trail where it meets SW 57th Avenue, four miles from downtown Miami.

Judging by the amount, even in this shabby part of town, it looked like he'd paid for a week's stay. The motel office manager had presumably insisted on payment upfront. RP had traced the address and given it to me.

If the Met had passed the same information to the Miami Police Department, they'd most likely be on their way there now.

I glanced at my watch. It read 3.30pm.

I told Lynne and Alisha the news. "Leave your bags in the car. We're not staying. We're going to the motel... now. We haven't got much time."

Lynne's face turned pale at the immediate prospect of putting on her Oscar-winning performance, as RP had described it.

"Do I have to do this? Isn't there another way?"

Before I could react, Alisha hugged Lynne tightly and said, "Lynne, this is it. Come on... we're close now. Remember what it will be like to see Georgie again."

"C'mon you two, the motel's only a few miles from here. Let's go," I urged.

Lynne had phoned her mother every day whilst we'd been in the US, trying to allay her fears. The previous night, Margaret asked to speak to me.

She said, "You know, having a child taken away is the most traumatic thing to happen to a mother. And now my pregnant daughter and her boyfriend are chasing Nick and Georgie all over Florida. Perhaps it's best if Lynne and Nick do get back together. At least they won't have these problems with abductions, courts, contact orders and harassment. Surely Nick's learnt his lesson?"

I exploded. "That's ridiculous! You've forgotten what Nick was like to live with. And we've probably heard only half the story."

I thought about telling her about Nick's drug dealing, but I didn't want to worry her any more than necessary.

She said, "You obviously love Lynne, James and I like you. I'm sure you'd be good for her and Georgie. But it's so *messy*, isn't it?"

"You could say that."

I worried that deep in her heart Lynne felt the same way.

★

I thought about what we'd do once we located Nick. The plan had to be foolproof or I'd lose Lynne. And Nick couldn't possibly know about my involvement. But I needed to be around to make sure he didn't do anything silly.

I drove to a car rental site, hired another car, transferred my case and gave Alisha the keys to the Ford Explorer. I followed her to the motel, parked in a bay away from the office and pulled a baseball cap low over my face. I watched Alisha and Lynne go inside and a couple of minutes later they emerged and made for Room 14.

The door opened, marginally at first, and then wider. Nick's face registered utter surprise. I heard Georgie whoop with joy at seeing his mother. They hugged for a good minute before all four of them went inside. I'd have given anything to be with them. I hoped Lynne's nerve would hold.

An hour later, Alisha came out with Georgie. I slid further down in my seat. As planned, she took him to a McDonald's, leaving Nick and Lynne to have their chat.

I remained in my car, imagining the conversation taking place which would change my life. I drummed my fingers on the steering wheel in frustration. I tried listening to the radio but got angry at the strident ads exhorting me to join a health club at 'never to be repeated' special rates, or take advantage of '*Twofers*' (two for one) dinners at a local diner.

Another hour passed before I saw Alisha's car return and draw up outside the motel room. She and Georgie knocked at the door and they entered. We'd earlier considered not returning Georgie to Nick but discounted the idea once I remembered he appeared on Nick's passport. They had to leave the US together.

A further half-hour dragged by. By now it was 6.30pm. I cheered internally as I saw Nick come out of the motel room carrying his case, followed by Alisha and Lynne, who held Georgie's hand. They made their way to their respective hire cars. If they headed for Miami airport, twenty minutes away, I'd know the plan was working.

I breathed a huge sigh of relief when they turned left out of the motel – heading in the right direction. I followed them.

My fallback plan if Nick didn't cooperate was to call the Miami Police Department and inform them of Nick's location. That wouldn't have been our perfect result by a long way and I was glad I didn't have to resort to it.

We'd planned for Alisha to return the hire car at the airport, go to the British Airways ticket office and get the return flights changed to one of the evening flights to Gatwick.

As I made my own way to the security check area, taking great care not to be seen by them, I spotted Alisha heading towards the ladies' rest room on her own. I was desperate to know how Lynne had managed to get this far.

As Alisha emerged, I pulled her to one side.

"How did it go?"

"James! You startled me!" She looked nervously around first and then spoke in a hushed voice. "I've never seen anyone so stunned to see us as Nick… he asked how the bloody hell we found him. We said we'd employed a hotshot private eye. We didn't go into details."

"Good. How did he react once he got over the shock?"

"Actually, I think he'd got stressed out trying to handle Georgie. He'd been unhappy and tearful ever since they'd left Disneyworld. He hated staying in motels… 'so boring', he said. And obviously, he's missing his mum, his grandma and his mates at school."

"Poor little bugger."

"I know. Anyway, we've changed the tickets. We're booked on BA 208 leaving Gate 21 at 21.45 and landing at 11am UK time."

"Good. How's Lynne?"

"Very nervous. We haven't had much time to discuss the finer details. But looks like she's pulled it off."

"Fantastic. Sounds like he's swallowed the possibility the police will drop any charges as long as Lynne's happy."

"Yeah. It wasn't easy, though. Her biggest problem was getting Nick to accept she was pregnant with your child. She said she'd told him categorically she'd finished with you. He fell for it. Look, I'd better go. They'll be wondering where I am." She ran towards the gates without a backward glance.

Half an hour later, I changed my ticket for a flight leaving later in the evening.

Before going through to security, I called DS Evans' landline even though I realised it was a few minutes after 2.30am in the UK. I left a message telling him about Nick's flight and urged him to be at Gatwick to arrest him. I hoped he'd pick up the message in time.

I called RP and left a message. I explained what had happened.

"Can you be there tomorrow to meet them, make sure everything goes according to plan? I'm worried that if DS Evans doesn't arrest Nick, it's going to be difficult for Lynne."

I bridled at the fact that Lynne had told Nick emphatically we were finished. I fretted that she might have had a change of heart.

Finding it difficult to sleep on the flight, I twitched and turned, never getting comfortable. I continuously ran through every likely scenario that may take place in the morning. Finally, I fell into an alcohol-induced fitful doze.

My flight landed on time and I called RP the second I emerged from customs.

He said, "I'm sure you'll be delighted to know the plan worked perfectly. Lynne told me the police intercepted Burrows and took him to an interview room with his baggage. Customs waved Alisha, Lynne and Georgie through. Lynne's mother met them and I arranged a driver and car for them. I presume they're home by now."

"Thank God! I'll call DS Evans later today. I'm assuming Nick'll be detained, won't he? I wouldn't like to meet him if he's back on the streets. He must be blowing a gasket."

"He won't be granted bail, James. What's to stop him trying to abduct Georgie again? And the drugs charge is serious. Mind you, strange things happen. Let's hope your DS has done his stuff."

I thanked him again, ended the call, and punched the air with excitement, yelling, "Yes!"

When I called DS Evans later, he confirmed that Nick had been arrested for abducting a child and for drug dealing. Police bail had been denied.

"Burrows realises he's been duped. If he could get hold of you two, he'd throttle you both to death. He's not a happy bunny."

He confirmed that he wouldn't be taking any action over my blackmail attempt.

A good day all round.

CHAPTER SIX

April 1996 – August 1998

I decided not to contact Lynne until the next day. It would give her a chance to get back to something approaching normal life with Georgie.

I called Margaret instead to get a handle on Lynne's current state of mind. She confirmed that Lynne and Georgie both needed rest and that the experience had affected them badly.

"Do you think they're up to seeing me soon?"

"I'd give it another few days if I were you. Lynne needs to get her head around what to say to you. She thought you were wonderful, James. You won her over. But then all this business with Nick. She can't help but think if she'd never met you, none of this would have happened. You can see why she's a bit confused, can't you?"

"Yes, I can," I said. "I understand. That's fine. Please give them my love. Tell her I'll call her soon."

Of course, it wasn't bloody fine. I ached to be with her, Georgie and the 'Bump'.

★

Later that day, I received a call from Peter.

"Can you pop in, James? Something's cropped up you should know about."

"What is it?" I said.

"It's best discussed in person, I think." He sounded on edge. I arrived in my office fifteen minutes later. Peter walked in looking hugely embarrassed.

"I'm sorry, James. I don't know how to put this… the auditors have finished their audit. They've discovered a problem."

"What do you mean? Everything's OK isn't it?"

"Well, no, actually it isn't. It's serious." He couldn't look me in the eye.

"What the hell's wrong, Peter?"

"I hate to have to tell you, but we've been the victim of a major fraud in our car leasing division."

He explained that the auditors had discovered that payments from the finance company we used to fund the cars we subsequently leased out never reached our bank. They'd been siphoned off to a number of separate bank accounts in different names. The computer records had been hacked into and amended to cover the shortfall. The auditors called it a classic case of 'teeming and lading'. Twenty cars were involved with a total value of well over half-a-million pounds. Just what I needed.

"Who did this, Peter?"

"There's only one person who could have hacked into the computer; John Hartley."

"What? Our leasing manager? Surely not. He did well in the first few months, didn't he? You, yourself described him as a born salesman. You said he could out-charm Prince Charming."

"I know. Maybe I trusted him too much. I let him get on with it. He appeared so… capable."

Suddenly it made sense. Two months earlier, in early February, shortly after our review meeting, when we'd praised his sales performance, Hartley had asked to see me.

In his cultured voice, he'd said, "I'm afraid I have to resign with immediate affect. I've got a personal problem I need to sort out. I thought I ought to let you know."

He'd sounded genuinely contrite – totally the opposite of his cocky self.

"I'm sorry to hear that, John. What problems? Anything we can do to help? I don't want to lose you."

"I know. I've enjoyed it here. I don't want it broadcast but my wife's been diagnosed with terminal cancer. I need to be with her at this time." His eyes welled up.

I'd suggested several possible solutions, offering to keep his job open or allowing him to work from home for a while, but he'd rejected my offers.

Although he'd proved a great success in the job, I never came to terms with his attitude. I now realised that when he'd bullied one of our staff it was probably to do with covering up the fraud.

Furious with Peter, I yelled, "How the bloody hell did you allow this to happen? You're the computer whizz. You should have ensured our programs were safe from hackers."

Staring down at the ground, he shuffled from foot to foot.

"Christ, Peter!"

"Do you want me to resign?"

"No, of course not. Can we cover the loss?"

"It'll be difficult. I'll have to talk to the bank, but I think so."

"What a bastard! Look, why don't you check on Hartley's whereabouts, try to contact him. It's probably a useless exercise, but it's worth a try."

My ego wouldn't let me admit I'd been fooled. It represented a giant blot on our stewardship of the business, which we coveted. If news got out, I couldn't face my fellow businessmen or the vehicle manufacturers. Bad enough that the bank had to be involved.

I persuaded Peter not to call in the fraud squad. "We don't need to magnify the problem and get unwelcome publicity," I said. "Anyway, the money's probably been spent or tucked away in a Swiss bank account by now."

Our auditors' role was to provide an audit report for the shareholders, Peter and me, so no one else was involved.

That evening, Peter visited Hartley's address, only to find the place locked up with the curtains drawn. He spoke to a next-door neighbour, Mrs Matthews, who knew the Hartleys well.

"Haven't seen them lately. They just disappeared overnight. It's unlike them not to let me know when they're away."

Peter asked about Mrs Hartley's health.

"Cancer? No, she didn't have cancer. She'd have told me. We shared a lot of stuff over the years."

★

Next morning, I couldn't wait any longer. I called Lynne. She sounded cool and matter-of-fact. I found it difficult to gauge whether she wanted to hear from me or not. But at least she agreed to see me that night.

Opening the door, she smiled weakly, nothing like the smile she usually reserved for me. She looked as beautiful as ever, but the sparkle in her eyes, her best feature in my book, was missing.

She still enthralled me. I hugged her and kissed her on the lips, taking her by surprise, pleased she didn't rebuff me. I'd brought flowers and a bottle of non-alcoholic fizzy wine.

Placing the bottle on the table, I said, "Thought we should celebrate your return by drinking fake champagne. What do you think?"

"Why not? I'm just glad to be home. Thanks for the flowers."

She'd clearly made an effort to look good, wearing a long flowing dress, disguising the fact that she was nearly six months pregnant. I asked her how she felt.

"Well, considering all that's happened, not bad. A bit tired, that's all. I'm going for a check-up next week. We'll know if everything's ok then."

"Good." After I'd poured the 'champagne', I proposed a toast. "Congratulations on all of us returning home safely. You did a fantastic job on getting Nick to cooperate."

"I don't know how I did it. Thank goodness, he believed me. On the plane coming home, I had a few anxious moments. He asked me whether the police really would drop the charges against him. 'Of course', I said. Then he made me promise him we'd be ok together."

She shuddered and continued, "Then I panicked. What if the police didn't arrest Nick? I'd be back where I started; living with someone I detested more than I did before."

She had no idea how pleased I was to hear her say that.

I held her hand and said, "Well, the main thing is you have Georgie back. He's been through a lot too, but hopefully when he gets back into the routine of home and seeing his mates at school he'll settle down. I want to help. If there's anything I can do, I will."

She nodded. "I know."

"What does Georgie think about his father now?"

"Well, I told him his father had done bad things and that it's most likely he won't see him for a while. He gave me the impression he accepted it, but he's hard to read at the moment."

"He needs time. I know this sounds daft, but actually, I'm feeling sorry for Nick. I'd have been perfectly happy for him to have as much contact as he wanted. But it wasn't enough for him. He wanted you as well. He's brought all this on himself. He's screwed up his life."

"Don't tell me. He's been doing that for as long as I've known him."

We chatted until the early hours. As I left, I turned to her and said, "Look, you and Georgie are back home, Nick's out of the picture and you're expecting my baby. Why don't we get married?"

"I'm not ready yet, James. I need a bit of time to get over this… Nick business."

"Do you blame me for what happened? Is that it?"

"No… not really. I'm confused, that's all. I need more time to sort myself out. Let's carry on as we are for a while."

I didn't push the point. "OK. If that's what you want."

I tapped her bump and said, "Look after that baby of ours," then hugged her tightly and kissed her neck. Her smile became broader and the sparkle in her eyes appeared brighter.

★

Two days later, as I arrived at my office, Peter rushed in. He thrust a photocopy of a press cutting from *The Times,* dated 20th February 1996, in front of me.

John William Hartley had been sentenced to five years imprisonment for embezzling funds from a charity organisation he'd worked for before his time with us.

The press cutting mentioned that he'd also been convicted of causing actual bodily harm to one of the organisers.

Peter said, "I've been digging around. Spoke to one of our customers who knew we'd employed Hartley. He remembered something in the papers about him. I checked back through the archives on various websites. It took me ages, but this is what I found. Don't know how we missed it. At least, it explains why he went AWOL."

"Didn't you check his references?"

"Well, as he'd been taken on by the Greenwich business before we took it over, I assumed they'd checked. I've since gone through his file and the references were impeccable. Obviously forged. We've been well and truly conned."

"You could say that."

I didn't blame Peter. Especially when I thought about the time I attended a two-day leasing conference in Birmingham with Hartley. Peter couldn't make it, but as it represented a good networking opportunity, I went in his place and spent a lot of time with Hartley.

We didn't talk about relationships or anything deep, men seldom do, more sports and business. I only knew he was married, no kids. Although he said he'd have liked one.

I found him tolerable enough, although his self-confidence could be overpowering. What separated him from anybody else I ever knew was his ability to draw people into his network – big hitters included. They attached themselves to him like steel pins to a magnet. Once under his control, he manipulated them at will. The ultimate salesman… or con man.

He had the balls to steal from me whilst simultaneously building my business. He'd got to me too.

★

For the next two months, we became a family again. Lynne's mood brightened and we got close to how we used to be before Georgie's abduction.

I talked to him a lot, but the chatty, ebullient Georgie I'd known before the abduction had been replaced by a brooding, quiet boy. Except when we chatted about his passion for football and his mates at school. Only then did he become animated.

I deliberately didn't raise the subject of his father with him; I thought he'd talk to me about it when he wanted to.

Just a matter of time, I reasoned.

★

At Nick's trial for abduction and drug dealing on Monday 23rd June at the Inner London Crown Court in Newington Causeway, on London's south bank, he pleaded guilty in the face of the overwhelming evidence against him. This meant a heavily pregnant Lynne wouldn't to have to face him in court. I imagined him vaulting the dock and carrying out his promise of throttling her to death.

DS Evans called me shortly after the trial.

"He got three years for the abduction and four years for drug dealing, the sentences to be served consecutively. We're pretty pleased with that. I'm sure you are too."

I thanked him for his help and understanding. I called Lynne with the news.

"Good. At least we can get on with our lives now without that bastard screwing it up!" I wasn't sure whether by 'our lives' she meant together or apart. But her feelings for Nick were abundantly clear.

With the trial out of the way, we focussed on the

arrangements for our big event. Our baby was due on 15th August. I couldn't believe how obsessed and excited I'd become about it, looking at families with babies in the street, inspecting and discussing with them the merits of the buggy they were using. It became a major topic of conversation between Lynne, her mother and me.

We had endless discussions about the baby's name. I favoured Jack or Josh for a boy and Lynne preferred Jess or Emily for a girl.

Emily's birth two weeks prematurely at the Royal Hospital in Whitechapel, at 2.24pm on 31st July, weighing six pounds two ounces, proved to be the most emotional experience of my life.

I regretted my parents hadn't lived long enough to see their granddaughter. As their only child, they'd often told me they looked forward to being grandparents one day. Their death in the car crash over twenty years ago still haunted me.

Gowned-up and present at the birth, the midwife asked if I wanted to cut the umbilical cord, which I did. I couldn't have been happier.

Then she handed the most precious blonde bundle to Lynne, whose joyous face made me want to cry. Then she passed her to me.

"She's gorgeous. What a beauty!" I said, as I peered into her tiny face. I'll never forget the warmth of her body steadily breathing next to mine and the indescribable smell of a brand new human being I'd help create.

★

Emily became the sole focus of attention for the following few months, to the detriment of everything else. Lynne's mother, too, devoted herself to her granddaughter's welfare. Emily took her milk from Lynne greedily and from week to week grew bigger, stronger... and noisier.

Georgie, despite at first liking the idea of having a baby sister, became more withdrawn, sullen and preoccupied. I thought it might be something to do with his father. I asked Lynne whether she'd told Georgie about Nick's offences and the sentencing.

"I said he'd be in prison for a long time and that Georgie wouldn't be able to see him until he was a grown-up. If he wanted to write to his father, I told him he could. He said he understood."

"You do know that Nick could apply to the family court to *insist* that Georgie visit him in Belmarsh, as long as he has an adult with him, don't you?" RP had mentioned this as a possibility.

She shot back, "Oh, really! Who's going to take him then? *I* certainly won't. And if you took him there'd be a prison riot. Nick can apply for as long as he likes. There's no way I want Georgie near *that* man. No, I think it's best the way it is."

Nick did apply to the court and, unbelievably, the judge sent round a court welfare officer to ask Georgie whether he would like to visit his father in Belmarsh prison.

Georgie's opinion, apparently, carried great weight in the judge's eyes. It must have been distressing for a nearly nine-year-old lad to have to make such a choice.

Lynne too, found it difficult to remain impartial, but didn't want to be accused of influencing her son – an impossible task.

In the event, Georgie told the welfare officer he didn't want to see his father. I don't think Georgie hated him, he simply chose to avoid him. I suspect he felt deeply embarrassed too, having a father serving time, although he never admitted it to Lynne or me.

I didn't have to be Einstein to guess Nick's reaction. He'd naturally blame Georgie's decision on us, fuelling his hatred of Lynne and me still further.

As the autumn leaves flittered down from the trees and the days grew shorter, Georgie's attitude to both Lynne and me deteriorated. He became monosyllabic; grunting one-word replies when asked a question. Rude, too.

His teachers at school had also seen a change. His erratic behaviour and non-existent concentration gave them cause for concern, which they shared with us.

It came to a head on a visit to the museum in Greenwich. He went missing for over four hours. I trembled at the thought that Nick had arranged for someone to abduct him again.

I tracked him down to the comic section of a bookshop in the town. I forcibly frog-marched him back to the car, where Lynne was beside herself, fretful and anxious.

Lynne yelled at him, "Where have you been? I've been worried sick."

Before Georgie could reply, I shouted at him too, pushing him into the back seat of my car. "Don't you *ever* do that again! See how upset your mother is?"

Georgie, his face contorted and eyes glaring defiantly into my rear view mirror, yelled back at me, "Who are you to tell me what to bloody do? I'll do what I want. You're not my father!"

Lynne turned to him, almost getting out of her seat and shrieked, "How dare you speak to James like that? And don't let me hear you swear again. Apologise at once!"

"Why should I? No one cares about me, anyway." Georgie glared at both of us, daring us to respond.

Still facing him, she shouted, "Don't be ridiculous. Of course we care!"

Emily, strapped in the car-cot next to Georgie, started wailing.

I said, "Look, this is hardly the time or the place to keep shouting at each other. C'mon, let's discuss this at home."

The car, heavy with silence on the short journey back to Lynne's apartment, felt leaden, as if in sympathy with the occupants' moods. Locking it whilst she and Georgie, his face flushed with an insolent expression, went inside, I followed, still seething.

Georgie ran straight upstairs to his room. After Lynne had settled Emily in her cot, she went to the kitchen to make tea.

I followed her and said, "What the hell was that all about?"

She sighed and shook her head. "God, you must wonder what you're taking on with this family." I put my arms around her.

"Of course I don't. It's just that he's acting so out of character. I thought he'd been abducted again."

She closed her eyes tightly and said, "Oh, please. Don't remind me."

*

Usually, I felt I could handle anything life threw at me, but this was fresh territory. I didn't have a clue. Then I had the bright idea of asking Pat for advice. She'd brought up two boys. She'd know what to do.

"So you're surprised Georgie's reacted the way he has, are you? I'd be more worried if he hadn't."

She sounded exasperated. "Think about it, James. He's had to cope with a lot over the last few years. His parents split up when he was just a little boy, didn't they? What age? Five? Six?"

"Six, I think."

"He only sees his father, who he idolises, every two weeks and then his mother has an affair with a complete stranger. Then he learns she's having your baby."

"Yes, but –"

"Hang on! I haven't started yet. He's abducted to Florida, wondering whether he'll ever see his mother again. Have you thought about how traumatic that must have been for him?"

"I know, Pat –"

She carried on as if I'd said nothing. "His father's arrested at the airport, convicted of abduction and drug dealing, and then he has to choose whether or not to visit him in jail, either upsetting his mum or facing not seeing his dad for years."

I'd never seen her so passionate before.

"Yes but –" this time I managed to get a word in. "What kind of father could he be? Someone involved in drug dealing and child abduction?"

She slapped me down. "Yes, but Georgie doesn't see any of that. All he knows is that his dad's in jail, he's got a part-time 'uncle'" – she made quote signs with her hands – "who may or may not be a long-term fixture and now he's ignored by most of the adults in his life, at the expense of Emily."

"Yes... I see that, now."

"And I expect when they were in Florida, Georgie's father stirred things up by telling Georgie that his mother abandoned him in favour or you. Nice."

Softening her tone, she continued. "You must remember that Georgie, until three months ago, was the *sole* focus of attention. His mother obviously doted on him. You were trying hard to win him over and even his grandmother, from what you've told me, spoilt him rotten. Now that energy is focussed on Emily. I'm surprised the poor lad's not gone mental."

Suddenly it made sense. Pat had made the case succinctly. I told her she should have been a barrister. How could I have been so blinkered? Why didn't I see this coming?

"What can we do?"

"Well, it's not going to be easy. The first thing that needs to happen is for the adults in his life to be aware of what's going on. Give him some TLC. It'll take time, but it's the only way."

"So?"

"I've learned what kid's value most above everything else is stability. They need to know that both their mum and dad are there for them, no matter what."

We chatted on, Pat telling me about the problems she'd had with her two. She could laugh about it now, she said, but at the time, it wasn't funny.

I told her I still loved Lynne and wanted to spend the rest of my life with her, Georgie and Emily.

"Well, that's the most important thing, isn't it?"

★

I thought deeply about Pat's comments and decided to do something about it.

I arranged dinner at Lynne's favourite restaurant near Tower Bridge. Pouring the last dregs of a bottle of *Multipulciano,* I came right out with it.

"Lynne, come on, let's get married. I think now would be a good time. What's stopping us?"

"I don't want to take advantage of you, James. Not with this business with Georgie going on."

"But that's my point. I think he'll respond well. He'll know we're serious about each other – give him stability. I think we're ready to become a family. We can sell our flats and buy a house with a garden. It'll be a fresh start."

She laughed. "Getting a bit ahead of yourself, aren't you?"

"Well, that's me, isn't it? Mr Persistent. Come on. Please say yes."

"Are you really sure?"

"Of course I am. I've wanted this for months."

After a few moments, she said, "Yes."

"Really?"

"Yes, yes, yes!" For the first time for ages, her eyes twinkled and I got that vivacious smile that always made my heart fly. I proposed a toast.

"Happy Families," I said, grinning, as we enthusiastically clinked our glasses together.

★

We married at Tower Hamlets Register Office in Bow Road on 5th March 1997, eighteen months after we'd met. It felt like a lifetime given everything that had happened.

I'd never been happier. We still had problems to overcome, of course, but they only served to strengthen our relationship.

Over the following months, Alisha, Margaret, Lynne and I worked hard to ensure Georgie wasn't ignored. His school reports and teachers' comments greatly improved too. Pat had been right. Marrying Lynne provided the impetus for him to believe we were in it for the long term.

We sold our flats quickly in a buoyant market and found a delightful double-fronted five-bedroom period house in need of improvement in the leafier and smarter part of Blackheath, close to the conservation area of Westcombe Park. I liked the idea of putting our own mark on the house and it gave us a chance to get back to something approaching a normal life.

We spared no expense on the improvements we made. We had great fun re-designing and decorating every room. Lynne had a real flair for it and I loved seeing her so happy, tackling the project with enthusiasm. Emily's bedroom gave the impression of a fairy grotto: pink, fluffy and twinkly.

We found a great new school nearby for Georgie and he settled in quickly. I think he enjoyed the idea of a fresh start as much as we did. We allowed him to choose how he wanted his room decorated. Cars and football were his passions. He wanted plain walls adorned with huge pictures of classic cars and, to my delight, he wanted photos of the Arsenal soccer team.

"Arsenal?" I said. "That's my team. I thought you supported your dad's team, QPR?"

"No. They're rubbish! I want to support a Premiership team."

I never discovered whether this change in his allegiance represented a vote for me or a sub-conscious effort to forget Nick.

Lynne acquired an unquenchable zest for life. She made a huge number of friends in our new neighbourhood and invited many of them to our house for either drinks or dinner. She loved playing host. It appeared as if a load had been lifted from her shoulders.

She got Georgie more involved in helping her bring up Emily. Despite his early resentment, he grew into the role of big brother. I told him, his job would always be to protect her as she grew older. He liked that.

We bought a beautiful holiday cottage in Lymington, a delightful coastal town in Hampshire, close to the New Forest, about three hours drive from home.

The cottage resembled the classic chocolate-box lid – a thatched roof crowning whitewashed walls softened by rambling pink roses around the door and pale blue racemes of wisteria reaching up into the eaves. The pretty garden, enclosed by a white picket fence, had several cherry trees, which carried stunning blossom every May.

When Lynne first saw the cottage she said, "Oh, it's beautiful! We must buy it." We hadn't yet set foot inside. I warned her not to be so enthusiastic in front of the vendor, but I failed. As a result, it made negotiating a decent price tougher. I didn't care.

When Georgie saw the marina, he said, "Wow! Look at those yachts. Can you teach me to sail? One of my friends' dads taught him. Said it's wicked!"

Whenever we visited, usually most weekends in the summer months, he and I went to the local sailing school. He proved to be a natural sailor and we spent many happy hours together tacking on the Solent before meeting up with Lynne and Emily for lunch or an early dinner.

Emily's gleeful reaction to the wild New Forest ponies, especially the foals tramping across the winding roads as if they owned them, made every trip worthwhile. I imagined her taking riding lessons when she became older.

Life couldn't possibly get much better.

However, on our last visit, Lynne became withdrawn and preoccupied.

"Is everything OK, Lynne? You don't seem your usual self."

"No, I'm fine. Just a bit tired, I suppose."

As I locked up that evening before we went to bed, I looked through the side window next to the back door and thought I saw movement in the garden. I opened the door and peered into the darkness, with the light from the windows feebly illuminating the immediate area. I called out, "Anybody there?"

No reply.

I thought it must have been a bird or a squirrel. Maybe I imagined it.

A week later, two police officers came to my office and told me about the arson attack.

PART TWO

PART TWO

CHAPTER SEVEN

August – December 1998

When DI Flood had asked me if I could think of anybody who'd want to murder my family, I had no hesitation in suggesting that Nick *must* have arranged it.

"I know he's inside, but maybe he arranged for a hit man or something," I said.

I explained Nick's background: the restraining order, the drug dealing, the abduction and the trial to the DI, whilst his detective sergeant furiously made notes.

"OK, I'll look into it," he said. "In the meantime, I'd like you to be available if we want to talk to you."

His earlier implication that I might have been involved with the arson simply because, for the first time ever, I didn't travel down to the cottage with my family unnerved me.

I racked my brains to come up with cast-iron evidence that would prove, beyond doubt, my innocence. Then I'd ram it down DI Flood's skinny throat, break my media embargo and broadcast it to the world.

Unfortunately, I couldn't think of anything. Except the fact it *had* to be Nick, the only person I knew with a motive.

★

The media stepped up their interest once the police released a statement confirming the fire had been started deliberately and asking the public for any information that could help find the perpetrator. I maintained my self-imposed media embargo and refused to talk to them.

I rarely left the house. My phone at home constantly rang but I never answered it, just checked for messages every couple of hours.

I parked away in my mind the hideous details of the fire and considered whether Nick planned to murder me too? Possibly, my business meeting saved my life.

Something else gnawed at me incessantly, feeding my guilt. Why didn't I install smoke alarms when we bought the cottage? I must have been stupid not to. Especially with a thatch. Would have saved their lives.

Stupid, stupid.

The post-mortem examination confirmed the cause of death; *Exposure to fire and fire effluents: toxic gases, smoke inhalation and heat.* The coroner sent me a letter informing me that he'd released the bodies and sent the relevant paperwork to the Registrar in Lymington. This meant I could register the deaths and go ahead with the funeral arrangements.

I couldn't organise anything. Since the fire, I acted on autopilot, going through the motions. Fortunately, Pat came to my rescue and, with Alisha's help, they made most of the arrangements.

PC Williamson, the family liaison officer, called.

"I thought you ought to be aware that Nick Burrows has applied to the Governor of Belmarsh prison for a Special Purpose Licence to attend his son's funeral."

"You are joking! He's the one who got someone to set fire to the cottage. How could he possibly think of attending?"

"We have no evidence of that at the moment, Mr Hamilton, and as Georgie's biological father, he has every right to attend."

"Do you know, I sometimes question whose side the police are on. I'll tell you one thing. If he does come, I won't be responsible for my actions. I'll bloody kill him!"

Maintaining her coolness, she said, "I understand how you feel, but I don't think that's going to help. And I should warn you about your threatening language. The Governor hasn't agreed yet. We'll have to wait and see."

Slamming the phone down, I yelled, "The fucking world's gone mad!"

★

The day of the funeral passed by in another blur. I barely remembered it happening, except for several scenes that remained in my head.

The huge number of people who came to pay their respects, many of whom I failed to recognise, surprised me. I assumed they'd read about the case or seen the media coverage on TV. Several of Georgie's school friends came too, many of them crying whilst carrying small bouquets or wreaths.

Margaret, weeping openly, had to be supported by Alisha. Especially when the three coffins, a maple one for Lynne, and two white ones for Georgie and Emily, were carried by the undertakers slowly into the crematorium.

Neither Lynne nor I belonged to a church. I'd asked a secular administrator to conduct the service. She'd sympathetically extracted information from Alisha and me and spoke in a reverend tone about each of their lives. She asked whether I wanted to offer a eulogy, but I wasn't up to it.

Just as well, because seeing Emily's tiny white coffin disappearing behind the curtain on its way to the incinerator, I felt my legs buckling underneath me and fought hard not to pass out.

Mercifully, I didn't have to face Nick Burrows. The Governor had carried out a risk assessment and decided not to grant the escorted visit on the grounds of public concern. Nick's short temper had resulted in a few scrapes with prison warders; he'd hardly proved to be a model prisoner. The Governor's refusal to grant him a Special Licence would have driven him mad.

When I got home, I read and re-read the many letters of condolence.

They helped greatly; a way of getting into my thick skull that my family were no longer around.

★

A week after the funeral, I received a phone message asking me to visit DI Flood and his sidekick at my local police station, Greenwich. He came straight to the point in his usual brusque manner.

"The scenes of crime officers have been busy. So have we. We've discovered the remains of a disposable lighter. Remarkably, the thumb wheel has survived and it's being checked for DNA. We'll get the results soon. We believe the perpetrator used this lighter to ignite a rag or paper and then posted it through the letter box."

"How on earth did any part of the lighter survive?"

"We believe the arsonist assumed it would be destroyed by the flames. The firemen tell us the fire developed rapidly, igniting the petrol vapours first, and then spread up the stairs, at the same time heating up the lighter on the floor. They said the plastic lighter casing enclosing the lighter fuel would have been under enormous pressure and they assume it burst, projecting the lighter away from the seat of the fire. We found it about eight feet from the front door under part of a collapsed ceiling. This protected it. The thumb wheel's in pretty good nick."

"I can't believe anyone could be so callous. It's such a cowardly thing to do." I slumped forward and stared at the ground.

"Can I get you a drink of water?" the DC said.

I shook my head. Flood carried on. "I'm sure you'd also like to know we've spent a considerable amount of time interviewing Mr Burrows at Belmarsh. We were especially keen to establish his current feelings. His ex-wife and you aren't his favourite people. He's certainly motivated."

"You could say that."

"We questioned him regarding the possibility that he arranged for a third party to carry out the arson attack."

"What did he say to that?"

"He emphatically denies any involvement. We're currently trawling through the phone calls and letters he's written since he's been inside. We're drawing up a list of candidates he may have met in Belmarsh and now released who could have been involved, directly or indirectly."

"I'm telling you, he's *got* to be behind this… no-one else could possibly have a motive." My hatred of Nick went off the scale.

"Well, maybe that's true, maybe it's not. We're digging as deeply as we can. We've found nothing out of the ordinary on your wife's computer, although it appears to be fairly new."

"Yes," I said. "Her old one became obsolete. I took it to the dump. I bought her a new one a couple of months ago."

"For the record, can you tell us which dump?" I told him.

The DS made a note in his book. Flood continued, "A search of her car has yielded nothing either."

I gave him a withering glare. "I could have saved you a lot of trouble. Of course there's nothing on her computer or in her car."

A thought struck me.

"What about this being a case of mistaken identity? Have you ruled that out?"

The DS spoke for the first time. "The previous owners rented it out and we've checked each of the occupiers of the cottage for the five years before you bought it. We also interviewed your closest neighbours. I'd say it's unlikely the arson attack was a case of mistaken identity."

DI Flood cut in. "As you know, we've also checked your computer at your office. Nothing's cropped up we can act upon. Can you think of anybody in your business dealings who might be a candidate?"

"No. No. We sell cars. Surely no one would do this if they simply thought they'd been sold a dud."

DI Flood stood up. "OK. If you think of anything else, please contact me." He handed me his card.

★

I had numerous telephone conversations with Flood and the family liaison officer, PC Williamson, over the following three months and she offered sterling support to Margaret during that time.

Despite a detailed investigation and questioning of potential witnesses, Flood discovered no link whatsoever between Nick and a possible perpetrator.

They'd checked out the list of prisoners whom he had access to and followed up everyone released from Belmarsh before the incident.

In one of our conversations he said, "We've got back the results of the DNA test on the thumb wheel of the lighter. Amazingly, it's intact. We've checked it against the current National DNA database set up in '95. Regrettably, there's no match."

He told me nothing had resulted from potential witnesses either. By the time our neighbours noticed the fire, the thatch no longer existed and the rest of the cottage had been destroyed. And CCTV didn't exist in this pretty part of Hampshire.

Flood asked, "We've eliminated Nick Burrows from any involvement with the arson attack, and a case of mistaken identity has also been ruled out. Is it possible your wife could have had a relationship with someone? And possibly that relationship had gone wrong?"

I couldn't accept he could be so brainless. I let him have it.

"I can't believe what you're suggesting. We'd been married for less than two years. We had a two-year-old daughter together. We lived a life of luxury. Why on earth would she have an affair?"

"Strange things happen."

"We were incredibly happy together – ask our friends. They'll tell you. Surely there'd be evidence… somewhere… Do you know what? You're clueless! You're *struggling* with this case, aren't you?"

He thrust his pocked face closer to mine and said, "As I've said to you before, Mr Hamilton, we're checking out *every* conceivable possibility."

★

I called RP, told him about Flood treating me as a suspect and that he wanted to pursue the idea about Lynne having an affair. He snorted down the phone. "Man's not for real. That's ridiculous."

I asked him to investigate any connections Nick may have made on the inside. I told him the police had followed up this line of enquiry, but I had more faith in RP's inimitable way of digging out a result by whatever method he chose, legal or otherwise.

I paid considerable sums of cash to RP over the next three months and he followed up numerous leads using his vast network of contacts.

But even the great RP got no nearer to solving the case.

★

On many days, I didn't bother to get dressed. There didn't seem much point. I'd pull on a dressing gown and spend hours with the curtains drawn, slumped in front of daytime television programmes.

Time had lost its relevance.

I put off sorting out my family's clothes, shoes and toys and left the bathroom cabinet exactly as it was.

I'd open the wardrobe, stare at Lynne's dresses hanging there, and then close the doors. The smell of Lynne pervaded my nostrils and I'd collapse back on the bed and roar with grief. It simply wasn't fair.

I missed her terribly. Night times were the worst. Often, I'd lay my pillows lengthways next to me in bed and sprinkle her perfume on the covers. I cuddled the bundle. I found it a comfort of sorts.

I hardly slept and rarely ate. I couldn't be bothered to cook anything. I lived on breakfast cereals mainly, the ultimate comfort food. I lost a couple of stone in three months and when I peered in the mirror each morning I barely recognised the face I occasionally shaved. I felt as if a woolly blanket enveloped me.

Alisha visited me once or twice a week. On one occasion, she exclaimed, "Look at the state of you! And the state of this place!" She yanked back the curtains, causing a shaft of sunlight to pierce the room.

I hadn't bothered to clean the house for well over a month. Dirty dishes covered the coffee table in front of the TV.

Several grubby glasses and a half-full bottle of Johnny Walker whiskey sat on a side table next to the armchair where I spent most of the day.

"You need help, James. You should see a GP. He'll prescribe anti-depressants."

She picked up the whiskey bottle, took it to the kitchen and I heard her pour the contents down the sink.

I remonstrated with her. "What are you doing? I'm fine."

"You won't be, carrying on like this. You'll kill yourself. C'mon, let's talk."

"I told you, I'm fine."

"This is you being 'fine' is it?" She looked around room. I followed her gaze. She had a point.

"Ok, perhaps I'm not fine. At least I got out of bed today. Usually, I pull the duvet over my head and stay there and don't talk to anyone or answer the phone."

"That's what I mean. That's not good."

"Yeah, but other days I do get up. I walk to Greenwich Park. We often went there together… all of us. I sit and watch other families with small children playing together."

"Well, that's better. At least you're getting out of this mess."

"Yesterday, I saw a father with his daughter skipping by his side carrying a bright pink helium-filled balloon. Her other hand tightly clasped her father's. Couldn't have been more than four. Suddenly she let go of the balloon. As it flew away, she became hysterical, realising she'd lost it forever. She started crying. Within a moment, she'd gone from joy to grief…"

Alisha hugged me as I watched my tears drip onto the back of her blouse.

She spent more and more time with me. She often held my hand and listened to my ramblings. She sometimes brought food which she cooked and stood over me insisting I eat it.

She must have been made of blotting paper, the amount of angst, pain and moodiness she absorbed. She never wavered in her support.

I felt close to madness.

Although the anti-depressants from the GP helped, they weren't the answer. Especially when mixed with alcohol.

Alisha realised I was stuck in a vicious circle of self-pity and guilt.

"I think you should get professional help. I know a counsellor. Let me make you an appointment."

"What's the point? Nothing can change the fact that Lynne and the children are gone. And after all we'd been through together…"

★

A few days later, Alisha bought me a book on dealing with grief. "If you won't see a counsellor, I suggest you read this. I'll go through it with you if you like."

The book identified the chronological stages of grief:

shock, disbelief, bargaining, anger, then ultimately, acceptance and re-energising.

I recognised these emotions from when my parents died. It took me a couple of years then before I acknowledged acceptance of their death. But that had been an accident, it wasn't premeditated. Now, I felt stuck between the disbelief and anger stages. I could never see me reaching acceptance… ever.

*

As time passed, I felt marginally better. I stopped drinking and, with Alisha's unfailing support, plus the 'happy pills', gained a semblance of normality in my life. But with no further information forthcoming regarding the murder investigation, I felt myself moving more deeply into the anger stage.

What the bloody hell were the police doing? I called Southampton police station every other day and spoke to PC Williamson. She always expressed her sympathy and empathised with my feelings. But regarding the investigation, her response remained the same.

"We're following up a couple of leads at the moment, Mr Hamilton. Rest assured we'll be in touch as soon as we have something to report." They could have employed a parrot.

Life for the rest of the world carried on as if nothing had happened. I found that difficult to accept. The sun still rose, night followed day and offices were packed with workers who commuted daily. Restaurants, pubs and cafes were full of happy, smiling people.

They still went to the cinema, to football matches or drove down to the coast at weekends with their kids giggling and shouting in the back seat.

I told Alisha, "Don't they know about Lynne and the children? Don't they care that someone amongst us is a killer?"

I wanted to scream at them. Sometimes I got as far as opening my mouth to do so.

I thought my pain might go away more quickly if I stopped constantly thinking about Lynne, Georgie and Emily. But I could never, ever forget them.

I went back to work and immersed myself in the business, becoming obsessed in every detail, more than I did before I met Lynne.

Some days it worked, some days it didn't. Pat and Peter understood my mood swings.

I met RP several times at his office to discuss progress. I noticed that he now swore and cussed a great deal, expressing his frustration. He didn't like to lose at anything. He was as convinced as me about Burrows' involvement. But the police had been down that road and closed the book on him.

I visited Lynne's mum regularly too. She acted as if her life had ended. She'd aged significantly; she looked as if someone had beaten her with a stick. I never saw her smile again.

Margaret sought solace in the church. Alisha and I were atheists. When the pain got to be too much, I wished I could have had something I could believe in.

Alisha nearly always came with me when we visited her. Margaret and I wallowed in the unfairness of it all, but Alisha would have none of it after the first few meetings.

"This is doing us no good. Let's try another approach."

She forced us to look at photos of Lynne, Georgie and Emily as cathartic therapy. "Let's concentrate on the *good* memories we have, shall we? It's what Lynne would have wanted."

The photos brought back joyful memories of Emily. She'd

inherited her mother's penetrating blue eyes, blonde hair and beaming smile. Friends teased me by saying they couldn't see anything resembling me in her features. I usually retorted, "That's a blessing."

I told them, "I loved taking her out in the pushchair to the local shops. It always took an age. Everyone was smitten with her. She'd reduce grown-ups to drooling idiots. All that goo-gooing, pulling faces and waving furiously in order to get a happy response. She always obliged."

I told Margaret and Alisha how, no matter how busy I was at work, I always got home in time for Emily's bath-time ritual.

"I'd turn the key in the lock of the front door and step inside. This energetic blonde bundle always rushed towards me with her arms stretched out in front of her, yelling 'Daddeee!' one of the first words she uttered. I'd whoosh her up in my arms and kiss her all over."

We all shed a tear…

But one question still dominated our thoughts.

Why would anyone want to kill my family if it wasn't Nick Burrows?

CHAPTER EIGHT

December 1998 – July 1999

We were dreading Christmas. We wanted to cancel it. Seeing jolly people drinking and eating themselves silly, wearing reindeer antler headbands and setting off party poppers didn't match our mood. And the ads on TV promoting kids' toys touched a particular nerve.

A week before Christmas Eve, I received a phone call from DI Flood.

"I've got good news, Mr Hamilton." He sounded upbeat for the first time.

"We've arrested someone we believe is responsible for the arson attack on your family."

"What! Who? Do we know him?"

"His name's Leroy Johnson. The Met arrested him last week for a drugs offence in Southwark, near Borough Market on London's South Bank. Although he hasn't been charged yet, we took his DNA as a matter of course and ran it through the National Computer. Early signs are that it looks like it matches the DNA found on the disposable lighter found at the crime scene."

Breathlessly, I spluttered, "Are you sure this is the man? Do we know *why* he did it?"

"No, not yet. We're waiting for confirmation from the

forensic bods, but I'm told if it's a complete match, the odds on misidentification are around seventeen million to one. We're bringing him down to Southampton nick and we'll question him this evening. I'll call you tomorrow."

I had so many other questions I wanted to ask. Did he know my family? Did he have a grudge against me? Did Nick employ him or did he act alone? I wanted to drive down to Southampton immediately, see what Johnson looked like. I fantasised about what I'd do to him to make him tell me the truth.

★

I spent that evening with Alisha at her flat in South Quay, near Canary Wharf, drinking and chatting about Johnson's arrest.

An eclectic mix of styles, mostly contemporary, adorned her living room. Ornaments and *objets'd'art* more suitable in a junk shop filled every corner.

We felt cautiously optimistic, but far from being in a mood to celebrate. Like my home, there were no decorations in the flat, not even a Christmas tree.

I didn't get any sleep that night; my mind raced, continuously examining the motive for the arson attack. At 9am the next morning, I received the promised call from DI Flood.

"We spent most of last night interviewing Leroy Johnson. There's no doubt now about the DNA evidence. It's a clear match. We're sure he did it. But the thing we're unhappy about is his apparent lack of motive. He's gone 'no comment' on us."

"He *must* be working for Nick Burrows, surely."

"If he is, he's not saying. As you know, we checked Burrows out thoroughly. Actually, we've eliminated *him* from the enquiry."

"That's crazy."

"I think it might be helpful if you came to Greenwich police station this afternoon, say three o'clock, for another chat. I'll be driving up later this morning. You can then tell us everything you know about Johnson. We can collect you or you can come in voluntarily."

"I'll be there. Although I know nothing about him."

My paranoia took hold. How would I know anything about Leroy Johnson? And Flood sounded convinced that Nick Burrows had nothing to do with the fatal arson attack.

I got to the police station in good time, and as he walked into the interview room with another detective, I yelled at him before he had a chance to speak.

"What exactly are you insinuating? I've never met Johnson. I wouldn't know him from the man in the moon."

"Let's sit down and discuss it shall we?"

Reluctantly I did.

"I'm sure you'd want us to follow up every possibility in order to get to the bottom of this case. So far, we can't find any link between Johnson and your family. So it's entirely credible that he worked on behalf of a third party. And I'm convinced it's not Burrows."

"Well, who else could it be, then?"

"We don't know yet. But let's start with you."

"Don't be ridiculous!"

"Let's deal in the facts, shall we? According to your statement, you told us that the night of the arson was the *only* time out of about twenty visits since you bought the cottage over a year ago that you didn't travel down to Lymington with your family. Your business meeting appears... *convenient*."

"Not *convenient,* as you put it. Just very important."

Ignoring me, he continued, "We checked your wife's

computer, there's not much on it. You told us you'd replaced it shortly before the arson attack."

Before I could respond, he flipped over his notebook and, reading from it said, "You told us you took the old one to the dump. Maybe there's incriminating evidence on the hard drive."

"That's absolutely crazy. I suppose you'll tell me next I paid Johnson or whatever his name is in used notes."

"Well, did you?"

"Don't be daft."

Both detectives remained silent.

"You'd have to provide a paper trail wouldn't you? You can check my bank account all day long if you want. You'll find nothing."

I realised I'd been trapped into appearing over-defensive on a theoretical point.

Flood carried on, "In the motor trade, as you well know, cash changes hands regularly, doesn't it? It would have been easy for you to get your hands on folding money. Petty cash to you, isn't it?"

"Are you seriously saying I paid Johnson in cash to murder my family?"

"Why not?"

"You cannot be serious!"

"I think there's a case to answer. The only thing missing is your motive. We're digging as deep as we can to discover what it might be."

"Dig as deep as you like. I can't believe you're pointing the finger at me. Are you going to arrest me?"

DI Flood stood and said, "Not at the moment. We'll carry on with our investigation. We'll be in touch when we get more information. You're free to go… for now."

I stumbled out of the police station in a daze. The police had obviously missed something — Nick desperately wanted revenge; he'd probably planned for me to be in the cottage as well on that fateful night.

★

Two days later, Flood called again.

"You'll be pleased to know that we've charged Leroy Johnson with murder and arson with intent to endanger life. He'll appear at Southampton Magistrates' Court tomorrow morning, 23rd of December, at 10am for the charge to be officially read to him."

"And what about me? I assume you've finally come to your senses?"

"We've taken advice about charging from the CPS. They think we have an excellent chance of getting a guilty verdict against Johnson. As far as you're concerned, we're keeping your file open pending further investigation."

"Not much I can do then, is there?"

"No."

I told him I wanted to attend the magistrates' court and sit in the public gallery.

"It's your call. It'll only last a few minutes. The case'll be adjourned and Johnson will appear at a Crown Court, probably Winchester, for a preliminary hearing after Christmas. After that there'll be a plea and case management hearing and he'll be given a trial date."

Nothing would stop me going. I wanted to see what he looked like, judge his demeanour, anything that might help me understand *why* he did it.

★

On the morning of the trial, a cold, blustery day, I caught the 7.39am train from Waterloo for the hour-and-a-half's journey to Southampton Central. I wore a thick overcoat with a high collar, which I turned up against the wind chill.

Unsmiling commuters scurried to their offices within the metropolis of London from the station. I negotiated my way to the train against this oncoming tide of human life and found a seat in an empty first-class carriage.

In the cab from the station to the Magistrates' Court, I felt the tension rising in my body; my mouth felt dry and my stomach had a knot in it.

The southerly gusts of wind from the Solent chilled the air more so than in London. As I arrived outside the court, a couple of men had gathered outside, braving the elements. I assumed they were reporters. The photographers were easier to spot with the tools of their trade swinging loosely around their necks.

I half-ran inside the modern steel and concrete building. I checked with the receptionist, who told me to go to Court Four upstairs. Panelled floor to ceiling in light brown wood and stylishly complemented by blue cloth seats, the courtroom appeared surprisingly light and airy.

Sitting in the public gallery at the back of the courtroom, facing the bench, by 9.45am, I watch the visitors taking their seats for the first case of the day. Half were taken by the time the magistrates filed in behind the bench. DI Flood entered with a colleague and offered me the faintest nod of acknowledgement.

I felt a surge of anticipation. I'd soon see the killer of my family. I forced myself to keep cool.

Without ceremony, Leroy Johnson appeared from a side door, handcuffed to a security guard, who led him to the dock.

Dressed in a pair of loose-fitting, faded blue jeans and a plain white T-shirt covering his black, scrawny body, Johnson looked in need of a good meal. He couldn't have weighed much more than ten or eleven stone. His sharply angular face and closely shaven dark head emphasised his large sticking-out ears and furtive eyes, which initially scanned the courtroom. I guessed his age at around twenty-five.

The magistrates, two middle-aged men and an older woman, each shuffled their papers in front of them. The Madam Chairman, addressing the defendant as Mr Johnson, asked him to sit down.

As she read out the charges, Johnson stared down at his feet in total disinterest. She asked him to confirm his name and date of birth. He answered in a thin, reedy voice. My guess had been spot-on.

Madam Chairman announced a date for the preliminary hearing at Winchester Crown Court in a week's time.

She remanded Johnson in custody and the security guard took him down. The whole scenario lasted under four minutes. I sat silently in the courtroom after Johnson had left the dock. As another defendant entered to face a charge of driving whilst disqualified, I stood up and filed out of the courtroom.

At last, I'd seen the man who'd created such a monumental difference in my life. Getting justice for Lynne, Georgie and Emily had finally begun.

Outside on the concourse, I asked Flood how long he thought it would take to get to trial. He told me curtly that with the current workload it should be around next July or August. A lot would depend on whether Johnson pleaded guilty or not.

He also said there was little point in me attending the preliminary hearing at Winchester, since they'd only be dealing with administrative matters and court management. And most likely, Johnson would appear in court via a video link from Winchester prison.

I asked him where I stood. He said, "We always keep an open mind until the result of the trial."

A week later, PC Williamson called to say that Johnson's arraignment hearing had been set for the 3rd March 1999.

★

Johnson's murder charge made little difference to my emotional well-being. I still wouldn't have any idea *why* he did it until the main trial.

But at least someone was in the frame.

I called RP. I wanted him to find out everything he could about Leroy Johnson. I assumed the police and the CPS would be checking him out too, but I'm sure they wouldn't include me on their circulation list. Especially as Flood hadn't ruled out my involvement.

I explained to RP Flood's insinuation that I'd been involved in the arson attack. "He really gets under my skin, you know?"

RP shook his head. "Sometimes, I wonder about our wonderful police force. Officers like him should investigate what's under their bloody noses, not go off on a hypothetical thesis."

"Do you want me to get background info on him too?"

"Can't do any harm, can it?"

★

Reminders of my loss were never far away. The whole of London appeared full of happy families looking forward to the New Year. On New Year's Eve, I didn't know what to do. I thought I'd stay at home, get a takeaway, try to read or immerse myself in business planning, wishing the night away. Instead, at Alisha's insistence, we visited Margaret.

She cooked us a meal, glad of something to do, I suspect, and I filled her in on the latest information regarding Johnson.

She said, "How could anybody do such an evil thing? It's beyond me." She grew close to tears as she shook her head.

As the witching hour struck, we watched Big Ben chiming twelve o'clock on TV and I proposed a tearful toast to the belief that justice would prevail.

Getting home in the early hours, I felt particularly mawkish, something that regularly happened. I looked through Lynne's dressing table drawers and our sideboards, containing all kinds of knick-knacks and photos, through fogged-up eyes.

I stumbled across a stopwatch Lynne had given me for my forty-first birthday. The inscription read, *To James. There's a time for everything. Love, Lynne. November 1996.*

The context then was keeping a record of my running times. Now the words had greater significance to me. Time to grieve? Time to get justice? Time to move on?

I thought 'moving on', as well-meaning friends had suggested, would constitute a gross act of betrayal. Even if I got the justice we craved, 'moving on' still didn't feel the right thing to do.

I often talked to Lynne, Georgie and Emily when I spent time alone at home. Ridiculous, I know, but it consoled me.

I particularly longed to hold Emily in my arms once again, imagining I could see her, smell her, hear her.

The thought of Johnson getting a significant prison sentence kept me sane. And there had to be a way of discovering Nick's involvement. He'd pay for it too.

*

A few weeks later, I visited RP's palatial office to go through what he'd discovered about Johnson and DI Flood. He reached inside a drawer and pulled out two files.

"Flood's got an interesting past. Here's a copy of his file you can keep."

I quickly scanned the neatly typewritten notes. Flood's CV showed him to be an ambitious model police officer, working his way through the ranks after joining as a probationer straight after leaving school. Along the way, he'd received several Commissioners' Commendations for outstanding commitment, courage and dedication.

The latest Commendation referred in glowing terms to Flood's role in dismantling a prolific south coast drugs network, resulting in lengthy prison sentences for the gang's leader.

RP had hand-written a lengthy note in the margin, I assumed because of the further enquiries he'd made. It referred to Flood's wife being the victim of a hit and run 'accident' a month after the gang leader's imprisonment.

As she cycled home from work one evening, a witness reported that a black BMW, complete with darkened windows, drove straight into her. She ended up in a coma in an intensive care ward for a month before Flood had the daunting task of turning off her life support machine. She never had a chance.

RP, noticing that I'd stopped flicking over the pages of the report at this point, said, "Poor bugger. To make matters worse, he's got two children, both girls, aged three and five at the time.

"The police are convinced that the gang were responsible. As you'd expect, they threw every available resource at the case for two years without success. Then the investigation ceased, due to government cuts in police funding. After that, my source tells me that Flood devotes every moment of his spare time trying to track down the perpetrators."

"That explains a lot," I said.

RP handed me another smartly bound folder. "Here's Johnson's file. He's certainly not had the best that life can offer, that's for sure." Considering it had only taken him a few weeks to put together, the exceptionally detailed dossier covered Johnson's entire life story.

"You can take this with you for more bedtime reading, but in essence he's been on the wrong side of the tracks most of his life."

As I flicked through the dossier, RP explained that Johnson was expelled from school and ended up, aged sixteen, in Feltham Young Offenders' Institute, renowned for its appalling treatment of inmates. He'd 'graduated' with little education and learnt no employment skills, despite the opportunities the Institute offered.

He'd drifted into ever-increasing levels of crime; burglary, drug dealing and had served three years from 1991 to 1994 at Pentonville for setting light to a warehouse. He claimed the owner had put him up to it, needing the insurance money to bail out his failing business. Fortunately, he'd harmed no one. The local police in the Elephant and Castle area in South London knew him well.

Shortly before Christmas 1998, nearly five months after the fatal arson attack on my cottage, the police arrested him on suspicion of drug dealing, but they didn't charge him.

Waving the folder in his direction, I asked RP, "Does any of this explain *why* he set fire to the cottage?"

"No. Except, obviously, he doesn't give a shit about anyone else but himself. I get the impression he'd do anything for money. You'll see the psychiatric report suggests Johnson felt empowered by the original arson attack; felt in control."

"That's sick."

"You're not kidding. It's obvious to me that, somehow, Burrows approached Johnson to be his hit man via a third party. No other scenario presents itself so clearly."

"Yes, I know. But Flood told me he'd followed up that line of enquiry. He's interviewed Nick several times and checked out possible links with Johnson, but none showed up. There appears to be no connection."

"Mm…" RP said. "Well I hope he tried hard enough. It wouldn't be the first time the police had screwed up."

★

I spent the evening going through Johnson's dossier in minute detail, looking for any clues that RP may have missed. Goodness knows how he got this stuff. He must have contacts everywhere in all sorts of places. I suspected he had one inside the Metropolitan Police Force with access to the National Computer.

The report made compelling reading. Johnson was born whilst his drug-addicted mother was on remand at Holloway prison. She'd bludgeoned another woman to death in a jealous rage whilst high on steroids and heroin. The jury found her guilty and the judge sentenced her to life imprisonment. A photocopy of Johnson's birth certificate read 'father unknown', although from Johnson's colouring, he was black. Johnson ended up in a care home, the first of many.

He'd suffered an unhappy, neglectful childhood. He got into drug dealing at ten years old, the same age as Georgie when he died.

How differently their lives had turned out. Through no fault of his own, Georgie, who had the possibility of doing something worthwhile with his life, was dead, and this scumbag, offering nothing to humanity, still lived.

The psychiatric report concluded that Johnson had difficulty empathising with people. He also possessed a craving for power, prestige and financial reward and possessed an inability to express remorse.

Motivated by a desire to feel important, he craved being the centre of attention. He wanted people to think of him as clever and useful.

When I finished reading the dossier, I threw it down hard onto the floor and kicked it to the other side of the room shouting, "Fuck you!" How could this apology for a man take the lives of three vulnerable, beautiful human beings without giving it a second thought?

I wanted to get into his prison cell and beat him up with a club until he turned to pulp, and when he couldn't take any more, I'd set fire to him.

Then he *would* be the centre of attention.

★

There wasn't much more we could do, except wait until Johnson's arraignment hearing on 3rd of March 1999. Despite the evidence against him, he pleaded not guilty and a trial date was set for later in the year, 28th July, at Winchester Crown Court.

If I couldn't get hold of PC Williamson, sympathetic as

always, I called DI Flood at least weekly during the next two months, ever mindful of his wife's tragic demise.

I tried to dredge up sympathy for him but without success. His fixation on finding a way for me to be involved in the arson attack beggared belief. I asked him every time we spoke if I was still under suspicion.

"I like to keep an open book, that's all. There's no further evidence I've discovered that warrants anything more than that... at the moment."

When I asked him about progress on the Johnson case, he told me more than I thought he might. Maybe he reasoned if he told me stuff, it would make me open up too.

He said, "The CPS are focussing on three issues: the DNA on Johnson's lighter found at the crime scene, his whereabouts at the time and the complete lack of motivation, other than something to do with his personality problems.

"Before going 'no comment' on us, Johnson said he'd mislaid his lighter and that someone else must have used it to start the fire. But he couldn't explain how it got from London to Lymington.

"He said at the time of the arson attack he'd been drinking in a pub near where he lived in Bermondsey but I'm not convinced by his alibi."

"That's good stuff, isn't it? Has he said anything about Nick Burrows being involved?"

"No. He hasn't. This is what's troubling the CPS. There's a total lack of motive for the killing. It's the missing link."

I fervently hoped the prosecution at Johnson's trial would apply enough pressure under cross-examination to make Johnson reveal Nick as the instigator. Then Flood would have to accept my innocence.

★

We tried to get on with our lives and dealt with it in different ways. I poured more energy into my business. Peter, still keen to atone for Hartley's embezzlement, suggested that now we knew Hartley resided in Belmarsh, we should visit him – try to recover the funds, if they hadn't been spent already.

I liked the idea. I didn't want to go down the route of informing the police, go through an endless investigation proving the fraud and it becoming general knowledge in the trade.

However, Hartley refused to see us. We estimated that with time off for good behaviour, he'd be released on parole around August 1999. We made a diary note to follow him up then.

Margaret was still a mess. Nothing would ever get her back to her usual sunny self. Alisha spent a lot of her time worrying about me.

I hoped that once Johnson was banged up and Nick's involvement confirmed, we could say justice had prevailed.

CHAPTER NINE

July – August 1999

Alisha badly wanted to come with me to Johnson's trial, but her boss insisted on taking his annual leave that week and she had to stand in for him.

"I want to go to see what the bastard looks like." Her anger matched mine.

I didn't trust myself to contain my emotions. I asked Pat if she'd come down to Winchester with me.

"Of course, James. I'd be happy to."

On Sunday, 27th July, we drove down to the beautiful medieval city, looking resplendent and majestic in the summer evening sun, and checked into the Hotel Du Vin boutique hotel at 7pm. The trial began the next day at 10am at Winchester Crown Court, with Judge Julian Carter QC presiding. Two weeks had been set aside for the hearing.

Lynne's mother couldn't face the ordeal of seeing her daughter's killer. We left her at home in the care of a next door neighbour.

Waking to another fine, sunny, cloudless day, we walked the four hundred yards to the Law Courts at the top of the city via an attractive cobbled courtyard. A sense of anticipation came close to overwhelming me.

Climbing the twenty steps to the imposing entrance of the

brick and flint four-storey building, I turned to Pat and said, "At last we'll hear *why* he did it."

"I hope so, James."

A cameraman and several photographers thrust their equipment in our faces as we reached the entrance. We pushed our way through them.

We checked the board, which confirmed the case was being heard in courtroom three on the second floor. A receptionist directed us to the public entrance and the fifty-seat gallery on the third floor which looked down onto the courtroom, directly facing the bench where the judge presided.

The first hour of the morning proved to be a non-event. Most of the time the lawyers spent empanelling the jury; selecting the twelve members from the twenty who'd been standing-by.

Reluctantly, we took the opportunity to sit outside, feeling the sun on our faces. I preferred to crack on. But at least we avoided milling about in the concourse with other people attending different trials. I climbed the stairs on more than one occasion to check with the court usher when the trial would start. I needed something to do.

By 11.15, we were sitting in the visitors' gallery, full to bursting point for the trial of Leroy Johnson for murder and arson with intent to endanger life. There'd been a great deal of media coverage, which I'd studiously ignored. Others were obviously intrigued.

The court official finally swore in the jury and Johnson, accompanied by a prison officer, whose bulk emphasised the defendant's gaunt body, sat in the dock.

He wore an ill-fitting dark suit and black tie, designed to add a modicum of respectability to the proceedings. He still looked in need of a good meal. As the court official read out the charges, Johnson wore the same expression and projected the same air of disinterest he'd shown at his first hearing in the magistrates' court.

I'd never attended a Crown Court case before. I'd watched the dramatic cases portrayed in *Kavanah QC* on TV. Everything was sorted within an hour. How different to the real world. The legal process, slow and laborious, examining every minute detail of the case, wasn't remotely like the TV programme. I almost screamed, 'Get on with it!'

The amount of paperwork involved staggered me. Each team of barristers had on their desks numerous Lever-Arch files with yellow Post-It stickers marking particular pages.

Judge Carter, every inch the stereotype of a High Court judge, bespectacled and resplendent in his red robe and parchment-coloured wig, peered at his laptop, occasionally prodding the keyboard with a single finger.

He invited the chief prosecutor to make his opening speech.

Mr Nigel Smithson QC, urbane, tall, elegant, in his late forties, with a shock of grey hair sticking out from under his wig, struck an imposing figure. He spoke with a public-school accent, conveying immense confidence.

Making eye contact with the jury directly, he said, "The prosecution case is straightforward. You will hear compelling evidence that will prove conclusively that the defendant is guilty of the sickening, pre-meditated murder of three people, including a two-year-old little girl.

"There are three key elements to this case which lead directly to this conclusion. Firstly, the evidence the prosecution will present will show that he knew a defenceless family lay sleeping at the cottage in Lymington on that fateful night."

He paused before continuing.

"Secondly, DNA on a cigarette lighter found at the crime scene has subsequently been directly matched to the defendant. An expert will inform us that the odds on misidentification are around seventeen million to one.

"And finally, the defendant has been given every opportunity to provide an alibi regarding his whereabouts on the evening in question. It is the prosecution's view that this alibi is not watertight.

"Putting these points together suggests there is only one suspect in this case. The defendant in the dock."

He expanded on each of these points for over an hour. His succinct, matchless performance significantly raised my confidence in getting a result. I couldn't possibly see how any jury could fail to convict Johnson. But we still were no nearer to finding out *why* he did it.

The defence barrister, Mr Quentin Renfrew QC, short, balding and paunchy with an arrogant manner, looked the complete opposite of the prosecutor. He stood and faced the jury, grabbing the lapels on his robe with both hands as he did so.

"I would take issue with my learned friend over his description of the evidence about to be presented as 'compelling'. We'll present a witness who will tell us that at the time of the arson, the defendant had been drinking in a pub in London.

"Another weakness in the prosecution's case is the defendant's complete lack of motivation. It defies belief that he'd commit this act for fun.

"Despite a great deal of investigation by the police, they cannot establish any connection whatsoever between Leroy Johnson and the Hamilton family.

"The police have also investigated whether the defendant worked on behalf of a third party, but once again, they have produced no evidence of this whatsoever."

I wanted to yell out, 'It's obvious he worked for Nick Burrows. They haven't looked hard enough'.

Mr Renfrew continued, "The only real evidence the prosecution have is the DNA on the lighter and this brings me to the circumstances of how it came to be matched to the defendant's DNA. The defence maintain this evidence should *not* form part of the prosecution case."

Judge Carter intervened. "Mr Renfrew, do I understand you correctly? Are you making the point that you don't think this evidence should be presented to the jury?"

"Yes, your honour."

"Then I'll hear your argument about the admissibility of the DNA evidence in their absence." Turning to the jury he said, "Please go to your room until you are asked to return by the usher."

To the gallery, he said, "The public and the press may remain, but I would remind you there can be no reporting of any argument in the absence of the jury."

As they shuffled out to the sound of murmuring from the gallery, I turned to Pat and whispered, "What's going on? This is ridiculous."

She held my arm. I think she thought I'd make a scene.

Mr Renfrew stood and spoke directly to the judge.

Speaking carefully and deliberately, he said, "Your honour, the defence believes the DNA evidence is inadmissible in this case. The current legislation states that the Forensic Science Service can retain only the DNA of people *convicted* of a recordable offence, not simply *arrested*. This is precisely the case with the defendant. His arrest never led to a charge for the alleged drug dealing offence five months after the arson attack. The DNA should therefore have been destroyed. It wasn't.

"Unfortunately, human error caused it to be left on the Police computer's hard-drive and, not unsurprisingly, Mr Johnson's DNA matched it." He paused, then emphasised, "*Illegally.*"

Mr Renfrew made this final point with a dramatic flourish, stabbing a finger several times at a file on his desk. The courtroom fell completely silent awaiting the judge's comment.

Before he had time to consider, Mr Nigel Smithson jumped to his feet and asked the judge for a brief adjournment to give his team time to respond. The judge agreed, stood, bowed and made his way to his chambers.

Clenching and unclenching my fists, I said to Pat under my breath, "I can't believe this. It's a complete joke."

The prosecution team animatedly discussed this latest development whilst we filed outside the courtroom in silence, wondering where this latest development would lead us.

Half an hour later, at 3.30, the clerk ushered us back into court.

Judge Carter asked for the chief prosecutor's response.

"Your honour, as I said in my opening speech, the evidence we shall present *is* absolutely clear, compelling and incontrovertible. However, I accept the law is also clear on this issue. May I request that you consider using your discretion in this case and admit the evidence? We are talking about an extremely serious crime with the loss of three lives, including a two-year-old. If this evidence is not admissible the case against the defendant will collapse and we don't believe that justice will be served."

The judge gathered his thoughts and spoke equally slowly and emphatically.

"Mr Smithson, I will ensure that justice is served in my court. I will adjourn now and make a ruling in the morning." He stood and bowed as the clerk shouted, "All rise."

The journalists rushed out of the court to file their copy – even with reporting restrictions in place, I speculated what dramatic headlines they'd conjure up.

How could the police and the CPS have screwed up in such a spectacular way?

I turned to Pat again and said, "How the hell did the case get this far? Surely, the judge can see as plainly as everyone else in the court that Johnson's guilty."

"I know, James. This is a farce."

We went back to the hotel after waiting on the concourse a while to avoid the press, although they knew as well as we did I couldn't comment on the trial.

RP had asked to be kept informed of developments. I called him and told him what had happened.

"For fuck's sake! I can't believe the judge would even need to *think* about it!" He thought Johnson's conviction was a formality.

Now Judge Carter had to make the call.

*

After a sleepless night, we arrived at the court early the next morning. I spoke to the prosecuting solicitor in the public area outside the courtroom to get an idea of the way the case may develop.

"The judge's decision is straightforward. According to the letter of the law, the defence is correct and the judge could accept the point. But we believe there's a strong case for him to use his discretion and common sense and allow the DNA evidence to be presented to the jury. We think he'll agree. I shouldn't worry too much about it."

As he entered the courtroom, he turned and added, "Oh, there's one other thing. I don't know whether you're aware of this. If the judge doesn't admit this evidence and Johnson's acquitted, under the existing laws of double jeopardy, he can't be tried again for the same crime. I don't think it'll come to that but I thought you should know the facts."

Again, the visitors' gallery filled to bursting point and I heard the usher turn people away. The air in the courtroom crackled with static. I expected a bolt of lightning and a rumble of thunder at any moment.

Johnson sat in the dock avoiding eye contact with anyone with his arms folded, a slightly puzzled expression on his face. The legal teams were chatting and shuffling their papers waiting for Judge Carter to appear from his chambers.

As he entered to the familiar words from the usher asking us to rise, the anticipation of his verdict on the admittance of the DNA evidence met with a resounding silence from the gallery and the lawyers.

Judge Carter peered down through his glasses to the laptop on his bench. After a moment spent scrolling, he looked up and said, "Under the 1994 Criminal Justice and Public Order Act, the law is very clear. If any person or persons are arrested but not charged or are acquitted, any DNA data and samples taken have to be destroyed."

He removed his glasses and addressed the lawyers. "I have given careful consideration to the facts surrounding this case and have concluded that because the defendant had only been rearrested on the basis of the *original* DNA test which should have been destroyed, the prosecution cannot present this evidence to the jury. We must be mindful of the defendant's human rights in this matter. Therefore I am directing the jury to acquit the defendant."

A united, audible gasp from the visitors' gallery, punctuated by shouts of 'No!' resounded loudly across the courtroom. I thought someone might start throwing things at the judge. The prosecution team glared at him.

Johnson's face broke into a supercilious smile.

Judge Carter invited Mr Smithson to comment. He stood and with a defeated expression on his face said, "We offer no other evidence against the defendant, your honour."

The judge asked the usher to recall the jury. Once they had settled, he informed them of what had transpired.

"Under these circumstances, I am directing you to pass a verdict of not guilty."

Two of the female members of the jury looked astounded. Their mouths visibly gaped in surprise. Other members looked perplexed. None of them expected the trial to be over so swiftly.

Despite the judge and both legal teams knowing that, given the overwhelming odds on Johnson being guilty, he'd walk free.

He could go to the football, have a drink down the pub and continue his nefarious trades in drugs, petty crime and vicious assault.

Judge Carter, speaking directly to Johnson, said, "You are free to go."

Every muscle in my body tensed up. I wanted to leap down from the gallery, rush at Johnson and squeeze his scrawny neck until his face turned puce. I'd hold my grasp until his life ebbed away.

Instead, I stood gripping the back of the seat in front of me so tightly, my knuckles turned white.

All the time I'd been in court, I'd absorbed every nuance, gesture and movement Johnson made. I never took my eyes off him. As he stood down from the dock, his smile grew into a wide grin. Finding my voice, I exploded, the words tumbling out of my mouth in a torrent.

"Does it matter *how* the bloody DNA evidence was collected? The fact is it exists and it's been matched to him." I jabbed a finger in Johnson's direction.

Pat tried, unsuccessfully, to pull me down back into my seat.

"You're all a disgrace. He's taken away my family. I can't believe he's walking free. You should be ashamed of yourselves. Do you call this justice? Never mind *his* human rights. What about mine? And how can you possibly defend a man like this?"

I spat the last remark directly at the defence counsel sitting in the well of the courtroom below me. The judge glared up at me and the rest of the gallery. He made a feeble attempt to get me to be quiet by waving his right hand up and down. He stood, bowed, and made for the sanctuary of his chambers.

The barristers and their clerks busied themselves clearing up the reams of papers and files from their desks and the defence team never once glanced up at me. The disempowered jury filed out of the courtroom silently, staring straight-ahead looking sheepish.

I'd assumed Johnson would serve at least twenty-five years in a maximum-security jail. I'd fantasised what life inside for a child murderer would be like. Not nice, I imagined. Now, he was out. Free. At large.

And I still didn't know *why* he'd set fire to my cottage.

★

We sat in the visitors' gallery for fifteen minutes whilst everyone else slowly filed out, like a funeral procession. Pat stroked my hand in an effort to calm me down. My whole body felt clammy.

When we left the court and made our way to the concourse, the prosecuting solicitor and the chief prosecution barrister were waiting for us. They ushered us to a quieter corner of the public area.

"I can't believe the case has collapsed," the solicitor said. "We were sure the judge would see it our way. I'm sorry."

Mr Smithson, the barrister, who'd appeared so confident in his opening address, appeared equally contrite. "I think Judge Carter's wrong in his assessment. He should have used his discretion. Do you want me to apply for an appeal?"

I responded, "What a fucking joke! Why bother? It's a complete waste of time. You can stuff the legal system. The Court of Appeal will find another loophole. Let's get out of here."

Turning my back on them, I ushered a shell-shocked Pat down the steps towards the exit, making our way back to the Hotel Du Vin. As we got closer to the door, DI Flood appeared, looking furious.

"What can I say? It's a shambles."

I shot him a withering glance as I strode past him and waved away the journalists who'd gathered outside.

They were shouting questions at me at the same time as a couple of photographers were firing away. I knew if I said anything more, I'd regret it and do something stupid.

I didn't know how to break the news to Margaret. Her heart had already been shattered. News of Johnson's acquittal might push her over the edge.

We checked out of the hotel. I asked Pat to drive back to London. I didn't feel in a fit state to do so. I was a strong candidate for being done for road rage.

Before leaving, I called RP. "Roger, the trial's over. We're driving back to London now. You can guess the outcome of the judge's verdict."

"You're not telling me the judge has acquitted Johnson?"

"That's exactly what he's done. Johnson's free. Apparently, *his* human rights outrank mine. Do you believe that?"

I explained the judge's interpretation of the law.

"Bloody hell! The man's not fit to judge a beauty contest. I'm sorry, James. Did they say you could appeal?"

"Yeah, but what's the point? Johnson can't be tried again. The law's crap."

I called Alisha, told her the news.

She couldn't speak at first. Then she exploded.

"God, I'm so angry! Is that it? Nothing's going to happen to Johnson? That's so fucking unfair!"

The journey back to London continued in angry silence. I devoted most of it to planning to get justice for Lynne, Georgie and Emily in my own way and to discover why they were murdered.

Over the following weeks, I had many imaginary conversations with Lynne. I knew she wouldn't want me to take the law into my own hands. She'd think it too dangerous.

I told her I'd never be able to live with myself until I'd dealt with the killer or killers of my family.

PART THREE

PART THREE

CHAPTER TEN

August − September 1999

I asked Alisha to come with me to Lynne's mother to explain that the judge had acquitted Johnson on a technicality. Margaret's body language and demeanour confirmed that the loss of her daughter and grandchildren had already destroyed her.

"Whatever happened to him, it wouldn't bring my daughter and the children back would it?"

Every flat surface of her living room displayed photos of Lynne, Georgie and Emily. I imagined Margaret holding conversations with them too, just like me.

Over the next few weeks, I saw Alisha a great deal. I asked her how she felt about Johnson. "I'd like to hang him up by his goolies and leave him to rot! I wouldn't mind doing that to the judge and the defence lawyers as well."

I thought as time passed, my rage, at fever pitch at the time of Johnson's acquittal, would evaporate and I'd slowly come to terms with what had happened. But I couldn't get through the fury phase, which grew stronger by the day.

I worked it off by punishing myself, going on ridiculously long runs and working out in the gym. My arms could hardly push open the front door when I got home. Every day felt as dark as night.

The feeling of unfinished business constantly resided in the pit of my stomach. Nightmares interrupted my sleep. Flashes of Johnson appeared before me, laughing, drinking and blowing cigarette smoke into my face.

Another horrendous dream witnessed the cottage engulfed by flames, fire engines' flashing blue lights and firefighters resolutely aiming their hoses at the charred remains. The sound track of Lynne with Emily in her arms and Georgie screaming in terror as they tried to escape whilst I stood by, helpless, played continuously.

Now I dreaded going to bed. Often, I didn't bother. I'd sit up scheming how I could end Johnson's life. I felt like getting a gun and shooting him dead, not caring what became of me. But then, my life would be over, spent sewing mailbags in prison for the next twenty years. I needed to dream up a cleverer way to take revenge and get away with it.

I reasoned that only then, the nightmares would end.

★

I decided to see RP. Although he specialised in surveillance, he came across as dependable, with a knack for getting things sorted.

His first words were, "I don't think I've ever known a case like this. For God's sake! The judge must be living in cloud cuckoo land. Upholding the law is one thing, but not using bloody common sense is another." He brought down a clenched fist onto his opulent desk with a thud.

I explained my increasing anger symptoms, the sleepless nights, the feeling of inadequacy and my hatred of that scumbag, Johnson.

"The only way I can carry on with my life is to get justice

for my family. I don't mean going through the courts either."

"James, I understand. Really, I do. However, you do realise the risk you'd be taking? Suppose it went wrong and you were caught?"

"OK, so what? My life's shit, anyway. I feel if I do something dumb and shoot him in broad daylight, in a funny sort of way, he's won. I want to be smarter than that. You're good at this stuff. You've been around. Help me sort this out."

He flipped his pen up and down, holding it between his first two fingers, weighing up my request. "Are you sure you *really* want to do this?"

"Roger, I'll go bloody insane if I do nothing. I can't simply walk away from this. I need to sort out Johnson and deal with Burrows once he's released. Otherwise, my life's not worth living. It's not fair that Lynne, Georgie and Emily are dead and this… this little shit's still around, laughing at us. You tell me what the scum-bag adds to civilisation. I'll tell you what, fuck all!"

"OK. I'll think about it. Give me a few days to put something together. I've a got a rough idea how we can sort this out."

★

RP's positive attitude encouraged me. I didn't care about the cost, which I knew would be considerable, or what methods he used to get results.

He called me a week later to set up a meeting back in his office.

"OK, I've come up with a plan. I don't know what you'll think about it, but, frankly, I believe it's the only option you've got."

"I'm all ears. If you can't get this sorted, no one can."

"Um, we'll see. I've got several ideas how we can deal with Johnson, but if we do, that's the end of the trail. We'll never know for sure if Burrows is involved."

"He must be."

"But there's no evidence, is there? Just a strong motive. I think we need to establish, finally, once and for all, whether there's a connection between Burrows and Johnson. The police have got nowhere and I've run out of ideas, apart from the one I'm about to propose to you. Johnson holds the key. We need to get up close and personal to him."

I frowned and said, "But how? I can't. He knows who I am."

"Well that's it. I propose we set a 'honey trap'."

"A what?"

"A 'honey trap'. Listen, most men lose their senses when an attractive woman comes on to them. They let their guard down. Their brains turn to mush. Another part of their anatomy takes over. I don't know why. Blame it on Adam and Eve. All I know is it works." RP's lips creased into a knowing smile.

"I suppose you're right. But who do you have in mind?"

"There's only one person that fits the bill perfectly. She's motivated, she's bright and she's not a bad looker."

"You don't mean …"

"I mean Alisha. I met her at your wedding and Lynne mentioned how close they were. She also told me they've been bosom buddies forever, which is why she went to Florida with her to help track down Burrows and Georgie. She's got balls, too. Do you agree?"

"Well, yes… She has, that's for sure."

RP continued. "I think she can get *very* close to Johnson,

get his confidence, learn stuff about Burrows, the arson attack and anything else that'll help us know who's behind this… mess." He raised a hand a few inches above his desk and waved it across his notes.

"I assume Johnson's never seen her?"

"Er… no. She never came to the court. Pat came instead. He'd know me for sure. I made a fuss there. But how far do you want her to go?"

"Well, I guess that's up to her. Only she can determine that."

"Won't Johnson be suspicious? Having someone come on to him?"

"It's possible. But believe me, men can be incredibly gullible when it comes to women. And at least Johnson and Alisha share the same ethnic background, don't they?"

He sat back in his chair, his customary pose after making a crucial point.

Then he sat forward again and stared at me intensely. "Why don't you put it to her, get a reaction? To be honest, I can't think of any other way forward. If she's up for it there are many advantages. We'd get access to his mobile phone, I assume he's got one, and email if he uses it. If not, we can bug his home if we needed to."

I knew Alisha felt as angry as me about Johnson's acquittal. As I made my way back to my office, RP's idea grew on me. The more I thought about it, the keener I got. If we'd simply sorted out Johnson – I speculated how RP would handle that aspect – there'd still be a feeling of unfinished business with Nick Burrows. He had a further four years to serve, assuming he didn't get time off for good behaviour.

I didn't know if I could wait that long.

★

Over dinner with Alisha at one of her favourite restaurants close to Canary Wharf, I broached the subject.

When we got to the coffee, I said, "If you do it, Alisha, think of the positives." I reprised RP's list. She sat silently for a while, contemplating my proposal.

"I can see what your brilliant private eye is trying to achieve. He's right about this being the only chance we've got to see if Nick's involved. The question is how far do I have to go to get the evidence?"

"That's entirely down to you, Alisha. No one else can decide. Why don't we take it a step at a time?"

"God, I'm so bloody angry about what happened! I can't believe that idiot of a judge let Johnson go free. But you're asking me to flaunt myself in front of a complete arsehole who'll do anything for money, even murder someone. I don't know… I loved Lynne… and the kids…so much. I'll have to think about it."

Feeling a pang of conscience about even considering RP's scheme, I said, "Look I'm sorry. Maybe it isn't a good idea." I reached for her hand across the table.

"No. No. I understand, really I do." She stared into the distance for a moment before turning to me again.

"I haven't flirted with anyone for years. Men haven't exactly been top of my agenda. Not sure if I've still got the knack." She smiled weakly at her self-deprecation.

"OK," I said. "Come on, let me walk you home. We can talk more next week." As we got closer to her apartment, she laid her head on my shoulder. I found it strangely comforting. No words passed between us until we got to the door to her apartment. She opened it and turned as I gave her a peck on the cheek. She returned the kiss, but softly on my lips before saying, "Goodnight, James. I'll call you tomorrow." She closed the door gently behind her.

I'd not experienced such an intimate moment since Lynne's death over a year before. I tried to understand her motive. Maybe she was practising her ability to flirt.

Maybe it meant something more ...

*

The next morning, whilst sorting out my laundry, my phone rang.

"Hi, James. It's Alisha. Thanks for supper last night."

"No problem. Did you think about what we discussed?"

"I've thought of nothing else. I've gone over and over it in my mind. Lynne and I were like sisters, you know. I'm like you... I couldn't live with myself if I did nothing. I'll do whatever it takes. I just hope I can live up to your faith in my skill as a *femme fatale.*"

"Really? Are you sure?"

"Yes. I'm sure."

"That's great. I'll arrange a meeting, the three of us. We can go through the plan in detail."

I called RP with the news. He sounded delighted and we arranged to meet at his office in the next few days. He said this would give him time to carry out surveillance on Johnson, get an idea on where he lived, the people he mixed with, which pubs he frequented.

A week later, we met up at RP's office. Alisha had already arrived. I barely recognised her.

She'd had her hair dyed bottle-blonde and cropped in an elfin style, highlighting her high, dark cheekbones. She wore glossy pink lipstick and thick mascara, emphasising her brown eyes. Black high heel boots and a black leather coat completed the effect.

Unbuttoning the coat, she revealed a figure-hugging cherry-red short dress, just the respectable side of tarty.

She gave me a twirl saying, "Well, what d'ya think? Do I pass the test?"

"Wow! Definitely gets my vote."

"Mine too," RP said, as he appeared at his office door and invited us in.

Alisha, clearly enjoying the attention, said, "Of course, I'll only dress like this once I come into contact with Johnson. I don't want to be arrested for being a hooker before we get going."

RP emphasised the fact that she could extricate herself at any time she thought she'd be in danger. I concurred.

He waved a folder in front of her and said, "You'll see from this dossier I've produced, Johnson's a piece of work, well-known by the gangs in south London. You'll need to be careful."

"I'm quite capable of sorting out any problems myself," she replied. "I've thought it through. If you think this is the only way we can get justice for Lynne and the kids, count me in."

Her feistiness resulted from the circumstances surrounding her deep distrust and loathing of men. She'd once told me about the bitter separation from her second husband, five years earlier. She'd already been through an acrimonious divorce from her first husband two years before that.

"This bastard sold our house and convinced me that he'd bought another property I'd set my heart on. Instead, he disappeared with the proceeds after paying off the mortgage and left me homeless. He actually called me on the supposed day of completion and told me it was over between us. He said he'd found someone new, poor bitch. I've never seen or spoken to him since."

"What sort of guy would do that? Did you try to find him?"

"Of course, but I couldn't afford to throw a lot of money at it, I was skint. It took me ages to get back on my feet. Lynne helped me out, not just emotionally but practically too, like giving me money for a deposit on my flat. I'll never forget her kindness."

"You both appear to have been unlucky with your choice of men. I'm sorry."

"Don't be, James. Lynne always said you were the exception." She stroked my arm.

"Stop it! You'll make me blush."

*

RP suggested a number of scenarios. Getting Johnson to admit to the arson attack wouldn't help much, since he couldn't be tried again.

Her sole focus would be to discover hard evidence implicating Nick Burrows – something Flood had missed. Once she'd achieved that, she could leave the matter of dealing with Johnson and Burrows to RP and me.

He handed Alisha a copy of Johnson's dossier. He'd added a schedule of his main haunts, many well-known for drug dealing. He asked her to study the document more thoroughly when she had time.

As Alisha flipped through the papers he said, "This'll help you understand Johnson better. But a warning; think about what you say to him. You don't want to appear to have anything on him or it'll give the game away."

Alisha stopped flipping on a particular page. She looked at RP and said, "One of these reports says he's uncontrollable and possesses a violent temper. Nice."

RP replied, "No one said this is going to be easy. As I've said before, if you want to pull out of the arrangement at any time that would be perfectly understandable. Right, James?"

"Yes, yes, of course." I couldn't keep my eyes off Alisha, trying to assimilate the change in her appearance.

Looking at both of us in turn, she said, "No, my mind's made up. Let's get on with it."

"OK. Well, I think the first thing to deal with is this." RP handed her a new lightweight digital mobile phone – a far cry from the 'bricks' we were used to.

These latest mobiles had taken the country by storm – I'd read that over half the population now had one.

"Only use this to keep in regular contact with me and I can update James. It would be too dangerous if Johnson found out you had James on your contact list. You can give the number to Johnson, too. That way, you'll know the only calls you get will be from him or me. OK?"

We both nodded. He continued, "It would be great to have access to his flat. You'd be able to plant a listening device in his home and possibly an intercept on his mobile." I tried to gauge Alisha's reaction. She looked excited and nodded in agreement.

"Oh, and I placed a tracer on it. We'll know where you are at any time. Make sure you always have it with you."

RP warmed to the task.

"Once in the flat, you'll be able to access his emails and maybe 'borrow' the SIM card in Johnson's mobile. A list of his contacts would prove useful."

"Wouldn't the police have done that?" I asked.

"Almost certainly. But there's no harm in me and my team checking out who he's been in touch with since his acquittal is there? Do you have any questions?"

"Actually, I have two," Alisha said. "What about Johnson's drug dealing activities? I assume he's still at it. I don't want to be caught up in that. If I get arrested, it's the end."

"Good point," RP sounded impressed. "Actually, you could pretend to be a user. Be a great way to get to know him. Just make sure you don't have stacks of the stuff hidden away at your apartment. And your second question?"

"What about this bugging? Is it legal?"

"I've got a top-notch solicitor on my team who tells me it depends; the more critical the issue to proving the case against the defendant, the less likely it is that the court will deem it inadmissible. However, it's not black and white. I wouldn't want to rely on it a hundred percent. But we've been here before, haven't we? The legal system's botched this case once already."

"You're right," Alisha said. "I needed to know where I stood. I suppose there is one other problem."

"Oh, what's that?" said RP, frowning. "I thought I'd covered everything."

"Suppose Johnson doesn't fancy me?"

"Not a chance," I said looking her up and down. RP shook his head furiously in agreement.

★

Within the week, Alisha visited the pubs and clubs listed in the dossier RP had produced. Sometimes she took her friend from work with her. She told her she needed to research locations for the criminal elements of a novel she wanted to write.

She told me that, although nervous at first, she enjoyed acting out this fantasy life. I suspected this would change when faced with Johnson's actual presence. I offered to be around in the background. I wanted to be on hand if anything nasty took place.

"Rather defeats the object doesn't it? Suppose Johnson recognises you? That would make it bad for both of us." I reluctantly agreed.

She told me she received and rejected advances from several men in the pubs they visited. I thought that once she opened her mouth to speak, many would think her too classy for them, out of their league. But then a number would like the idea of pulling a black, middle-class, sexy, well-spoken, attractive thirty-five-year-old.

I expressed my fear on more than one occasion that this might be too dangerous, but she responded in typical fashion.

"Don't worry. I can take care of myself. My contempt for men knows no bounds. I've a good idea how a man's mind works. If it got a bit heavy, I've learnt that a knee in the bollocks can render a man completely useless."

I winced at the thought and said, "You should carry Mace, or whatever it's called, in your handbag. I'd be a lot happier if you did." She agreed, I think, just to please me.

★

Meeting Johnson for the first time proved a revelation. It happened in a pub, one of those noted in the dossier, appropriately called, *The Rat's Castle* in Kennington Park Road, near the tube station and frequented by the local lowlife, villains and gangs.

Alisha told us they used the pub as somewhere to network

and do business in drugs, contraband cigarettes and counterfeit designer goods.

Surprisingly, the pub had a room they used as a singles club every Tuesday night. Given the name of the pub, I didn't think it would be successful. But Alisha said several men and women attended regularly. She felt comfortable there and went alone. The arrangements were casual; no membership forms or special introductions and you could drop in at any time. She met Johnson there. He unromantically told her later that he often picked up girls at the club.

"Well, how did it go?" I couldn't wait to hear about her first encounter. I'd gone to her flat in Canary Wharf and we were sharing a Chinese takeaway.

She shook her head in contempt and said, "God, this is going to be difficult. He has no conversation except when he's talking about himself. And he's the biggest bullshitter I've ever met. And believe me, I've met a few." She flicked her head up in derision.

"But do you think he fancied you?"

"I think so. He asked for my number. I gave him the one for the mobile RP gave me. We'll have to wait and see, won't we?"

She didn't have to wait long. The next day Johnson had texted and arranged to meet her for a drink in one of the other pubs on RP's list of his regular haunts the following night.

Now the honey trap had been sprung, I felt nervous. I had every faith in Alisha but she'd entered a different league.

She and Johnson started dating regularly. Access to his flat became the next focus. He lived in Bermondsey, close to Jamaica Road. She told me he'd asked her back a few times, presumably for sex, but Alisha had played hard to get.

RP had told her, "You only need to go as far as you're

comfortable with. In fact, the greater the tease, the more likely you are to get the info."

I asked her, "What do you feel about this, Alisha, the sex thing with Johnson?"

She shuddered. "I like sex… with the right man, of course. I really don't think I can do it with him. But if that's the *only* way we can get the information we want… I've only got to think of those white coffins at the funeral." She closed her eyes at the memory.

She continued, "He just can't be allowed to get away with what he's done."

"But you're the one taking the risks. I feel so useless."

"Yes, but you'll have enough on your plate once we know the score."

I reiterated, for the umpteenth time, that if she didn't want to go through with the plan she could walk away and we'd think of another way forward.

I asked whether Johnson had offered her any drugs. She said he had – ecstasy tablets and amphetamines. She told him she occasionally used them at weekends and parties. Eventually, she'd have to negotiate that situation too.

She'd followed our plan by not appearing to be too inquisitive for the first few weeks, needing to gain his confidence.

She said he loved showing her off to his cronies, acting and bragging cockily. One of Johnson's gang had told her they'd never known him have a relationship lasting more than a one-night-stand before and most of those were with, in their words, 'dogs'.

She got the impression his mates regarded her as his 'posh totty' adding considerably to his status among the rest of the south London gangs.

She said he wore a permanent, supercilious smile. And his jaunty gait drove Alisha mad.

CHAPTER ELEVEN

September 1999

Although pleased we were now getting somewhere with our plan, it was far too slow a process for my liking. It would be another few weeks or possibly months before we could get a fix on the Johnson/Burrows relationship.

My frustration festered like a virulent disease and wasn't helped by the thought of Alisha getting up close and personal with that jerk. I couldn't wait until we had firm evidence, one way or the other, and then she could back off and leave RP and me to deal with the murderers of my family.

*

I found it difficult to move onto the 'acceptance phase' of my grief.

I did silly things like leaving the radio on when I left for the office each day. When I returned, often with a take-away, I needed to hear sounds in the house. I always had it tuned to either the classical music channel or Radio 4 – I couldn't bear to hear the lyrics of romantic songs.

I swear I heard Lynne call out my name at least once a day. Or, I'd catch a glimpse of her disappearing upstairs or into the kitchen. Occasionally, I could smell her evocative perfume.

With Alisha's help, I faced up, finally, to clearing out Lynne's wardrobe. It had been just over a year since the murder of my family.

Alisha and I tearfully bagged up her clothes, shoes and dressing table contents. A week later we dealt with the toys and other paraphernalia the kids had collected. I stripped Georgie's room of his posters and got a man in to redecorate. But I kept the replica Dennis Berkamp Number 10 Arsenal football shirt I'd given him when we first got together. I felt his change of allegiance from Queen's Park Rangers to my team, Arsenal, marked a significant turning point in our relationship.

Despite clearing the decks, the rawness remained, especially regarding my lovely Emily.

I remembered having her room decorated with pink wallpaper, pink paintwork and pink hanging mobiles over three years ago, before Lynne brought her home from hospital. I left it as a memorial to a remarkable little girl who deserved better than to be callously murdered by that monster, Johnson.

★

Three weeks into the honey trap, Alisha told me Johnson got increasingly frustrated at not having sex with her. It signalled a step up in the relationship.

She visited his flat a few times. I imagined it to be dirty and squalid, but Alisha told me the opposite. She said Johnson suffered from borderline OCD. It manifested itself into an obsession with cleanliness, both personally and in his flat. He washed his hands frequently and everything had to be immaculately clean and in place.

"I can't go on refusing him. I'm running out of excuses."

The thought of her having sex with Johnson abhorred me too.

I told her, "If you feel that you're getting in over your head, then you're out. You need to get the info soon."

She told him her job as a sales rep meant her travelling all over the country. This gave her the excuse of having to work odd hours from time to time and gave her some respite.

His chaotic lifestyle helped. He made enough money dealing in drugs and doing an occasional 'job' to get by. Some weeks he appeared to be flusher with cash than others.

I needed to know whether he knew Nick and asked Alisha several times whether she'd asked him yet.

"That's a big issue. I need a reason. It can't come out of the blue. If he does know him he'll want to know why I ask."

"I'll think of something," I said.

Silent and thoughtful for a moment, finally, she said, "Well… Johnson drinks a lot… and I mean a lot. He takes amphetamines too. That's the best time to talk to him. He's bragged about a few of the deals that he's done when he's like that and he often passes out. I'll have to choose my timing carefully."

★

We mentioned the sex thing to RP at one of our meetings. He understood our concern.

"There is a way we can speed up results from the honey trap, Alisha." He pulled open a drawer to his desk and produced a small torch.

"Here," he said. "Keep this in your handbag. It's not

unusual for women to carry torches. No one will suspect it has a tape recorder inside. When you push the light switch, the tape starts. Be good to record your conversations."

"Bit James Bond, isn't it?" she said, picking it up.

RP smiled and replied, "It's got a powerful microphone. You can leave it switched on inside your handbag. Remember to always keep it charged."

Alisha pressed the switch. Silently the tape started and ten seconds later, she pulled the switch back and we heard RP's voice.

He said, "I picked up a few of these prototypes in the USA. Clever, eh?"

He reiterated that he also wanted Alisha to 'borrow' Johnson's mobile for a few hours.

She'd already discovered that he had one but didn't use email. He loved texting where spelling and grammar weren't required.

Alisha, at first, thought it too dangerous, but when RP pointed out that these actions may cut short her relationship with Johnson, she agreed.

"In that case, I'll take the risk," she said.

★

Within the week, she'd succeeded in 'borrowing' Johnson's mobile. She delivered it to RP the next day. His techies copied the contacts file from the SIM card using a SIM card reader.

She dropped the mobile back in Johnson's jacket when she saw him the next day. He never missed it.

"Easy-peasy," she told me. "He went out like a light after a heavy drinking session. I hope RP can get something from it. I don't think I can carry on with this much longer. He's still a child in here." She pointed a manicured, vividly varnished finger to her head and tapped several times.

From the SIM card, RP followed-up Johnson's list of current contacts, about thirty in total. It took his team a week of intensive investigation into their backgrounds, but none of them pointed us in the direction of Nick... except one... someone by the name of Colin Greenland.

RP's thorough research turned up the fact that Greenland had been in Belmarsh prison at the same time as Nick and had been released in December 1997 after serving a four-year sentence for drug dealing. RP called me with the news.

"You're telling me this guy was out of prison at the time of the arson attack and he knew Johnson?"

"It would appear so, yes."

"He's surely the link we've been looking for, isn't he? Nick could have asked him to find someone like Johnson to carry out the arson attack on the cottage, correct?"

"Yes... he could." RP implied a note of caution. "But it's not definite. Greenland's a drug dealer, so is Johnson. That may be the only connection, and the fact that Greenland just happened to be in Belmarsh at the same time as Nick could be pure coincidence."

"Where does that leave us?" I said.

"I'll try to get more information from my contacts. You might want to tell Alisha about this. Perhaps she can find out more from Johnson."

★

I mentioned Greenland's name to Alisha. She frowned, whilst searching her memory.

"Yes... yes ...Colin... Colin Greenland. I think he's the

guy I've met a couple of times at the pub we go to. Big guy, not bad-looking, actually. I think he fancies me. Doesn't miss a chance to chat me up. Gets right up Johnson's nose. He's like a horny stag at the moment."

"Do you think you can talk to Greenland? Find out whether there's more to his link with Nick, other than being in Belmarsh at the same time?"

"I'll try."

"Don't forget your little friend, the torch. You can use it when you're with Johnson, too. Are you OK with that?"

She nodded in agreement. "OK. I'll have to be bloody careful, though. Johnson's getting to be a bit of a handful."

"Don't take any undue risks, Alisha. To be honest, if we'd don't make progress soon, I'm all for sorting out Johnson now and wait for Nick to leave prison and deal with him then."

"Yes, but we'll still be no nearer finding the truth, will we? And we can't be one hundred per cent certain Nick's behind this. I'll do another week, yes?"

Reluctantly, I agreed.

★

Using the torch digital recorder proved a masterstroke. A few days after our conversation, Alisha and I sat in RP's office and listened to a recording between Alisha and Greenland.

Before turning on the tape, Alisha explained that they were in *The Rat's Castle* pub. Johnson conducted most of his business there. He'd left her in the main bar whilst he met up with other villains in a small bar at the rear of the premises known as the 'Snug'. Greenland, never one to pass up an opportunity to chat up Alisha, had sidled up to her.

Despite clattering glasses, a general hubbub of chatter and the sound of a football match on the TV, we heard the voices distinctly.

Following inane banter, Alisha fast-forwarded to the vital dialogue.

Alisha: A little bird tells me you've done time.
Greenland: Who told you that? Your boyfriend?
Alisha: That would be telling, wouldn't it?
Greenland: It's no skin off my nose. Yeah, I 'ad an 'oliday in Belmarsh as it 'appens. Couple a years ago.
Alisha: Belmarsh? Oh, I know someone there. Don't suppose you've heard of him? His name's Burrows, Nick Burrows.
Greenland: Burrows? I might have. Big place, Belmarsh. What's 'e to you?
Alisha: Oh, just a boyfriend.
Greenland: One of many, I bet.
Alisha: Oh, yes. Loads. Anyway, how did you get to know Leroy?
Greenland: Leroy? I've known 'im ages. Now there's a bloke who should be inside.
Alisha: Really? Why do you say that?
Greenland: Doncha' know? 'E was all over the papers a few months ago. Burnt down an 'ouse wiv a woman and two kids in it.
Alisha: Why? What happened?
Greenland: Someone put 'im up to it. Leroy'll do anything for money. Anyway, he went to court and somehow 'e got off, jammy bugger!
Alisha: But who on earth would want to set fire to a house with a family in it?

Greenland: *All I know is this geezer wanted to get his own back. A lover's tiff, summin' like that. Said if he couldn't 'ave 'em, no-one would.*

Alisha: *That's terrible!*

Greenland: *It's called life. Anyway, d'ya wanna a drink or somethin'? My norf and souf's like the bottom of a birdcage.*

Alisha leaned over and switched off the recorder.

I let out a low whistle. I asked Roger, "What do you make of that?"

"Let's hear it again," he said, and motioned to Alisha to rewind the tape. This time he listened more intently.

When it had finished, he sat back in his chair and said, "Well, I thought he sounded a bit cagey about knowing Nick. And he appeared to know a lot about the arson attack. I got the impression he didn't rate Johnson much."

Alisha answered, "No, he doesn't. There's a lot of rivalry there. What do you want me to do next?"

RP thought for a moment and said, "Well what's good about this is that it leaves the way open for you to raise the subject of the arson with Johnson. You can tell him Greenland told you about it."

He continued, "What we really need to know is whether Burrows got Greenland to approach Johnson."

I looked at them both and said, "I'm sure he did. Lynne carrying my baby must have screwed him up. So screwed up, he took Georgie three thousand miles away."

"Could be, James," RP said. "Are you still happy to carry on, Alisha?"

"Yes. Yes, of course. I think we're getting somewhere at last."

RP replied. "OK. Be careful now."

CHAPTER TWELVE

September 1999

I wanted to be the proactive driver in our plan. Instead, RP and Alisha were still the leading players. This didn't sit comfortably with me.

I couldn't get involved with Johnson; he'd have recognised me instantly as the person staring at him incessantly when he sat in the dock at Winchester Crown Court. And my outburst had been particularly dramatic and memorable.

Two days later, Alisha called me at home. Breathless with excitement, she said she'd got a break-though. I pressed her to tell me what she meant but said it would be better if we met at RP's office as soon as possible.

Within the hour, I walked into his office in St James's Street.

Alisha beat me there by a few minutes. RP's glamorous PA ushered me into his office. RP poured me a cup of tea as I entered and waved a hand in the direction of a chair opposite Alisha, who smiled up at me.

As I sat, he said, "You've some news for us, Alisha?"

She placed the torch tape recorder on RP's desk.

"Well, I hope so. The recording's a bit indistinct in places and you'll hear Johnson talking fast. We're in his flat. Look, parts of this are a bit embarrassing… he's drunk and excited. I worked hard to get him in a good mood; you know what I mean …"

I didn't want to think about it.

RP glanced at me and said, "We're both big boys, aren't we, James?" I nodded, concerned about what I was about to hear.

Alisha pushed the switch and fast-forwarded to a pre-determined point. I could only guess at other parts of the conversation she'd concealed from us.

Alisha: Colin Greenland tells me you're famous.
Johnson: Why, what's 'e been saying?
Alisha: Says you were charged and tried for an arson attack and got away with it?
Johnson: Yeah. I did. It was in all the papers. Bit of a star, me. Trouble was I spent eight months on remand. Time I'll never get back.
Alisha: Did you do it?
Johnson: Yeah. It was a job, weren't it. Down on the south coast. I didn't ask questions. Got well paid though. Ten grand in cash.

RP and Alisha looked to me for a reaction. I stared at the torch, my hatred of Johnson intensifying. Is that all my family's lives were worth? Ten grand.

Alisha: Who paid you?
Johnson: Never mind that, come 'ere! Let's ...
Alisha: No, this is interesting. I want to know everything about you.
Johnson: Can't tell you. No one knows. 'E'd kill me if I told anyone.
Alisha: Yes, but when you were caught surely the cops put pressure on you to find out whether you were acting alone or not. Otherwise, what would have been your motive?

Johnson: Yeah, they did, big time. If I'd told 'em, my life would 'ave been 'ell inside. I ain't no squealer. Bad enough being on remand. No one likes a child killer. It weren't an 'appy time for me in that place.

Alisha: But supposing you hadn't got off? You'd be banged up for twenty years or more and your man would be free. Didn't that worry you?

Johnson: Yeah, 'course it bloody did! But if I squealed, I told you, 'e threatened to kill me. 'E knew some 'ard cases inside – 'e'd fix it, believe me. 'E's a nasty bastard. Doing time was better and there was always a chance I might get off, an' I did.

Alisha: Do you know why he wanted to murder that family?

Johnson: Summin' to do with 'er finishing with 'im… I dunno… you'll have to ask Greenland, 'e's the bloke who knows 'im better. 'E's done business wiv 'im before. 'E's the one who set up the meet when 'e told me about the job.

Alisha: Do you still see the guy?

Johnson: Yeah. 'E's still worried I might let summin' slip. 'E pays me a bit of insurance once a month just to be sure.

Alisha: How much?

Johnson: A monkey. Cash.

Alisha: How much is that?

Johnson: Five 'undred quid.

Alisha: Is that all? He's got off cheap if you ask me. He could be rotting in jail for a long time and you're the one keeping him free.

Johnson: Yeah. But it's nuttin' to do with you, is it? I dunno why you're so interested.

Alisha: No, you're right. I just think he's had you over, that's all.

Johnson: *No one's 'ad me over... now come on ...'ere! Let's 'ave some fun!*

Alisha leant over the desk and turned off the recorder. "I don't think you'll want to hear the rest."

We sat quietly for a few seconds, considering the implications.

RP broke the silence. "If I've heard correctly, Burrows isn't behind this." Even the great RP sounded incredulous. "Johnson clearly said he meets whoever it is once a month to pick up his insurance money. It has to be somebody else, unless Burrows got another guy to do his dirty work, which, I suppose, isn't out of the question."

"That's what I felt. I couldn't believe what he said." Alisha sounded excited.

I finally found my voice. "If it is someone else, who the hell is this guy? Why would he want to do this?"

RP stroked his chin with his right hand several times, his usual affectation, whilst his mind processed various scenarios.

Eventually, he said, "At least now, we've got a direct line on whoever it is. Alisha, if you can find out when Johnson next goes to meet Mr Mystery Man, we can get a look at him – shake him down, find out the connection."

"I'll try, but as you heard on the tape, I need to be careful. Johnson's getting a bit wary of me asking too many questions."

I asked RP, "What about getting to Colin Greenland? He's the one who set up the meeting to discuss the job, according to Johnson. He'll know who it is, won't he?"

"Good point, James," RP replied. "What do you think, Alisha? Can you work a little magic there?"

"Well, Greenland's definitely keen on me. Johnson hates me talking to him. I'll have to choose my moment carefully."

RP said, "A list of Greenland's contacts would be useful.

Do you think you could repeat the mobile phone trick you pulled on Johnson?"

"I'll try."

RP said, "OK. Well, we can't go much further forward until we know who this mystery man is."

I nodded in agreement, despite being conscious that Alisha remained in the driving seat.

RP considered putting Johnson under surveillance 24/7 but decided against it. Apart from the cost, although I didn't give a toss about that, he decided it wasn't going to be particularly effective. It would be a chance in a million that one of us would recognise the mystery man.

This proved not to be one of RP's better decisions.

★

Three days later, in the early hours of Saturday, my mobile's shrill ring tone jarred me awake. I peered at my luminous alarm clock. It read 1.10am.

"Oh, James! Can you pick me up? Now? I'm in a late-night cafe, *The Hide Bar* in Bermondsey Road. I'm in a bit of a state!" I heard Alisha snivel into the phone.

"Of course! What's happened? You sound upset."

"I can't tell you now. Just get here quickly, can you?"

"I'm on my way."

I tore through light traffic on the A2 and The Old Kent Road, aware of speed cameras and traffic lights, and worried about Alisha's anguished call. Less than twenty-five minutes later, I spotted her in the window of the cafe.

Heavy eye make-up streaked down her face; she had a cut lip and a bruised swelling under her left eye.

Her dyed-blonde hair was a mess and one of the heels of

her shoes had snapped off. Dabbing her eyes with a tissue she'd taken from her handbag, she looked a million miles away from the ballsy woman I knew.

As I approached her she fell into my arms with relief. I hugged her tightly for an age, before saying, "What the hell happened?"

"I… I suppose it's my own fault. We were drinking in the *Apollo club* near *The Rat's Castle* pub. Me, Leroy and a few of his mates. Colin Greenland was there too. Leroy went outside to do a bit of dealing. That's when I took the chance to chat up Greenland – "

"And …"

"Maybe I went a bit too far. Leroy returned and caught us snogging. He went mental. Dragged me out of the club and into an alleyway. He punched me in the face. Then he kept slapping me, called me a prick teaser and tried to rape me."

"Oh, Alisha!"

I held her tightly again.

"I tried to stop him. I caught him in the bollocks once with my knee but it only made him angrier. I couldn't match his strength. I didn't have time to use the Mace in my handbag. Then somebody from the club loomed from the darkness and shouted at him. He stopped and stormed back into the club in a strop."

"This is crazy. That's it. You've done enough." I shepherded her to my car.

"I'll take you back to my house. Don't even *think* about arguing with me."

In a barely audible voice, she said, "OK."

She laid her head against the headrest and sighed in relief. As I sat beside her on the driver's side, she opened her handbag and produced a mobile phone. I thought she wanted to call someone but she sat there staring at it.

"At least I didn't leave empty-handed," she said, a hint of a smile crossing her face.

"Is that ...?"

"Yes. It's Colin Greenland's mobile. He was so out of his head, he won't miss it for a while."

"Alisha!"

"What? That was the idea wasn't it? Let's hope RP can find out who our mystery man is."

When we got home, I made some coffee. Bathing her swollen eye with tepid water, I said, "Alisha, I'm proud of you. But look, this really is the end for you, OK?"

"Maybe. Let's see what happens next?" There seemed no point in discussing it further. I showed her to the spare bedroom, hugged her once more and kissed her tenderly on the cheek.

"Try to get some sleep. We'll talk about it in the morning."

I returned to my bedroom.

★

Next morning, over a late breakfast of boiled eggs and strong coffee, Alisha, looking as if she'd gone three rounds with Mike Tyson, passed over the mobile RP had supplied. It showed half-a-dozen text messages from Johnson, all expressing how sorry he felt about last night and urging her to get in touch.

"What should I do about these?" Alisha said.

"Nothing. You're not going back, Alisha. It's over. Does he know where you live?"

"No, I was careful not to tell him. I just gave him a general area."

She handed me Greenland's mobile.

"Good. I'll discuss this with RP on Monday. He'll have a few ideas."

We spent the rest of Saturday and Sunday together. I bought food from the market and we shared a lunch of cold chicken and baked potatoes washed down with a bottle of *Sancerre*.

Late on Sunday evening, I drove her back to her flat. By the time we arrived, Johnson had texted a further four times, and left countless messages imploring her to forgive him.

"Don't reply, will you? Let's agree what to do next tomorrow, promise me?"

"I promise."

★

RP made a few changes to his diary appointments to accommodate my visit first thing Monday morning, after I'd stressed the urgency. He was so into this case now, like a terrier with a slipper.

He expressed great pleasure about Alisha getting hold of Greenland's mobile, although he was concerned about the violence used.

"I knew she had balls, that girl. I'll give her that."

"Is it worth Alisha reporting this attempted rape to the police?"

"She could. But can't see where it would get us. She'd have needed to go to the police straight after it happened to preserve any DNA evidence. As it is, it'll be her word against his. Even then, say the police believe her; he'll get put away for a while. Then what?"

"I suppose you're right."

"I'm more interested in this." RP had Greenland's mobile in his hand. He acted like a kid with a new toy, tapping away and scrolling through the content and list of contacts. "These messages and texts look interesting. My techies next door can get access to deleted stuff too. This is Pandora's Box!"

I explained my uneasiness about Alisha getting back in touch with Johnson. He agreed, but as usual, his brain had assessed the likely pros and cons.

"I know you don't like it, but if Alisha's up for it, I think she should get back with Johnson one more time."

"No Roger. Enough is enough."

"But look at this way; if I can get closer to our mystery man from Greenland's mobile, I've got an idea that'll flush him out." He shook the mobile under my nose. "The fact that Johnson's keen to make it up to Alisha will play into our hands."

RP was never more persuasive than when he had a plan in mind.

"No, I don't like it Roger. It's not fair on Alisha. Christ, Johnson nearly raped her!"

I stared out of the window at the drab, late autumn day.

To my back, he said, "Why don't we ask her to see him just one more time?"

I turned and said, "I'll advise her not to."

Putting his hands up in mock surrender, he said, "OK. I understand. Anyway, I'll see if I can get somewhere with this mobile later today. Why don't we have a chat then?"

★

RP called later that afternoon and suggested Alisha and I meet up with him as soon as possible, said he had interesting information to share. We arranged to meet at his now familiar office later that evening.

She arrived at the office still wearing sunglasses. I asked

her to take them off so I could see her face. She obliged. The swelling had gone down slightly, but there remained a deep purple bruise under her left eye. Her split lip had crusted over.

RP offered words of sympathy to Alisha, before getting straight to the point. He looked pleased with himself.

"We've been working overtime on this and we haven't totally completed our search into all of Greenland's contacts but there's one name on the list that needs further investigation. I don't believe it could be another coincidence."

RP sat back in his chair and pointed his hands together, prayer-like. The tips of his fingers met his chin.

"If I remember correctly, Greenland said on the last tape that he'd done time in Belmarsh, but didn't admit to knowing Burrows. Well I've come up with another person who'd done time in Belmarsh at the same time as Greenland. In fact, according to my contact, they shared a cell together whilst they were on remand."

Before I could ask who it was, RP raised his palm to me and continued.

"Also, there's a note indicating that this person happened to be visited several times by Greenland after his release in December 1997."

"Go, on," I said, eager to get to the point.

"The most important thing I discovered is that this person began his sentence on 10th February 1996 and was released on parole on 3rd July 1998, a month before the arson attack."

RP looked at Alisha and then me.

"His name is Hartley, John Hartley."

CHAPTER THIRTEEN

September – October 1999

Before I could react, Alisha put her hand to her mouth and said, "Oh my God!"

"What do you mean?" I asked her. "Do you know Hartley?"

"Oh, James! Yes, I do know him. Maybe it's best if I talk to you privately."

I looked her straight in the eyes and said, "Alisha, if we're going to sort this out, we'll need to know everything, otherwise we can't fill in the gaps. What do you know about him that I don't?"

Looking nervous, her eyes darted between RP and me.

"Well… if you're sure you want me to. Lynne made me promise I'd never tell anyone… ever. It was her secret."

I yelled at her, "What bloody secret? What the hell has Lynne got to do with Hartley?"

Alisha avoided eye contact with me and said, "I don't know where to start… it's all so… complicated."

Looking up and facing me, she said, "How can I put this…? Before you came on the scene, James, Lynne and John Hartley had an affair."

"What? Are you sure? I'd never put them together."

"It's true, James. I hate having to tell you this. It started in

October/November 1994, I think. They met at the Mercedes dealership you bought. At first, despite being worried that Nick might find out, she became excited. He treated her well. He always had loads of money and spoilt her rotten. But as time wore on, he showed his true colours."

"I had no idea. She never mentioned him," I said.

Alisha continued. "He was married. Their meetings were clandestine affairs. As far as I could tell, no one else knew about it apart from me."

Inspecting his notes, RP interrupted. "Yes, married three times, the last time in 1989." He waved a hand towards Alisha, signalling her to carry on.

"I first met him at Lynne's flat. She wanted my approval. But something about him, I don't know… I didn't like." She shook her head.

"I had to admit he came across as charismatic and charming. He'd hooked her. But to me, he appeared over-confident, a bit smarmy, thought he was God's gift to women."

She brushed an imaginary piece of cotton from her leggings before adding, "Believe me, I've met a few of those types in my time.

"Actually, later, I hated him. Lynne told me that he didn't like her going out with make-up on or dressing provocatively. She told me that, on many occasions, he completely lost it if she didn't agree with him and sometimes he hit her. Then he'd be full of remorse. Talk about out of the frying pan and into the fire."

"Just like Nick," I said.

"I know. She'd swapped him for Hartley, except Hartley controlled her more psychologically. He really messed up her mind."

I said, "But why did Lynne put up with it? Surely she'd learnt her lesson?"

"My sentiments exactly. She was hopeless with men... a sucker for anyone showing her attention. And useless at getting herself out of these situations."

"Did Hartley know what you thought of him?" RP asked.

"You know me. I couldn't stand by and watch Hartley mess her up. I called him once. Told him to back off and not treat Lynne so badly. He tried to turn his charm on me. Made me feel sick."

"Did he respond?" I asked.

"You're joking. He completely ignored me. I begged her to end the relationship."

"Are you saying he was seeing her at the same time as me?"

"Yes, but only for a short time, a couple of months at the most. She tried hard to extricate herself, but he wouldn't have it. He's a clever bastard."

"I can't believe Lynne had been cheating on me!"

"No, it wasn't like that. Lynne tried desperately to get Hartley out of her life, especially after meeting you. But she fell under his spell. Even more so than Nick, and we know he's bad news. He's thuggish. Hartley's in another league. He's a smooth, manipulative charmer."

Anger grew in her voice as she said, "He kept putting her down all the time, telling her she was useless, didn't know what he saw in her, that kind of thing, to the point where she'd burst into tears. Then he'd treat her like a Goddess before knocking her down again. This became the pattern. That way, he had total control of her emotions. She thought she was going mad."

"Bastard!" I muttered. Alisha looked at me sympathetically and continued.

"I felt so sorry for her. After she met you, she tried even harder to get rid of Hartley. Then, around the same time, she had to deal with all that stuff with Nick abducting Georgie to Florida. She'd replaced one problem with another."

I asked, "Did she finally end the affair?"

"Well, suddenly, I think about the beginning of February '96, a few months after you and Lynne got together, he disappeared and she never saw him again, at least, not to my knowledge. Lynne thought that, at last, Hartley had given up, that you being on the scene had got in the way of his plans."

She turned to RP. "You said he went to prison about then."

Inspecting his notes, he said, "That's right, 10th February 1996."

"I'm so sorry, James." She reached for my hand.

After a moment's silence, RP asked me what I knew about Hartley.

I told them about his job with us and the embezzlement.

"He left us after giving us a cock and bull story about his wife having cancer before we'd discovered it. Later, we traced him to Belmarsh prison.

"I didn't realise he'd been released. He was due out in 1999, at the earliest. I planned to visit him then, try to get what was left of the money back."

RP checked his notes to confirm the dates.

"Looks like he appealed against his sentence. Got a year knocked off."

I shook my head and said, "This is unbelievable."

RP nodded and studied his notes again. "I think I've got an accurate time frame for the Lynne/Hartley relationship which appears to fit. What we don't know is what happened after Hartley's release on parole from Belmarsh in July 1998."

I turned to Alisha and asked, "Did Nick know about Hartley?"

"I don't know."

"Well, if he did, that would have inflamed his hatred of Lynne even more, wouldn't it? Make him more determined to take revenge."

RP stopped scribbling and said, "There are still a few gaps here. To be sure whether Hartley's our man we have to find a link between Hartley and Johnson. "

"How can we do that?" I asked.

RP, stroking his chin yet again, said, "It looks like Hartley's been using Greenland as the go-between. Hartley's not unintelligent. If he did use Johnson as a hit man he wouldn't want any evidence like text messages or calls from him on Johnson's mobile. One possibility is that Hartley texts Greenland and he tells Johnson where to meet up for the monthly 'insurance' payment."

RP placed his pen on the desk and sat back in his chair.

"Why don't we take a time-out now? I'll give this more thought. Let's meet again tomorrow morning. Are you happy with that, James?"

"Er... yes... sorry... bit shell-shocked, that's all. I wasn't prepared for this."

Alisha said, "I'm so sorry, James. Lynne swore me to secrecy."

I couldn't help but feel sorry for Lynne. She'd got herself into an intolerable situation. Perhaps she thought that adding the complications of an affair with Hartley to her problem with Nick would drive me away.

★

Next morning, a cloudless autumn day, we met at RP's office again.

He went straight to the point after pouring the ubiquitous coffees.

"Any more thoughts?"

Alisha, who'd taken a few days' sick leave, still wore her sunglasses. She shook her head. I think she thought she'd already said too much.

I shook my head, too. I felt numb.

RP, looking at us both in turn, said, "OK. Alisha, what's the situation with Johnson? Is he still texting you, begging forgiveness?"

"Er… yes. I got another one yesterday." She fumbled inside her handbag and produced her mobile, lifted her sunglasses onto her forehead, scrolled though the texts for a few seconds and read out, "*'get in touch alisha. miss u. really sorry 4 what I done. wanna make up Ill do anything. Call me. Leroy.'*"

"That's about the fifteenth one he's either sent or left as a message."

"Excellent. Obviously, he's still interested. We can use him to flush out Hartley."

I spluttered, "How? Are you still suggesting Alisha gets in touch?"

"I think it's the only way."

Before I could respond, he turned to Alisha and said, "You remember you put in Johnson's mind that the £500 per month insurance money is peanuts? And you implied Hartley took him for a fool settling for so little?" Alisha nodded.

"I've got an idea. It'll need you to get back with Johnson, but only for a short time, I promise."

I slammed my hand on RP's desk. "No, I'm sorry Roger. You weren't there when I picked Alisha up after Johnson had beaten her and tried to rape her. It wasn't a pretty sight. It's not fair she should run that risk again."

"It's OK James," Alisha said, putting her hand on my arm. "I acted stupidly. I asked for it. Let's hear Roger out."

"Thank you, Alisha. Well, my plan is this; call Johnson, say you'll continue the relationship but you won't stand for any more violence. And tell him that you're fed up spending time with him holed up in his flat. You want him to take you to fancy restaurants, travel a bit, and have a good time."

"Then what?" Alisha said.

"Well, we have Greenland's mobile with Hartley's contact number, don't we? You can tell him that you've found out from Greenland who the mystery man is and his mobile number. He may not believe you, but the way I see it, he'll be gagging to impress you. I doubt he'd worry about where the info came from.

"Get him to text Hartley saying the 'insurance' money needs to be greatly increased — suggest he wants a big lump sum upfront, say twenty-five grand. Get him to imply that he's written a statement involving Hartley and if he doesn't play ball, he'll pass it over to the police."

"And then?" I said.

"Well, first Hartley'll be beside himself with the fact that Johnson knows his mobile number. Remember? I'm certain the contacts between them were via Greenland." RP waved Greenland's mobile at us.

"Hartley would want to ensure there's no evidence linking him directly to Johnson. If Hartley bites, his response could be the evidence we need."

"Is that it?" I said.

"It's the first stage. I've got an idea where this'll lead. Ultimately, we'll need to deal with Johnson *and* Hartley if he's the one, won't we?"

Alisha and I both nodded. "What do you think, Alisha?" I said. "Are you sure you want to carry on?"

"Too right, I do! We've come this far, haven't we? I'll get in touch with Leroy. I'll try to persuade him to get more money out of Hartley. Be interesting to see Johnson's reaction."

"Well, I'm still not happy. It's far too risky," I said.

RP responded, "It is. However, there is one other point Alisha can make to Johnson. Remind him he's immune from prosecution for the arson attack, but Hartley's not. If he's banged up, he can't hurt him. That may strengthen your hand." Alisha nodded again.

I said, "Roger, there's one thing I couldn't get out of my mind last night. Do you think Hartley ever saw Lynne again, you know, after his release from jail?"

RP turned to Alisha and said, "Did Lynne ever mention it to you?"

"No, of course not, I'd have said so." She sounded affronted.

RP said, "I think I should visit Greenland with one of my guys. Put a bit of pressure on him. Get him to tell us more about Hartley."

"No, Roger. I want to be involved. I'll go. I can handle myself."

"Are you sure that's wise?"

"Positive." I needed something to feed my hatred of the low-life scum we were dealing with.

"OK. Here, take Greenland's mobile. You'll need it to prove the connection with Hartley and Johnson."

RP, in his usual meticulous way, then gave me a master-class in how to approach the situation. I felt like a sleuth's apprentice.

CHAPTER FOURTEEN

October 1999

Alisha called me at home the next day. "I've done it. I called Leroy and we met up last night. He's swallowed the bait. I told him there were two conditions if I went back to him. The first, no more physical stuff. I told him if he so much as slapped my arse, I'd be off!"

Typical Alisha.

"And the second, I told him I wanted to be better off. He totally bought the blackmail line. I think he'd been thinking about it since I pointed it out a couple of weeks ago. He's a greedy bugger. Wants to prove to me how tough he is. I told him straight; I want to wear expensive jewellery, go travelling to nice places and all that. Whether he believed Greenland had given me Hartley's number or not, he couldn't wait to send the text. The power of love, eh?"

"Yeah, right. Power of lust, more like. Did you mention he can't be tried again?"

"Yes I did. He said his solicitor had already told him after his acquittal."

"Be careful, Alisha. I don't want you to get beaten up again... or worse."

"I will, I promise. We're getting close to knowing what happened, aren't we? I can back off soon. Then it'll be up to you and RP."

★

Greenland's mobile buzzed in my jacket pocket immediately after Alisha had called. I didn't answer it, hoping the caller would leave a message. He did.

I couldn't mistake the bass timbre of Hartley's newsreader's voice.

'Colin, it's me. What the fuck's going on? Just got a text from Johnson. I'm not happy about it. How the bloody hell did he get my number? I hope that for your sake you didn't give it to him. Call me, pronto.'

I called RP immediately and read the message to him. Then I said, "Hartley sounds rattled."

"Good. Tell Alisha to persuade Johnson to send another text. Keep the pressure on. This time give Hartley an ultimatum; either come up with the readies in twenty-four hours or he'll hand over to the police the written statement confirming Hartley's involvement in the arson attack. See what that brings."

I called Alisha and relayed RP's idea. "OK. I'm seeing Johnson tonight. I'll let you know how it goes."

She called the next morning. "He didn't need much persuading. He sent the second text last night. Johnson's liking being in charge of the situation. He's convinced Hartley'll cough up. He's promised me a huge diamond ring when he gets the money."

"Yeah, right," I said.

I decided to visit Greenland that afternoon. RP had already given me his address, which was a first floor flat above a shopping precinct in Abbey Street, Bermondsey. He thought afternoons would be a good time to find him home.

I loitered outside the shops for a good hour, checking that he didn't have visitors.

Greenland's mobile bleeped several times, indicating messages, which were all from Hartley.

The last highlighted his level of frustration.

'Colin. I'm getting really pissed off. Why the fuck aren't you returning my calls? I need you to call me back urgently.'

The entrance to Greenland's flat was via a stairway at the rear of the precinct where all the wheelie bins from the shops laid strewn about haphazardly. I rang the bell, aware of the pungent smell from the decaying fruit dumped by the greengrocer, combined with the spicy odour of an Indian restaurant.

Greenland opened the door only wide enough to see my face. Before he had time to register what was happening, I thrust my shoulder hard at the door, taking him completely by surprise. Despite being over six feet tall, he almost lost his balance. I stepped inside the cramped, cluttered room. A barely audible ancient flickering telly in the corner lit up the gloom. The drab curtains were fully drawn. Peeling wallpaper and threadbare carpets completed the sense of decay.

He wore a pair of grey sweat pants, trainers and a grubby white T-shirt with a picture of Che Guevara on it. I flashed my open wallet at him containing something, which appeared surprisingly like a police warrant but was my health club membership card. He only had time to snatch a glance at it before I returned it to my pocket. I said, "I'm investigating an arson attack which we believe John Hartley instigated. You know him, don't you?"

"No. Never 'eard of 'im. Now piss off!"

I held up Greenland's mobile close to his face, pointed at Hartley's name in the list of contacts and played his latest message.

"Where the fuck did you get 'old of that?"

"It doesn't matter. I also have a record of your prison visits to Hartley. So don't fuck me about. Let's sit down and discuss, shall we?"

He did. I expected him to be violent. If it got rough, I hoped my martial arts training would literally kick in.

RP had explained to me how powerful initial aggressive behaviour could be. "It disorients the victim," he'd said. "Gives you a head start."

In truth, Greenland turned out to be a pussycat.

"Who are you? What d'ya want from me?" His eyes revealed panic.

We sat down on opposite sides of a low coffee table covered with a jumble of crumpled newspapers, magazines and empty beer bottles. The remains of a takeaway lay perilously on top of the heap.

"I'll tell you what I want soon enough. Listen to this first."

On my Dictaphone, I played him a copy of the conversation Alisha had recorded when Johnson admitted Greenland had set up the meeting with Hartley, resulting in the arson attack. His jaw dropped open.

"Unless you tell me everything you know about Hartley's involvement, I'll hand your mobile and this tape to the police. I'm sure you'd agree they'd have a strong case for charging you with being an accessory to murder."

He trembled at the word murder.

"So you're not the filth?"

"Let's say I'm helping them with their enquiries. Once I'm satisfied with your answers you can have your mobile back." He sighed with relief.

"OK. How do you know Hartley?"

"We became mates after being banged up on remand. 'E kept going on and on about 'is affair with someone from work called Lynne. 'E couldn't stop talking about 'er. 'E learnt about 'er having a baby and got 'imself wound up about being sent to prison four or five months before she was due. 'E was convinced it was 'is. 'E said she'd met another geezer and the thought of them bringing up 'is kid drove 'im nuts."

Certain I hadn't heard correctly, I asked him to repeat what he'd said. He did. I wanted to yell at him, 'That's fucking ridiculous!'

"Let's get this absolutely clear. You're telling me Hartley believed he was the baby's father?"

"Yeah, that's what 'e told me. 'Artley went mental every time 'e thought she was going to marry this prick. An' he couldn't do nuffin' about it."

"Don't lie to me!"

"I'm not. That's the truth. 'E told me that before being banged up, 'e wanted to go abroad with 'em, start a new life together. Said 'e 'ad plenty of dosh stashed away."

I wanted to smash my fist in his face, but I needed more information.

I recovered enough composure to ask, "Why did you visit him in Belmarsh after you were released?"

"I told you. We became mates. 'E wanted to know everything about 'er. 'E paid me well enough. 'E asked me to tell 'im, you know, where she moved to, where she went at weekends, that sorta stuff."

"What happened on Hartley's release from prison?"

"'E told me 'e'd stalked 'er in Blackheath and 'accidentally' bumped into to 'er when she was walking with the kid in the buggy."

I bit my lip. I wasn't sure I could take any more revelations.

"'E said they 'ad a slanging match in the street. Apparently, she made it clear she didn't want nuffin' to do wiv 'im. She really wound 'im up by saying the baby wasn't 'is and 'e should get lost."

"Then what?"

"'Told me 'e'd followed 'er and 'loverboy' down to Lymington on the souf coast. I'd found out the address. They went down most weekends in the summer. So did 'e. 'E was so wrapped wiv 'er. "

I recalled, on the weekend before the arson attack, seeing movement in the cottage garden when I locked up at night. I shivered at the thought that Hartley had been yards away from my family.

"How come you got hooked up with Leroy Johnson?"

"I don't wanna say any more. I dunno who you are, but if 'Artley knows I've told anyone about 'is love life, 'e'll go bloody bananas."

I stood, reached over and grabbed his T-shirt, pulling him out of his chair. I drew his face as close to mine as I could. Putting on my most aggressive expression, I snarled, "*I'll go bloody bananas if you don't tell me everything!*"

His eyes gave away his fear again. "OK. OK." I released him and he slumped back down into the chair.

"'Artley asked if I wanted to earn a big 'wedge'. 'E wanted me to set fire to the cottage. Wipe 'em all out. I told 'im, it wasn't my bag, but I knew a geezer who'd do it if the price were right."

"And who's that?"

"It's no secret. It was splashed all over the papers. Leroy Johnson."

More questions filled my head. But one thing became clear; Nick Burrows wasn't responsible for the arson attack.

I gave Greenland back his mobile after deleting Hartley's messages and texts, as advised by RP. He'd already taken copies. I told Greenland I had no use for it anymore. I didn't tell him one of RP's techies had installed a clever piece of software on it which would hack into his calls and messages. Every time he used the mobile from now on, RP's team would get a text or could listen in and record the conversation. The wonders of digital telephony.

"It's very new, not perfect, and possibly illegal, but bloody useful," he said. Was there anything RP couldn't fix?

I left Greenland's flat with my mind in a whirl. I urgently wanted to speak to RP and Alisha. I called them and arranged to meet later that evening. Alisha said she could get away from Johnson for a few hours. He went out most evenings peddling dope, but after the scene with her and Greenland, he'd become much more inquisitive about her movements.

★

RP's office appeared even more striking at night. The lighting provided by the multi-coloured glass chandeliers and exotic wall lights were more in keeping with a London club; he had an aversion to the fluorescent strip lights found in most of London's offices. He'd organised a Chinese meal, which arrived shortly after we did.

I'd lost my appetite and picked at the food, but as RP and Alisha chomped their way through chop suey and crispy duck, and drank chilled bottled beer from the fridge behind RP's large desk, I explained what happened at my meeting with Greenland.

When I'd finished, a stunned silence ensued, before Alisha said, "I had no idea John Hartley believed the baby to be his. If Lynne knew, she kept that to herself."

"Good work, James. Welcome to the detectives' club. So now we know." RP stared at both of us in turn.

I slumped back in my chair and said, "I still can't believe any of this."

Alisha gazed down at the ground and, shaking her head, said, "I had absolutely no idea Hartley would go that far. He's a lunatic!"

Slamming my fist down of the desk, I said, "I can't get out of my head that it appears that whilst Lynne carried *my* child she was still seeing Hartley?"

Alisha put her hand on my arm and said, "It wasn't what you think, James. She tried everything she could think of to get out of the relationship. He terrified her. She grew afraid of what he'd do if she ended it. He threatened to tell Nick."

I opened my mouth to respond, but before I could, Alisha continued.

"It brought matters to a head when you appeared on the scene. You made all the difference to her. But it took her a long time to accept that you loved her so much; she doubted her ability to ever be happy with a man. I know that in the end she truly loved you."

I wanted to believe her, but Hartley's claim had rocked me. I couldn't think straight.

RP broke the silence.

"There's something else you both need to know. The spyware on Greenland's mobile worked a treat."

He retrieved his mobile from his jacket pocket, laid it on the desk, and stabbed a couple of keys. "Listen to this conversation between Greenland and Hartley after you'd left him."

Hartley: *Where the bloody hell have you been? I've been trying to get hold of you for days.*
Greenland: *What d' ya mean? I've been around.*
Hartley: *Yeah? So why didn't you return my texts?*

Greenland: What texts?

Hartley: You know what a text is, bonehead! I sent you several in the last few days. All bloody urgent.

Greenland: Didn't get 'em. What did you want?

Hartley: I wanted to know how Leroy Johnson got my mobile number. He's trying to blackmail me over that arson business. Did you give it to him?

Greenland: No, of course not. I know 'ow you feel about 'im.

Hartley: This is exactly what I didn't want to happen.

Greenland: I think I know 'ow Johnson got your number. I mislaid my mobile for a while. Got it back now.

Hartley: I worked that out all by myself.

Greenland: Johnson's got a new bit of totty. Met 'er a few times. She's been asking a few questions. She may 'ave nicked my mobile. Possible she's gone through my contacts an' told Johnson. 'Ad a geezer round my place asking questions.

Hartley: What geezer? What did you tell him?

Greenland: A sort of private dick, not the filth. I told 'im nuffin'. Whatdya take me for?

Hartley: What's this woman's name?

Greenland: Er… Alisha, yeah, that's right… Alisha. She spends a lotta time with that waste of space.

Hartley: Oh, great! Alisha? That's all I need! Call me if you hear anything.

"That's it," said RP, leaning over and turning off his mobile. "Now Hartley knows you're involved, Alisha. He's probably already worked out that you are too, James. Obviously, this puts you both at risk."

Alisha, for the first time since I'd met her, appeared concerned. She looked at me first, then RP and said, "Now what do we do?"

"Well, it's pretty obvious now, that Hartley and Johnson were responsible, isn't it? Clearly, Greenland had a role in it too."

"I should have sorted him out when I had the chance!" I spat out.

"No, you did well. We may need him," RP said.

He continued, "We could consider going to the police with this evidence. Trouble is, the court possibly won't admit much of it. We know all about that don't we? And even if the police did get a result against Hartley, Johnson remains free. And he can't be tried again."

RP had struck a raw nerve. I couldn't bear the thought of Johnson still being at large.

"That can't be allowed," I said, shaking my head.

RP, stroking his chin yet again, said, "Listen, I've got a plan to deal with Hartley *and* Johnson."

I said, "Aren't things a bit more complicated now? Hartley knows Alisha's directly involved." I turned to her and said, "Will he remember you as Lynne's friend?"

"Oh, he will. You know me. As I told you, I wasn't backward in coming forward. He knows I didn't approve of him."

I said, "Look, you've done your bit, Alisha. Leave this to Roger and me now."

She glared at me. "Absolutely not! I've come this far. Lynne meant a lot to me too, you know. I don't care about myself. You're not getting rid of me that easily. Tell us your ideas, Roger."

★

We left RP's office at midnight. I didn't feel like going straight home. I persuaded Alisha to stop off at a bustling late night bar in Piccadilly.

Alisha stressed what I'd meant to Lynne.

"You know, I don't think I'd ever seen her happier than when you two got married. She loved you so much. Proud of you too; you'd been through loads of stuff together."

"I know, I know. And I loved her too. But I just can't get out of my mind Hartley's claim to being Emily's father." She leant forward and held my hand.

"Yes, but you were there at her birth. And you brought Emily up from the start. You saw her every day of her short life. You were a *real* father to her. Hartley played no part in that whatsoever, even if his claim is true, which I don't believe, incidentally."

"Yeah, you're right, I suppose." My eyes welled up. I fought to contain my tears. I presumed I'd always feel like this whenever I thought of Emily.

"I'm missing them terribly…"

We both fell silent for a few moments, the vacuum filled by the sounds of bubbly conversations competing with ubiquitous background music.

Alisha placed her face closer to mine, ensuring I could hear her.

"Lynne always told me how kind you were, not just to her but other people. Something she didn't expect from a high-powered businessman."

"What do you mean?"

"Well, didn't you once pay for an airplane ticket for a stranger? A waitress you'd only just met who needed to visit the dying grandfather who'd brought her up. Where was it… Spain?"

"Yes, but…"

"And she told me you once bought a specially adapted van for a badly disabled guy so that his carer could drive him around. He hadn't left home for three years."

"Stop it. You're embarrassing me. That's all Lynne's influence."

"Well, she loved you for it."

I changed the subject.

"What do you think of Roger's ideas?"

"Very good. Total professional, isn't he? We're doing the decent thing, James. Bloody legal system's kaput. This is the only way to get things sorted."

She took a sip of her wine and said, "I'll text Johnson and arrange to meet up. I'll let you know how I get on."

"Please be careful, Alisha. If Greenland's told Johnson about you 'borrowing' his mobile, you're in big trouble."

CHAPTER FIFTEEN

October 1999

In the darkness of the early hours of the next morning, sitting at home clutching a can of beer, I analysed Greenland's information.

The thought of Hartley being Lynne's lover before I came on the scene and the repellent claim that he was Emily's father made me physically sick. I didn't know which was worse – the thought of Lynne fucking him, or Emily being the result. Either notion made me want to retch.

Other thoughts troubled me. Did Nick Burrows know about Lynne's affair with Hartley? It's possible that Georgie may have let something slip. Nick would have been incandescent with rage, adding impetus to Georgie's abduction.

And I couldn't understand why Lynne, my beautiful Lynne, who could have had anybody she wanted, put up with such arseholes as Burrows and Hartley. They destroyed her.

She'd told me she always felt the need for a man in her life – any man. Having a father and stepfather fail her when she was so young led to her insecurity and lack of self-worth.

We discussed it many times. It was a big issue for her, but I always told her my role in her life was to compensate for them.

I fantasised about how our lives would have turned out if

I'd met her first. We'd have brought out the best in each other. We'd have been a perfect match.

However, the trouble with fantasies is that they don't last. Inevitably, reality kicks in, and when it did, I became inconsolable.

Sometimes I went into our guest room, took the mattress off the bed and placed it against the wall. I'd spend an hour punching away in manic fury at my impromptu punch bag, shouting out obscenities at the top of my voice. Good job I lived in a detached house.

My biceps ached afterwards. I could hardly lift a glass of wine.

*

We spent most of the next afternoon and evening in RP's office tossing ideas about. He loved scribbling notes, drawing diagrams and sometimes doodling whilst considering the merits of each idea. His style replicated the deliberations I made in acquiring new businesses.

Given our previous experience of the justice system, we wanted to make certain Johnson and Hartley would pay for what they did.

We eventually settled on a plan to ensure that Hartley couldn't possibly escape the full force of the law. It had three key goals: disposing of Johnson, setting up Hartley as the killer and providing overwhelming proof that he'd arranged the arson attack.

I didn't care about the money he'd embezzled from me. But I cared deeply about taking revenge for the loss of my family.

RP questioned me directly. "Are you sure you're up for this?"

"Yes, I am. I *need* to be more involved, you know that. I'll go bloody insane if I don't *do* something."

"OK, I understand. But I'd be happier with the plan if you worked closely with one of my contractors. He's worked for me before. He knows his way around and he's excellent at what he does. If you're happy with that, I'll brief him separately. It's not a good idea for you to know all the details, in case something goes wrong. Is that OK?"

"That's fine."

We finally called it a day at around 10.30pm. We'd checked and rechecked the details of the plan and decided to sleep on it. We agreed to confer the next day to see if we'd had second thoughts or come up with any modifications.

Next day, I called him to confirm that, after speaking with Alisha, we were both up for the plan as it stood.

"Good," he said. "I'll set the ball rolling. We don't have a lot of time. I'm worried something might happen to Alisha. We're dealing with dangerous men. I'll call you back later with the details."

★

We'd covered every angle to the *n*th degree and with military precision. I had complete confidence in the plan. I'd built my business empire on similar principles.

We needed to convince Johnson that Hartley wanted to meet to hand over the cash Johnson had demanded. I called in on Greenland again and asked for one more small 'favour', reminding him of the serious shit he was in.

I told him to text Johnson saying Hartley wanted to meet up. The venue, chosen by RP, was a disused railway arch, formerly used for car repairs in St James's Road, close to Southwark Park.

He sent it whilst I watched. He couldn't have been more helpful. The threat of being charged as an accessory to murder spooked him.

Alisha told me later that Johnson fired up with excitement when he received the text.

"He truly believes he's enticed Hartley into meeting his demands. He's unbelievably smug about it."

"Great," I said. "That's it, Alisha. You don't have to see Johnson again. It's my call now. I can't thank you enough for what you've done." I hugged her tightly.

★

It hadn't rained for two months and the last few days had been humid, almost tropical. As I left home to meet RP's 'contractor' at a busy pub, *The Chalk and Cheese,* less than half a mile away from the meeting place, the heavens opened after an extended period of thunder and lightning.

The 'contractor', a British Afro-Caribbean, aged around thirty-five, well built, over six feet tall and with a day or two's stubble on his face emphasising his blackness, made himself known. His expressionless eyes matched the clothes he wore; a black beanie hat, dark trousers and a black bomber jacket. I wouldn't have enjoyed meeting him in a dark alleyway.

He spoke few words. He asked me to call him 'Bruno'. After a drink, we walked the short distance to the converted railway arches, holding up our collars against the driving rain. The archway building, covered in graffiti and with a dilapidated 'To Let' sign hanging loosely from the wall, had clearly been on the market for a while. In the otherwise empty car park, a single car was parked out of sight of the main road and close to the building.

Arriving a good half-hour before the appointed time of 11.30pm, Bruno made for the car, a 1997 maroon Toyota Avensis, before going to the archway door. He fumbled inside his coat pocket for the keys and opened the driver's door, reached in and produced a large black holdall.

Heading for the archway entrance, he produced another key and unlocked one of the doors. From his familiarity of the layout, I guessed he'd used this venue before. I asked Bruno about the possibility of CCTV cameras covering the arches.

He spoke with only a hint of a Caribbean accent – more Essex than Barbados. "Don't worry 'bout that. They've been dealt with."

The building smelled of engine oil and was windowless except for two skylights above the double doors. Bruno reached inside his holdall and retrieved two heavy-duty torches, which he switched on and placed on a workbench. The beams shone upwards, rebounding around the arch, producing a halo effect. Several workbenches, a desk and four chairs sat on the painted concrete floor.

Occasionally, the building rumbled with the sound of trains passing over the arches.

Bruno opened his holdall again and handed me a plastic bag containing a pair of white paper overalls, complete with a hood, like the ones I'd seen forensic teams wearing at crime scenes on TV.

"Take off your jacket and trousers. Put these on," he said. When I'd done so, he handed me a dark blue jacket, a pair of grey trousers and a blue baseball cap, which he also took from his holdall. He motioned for me put my clothes in the plastic bag and to put the replacement clothes on over the overalls.

They were a tight fit. I struggled, but managed it with difficulty.

He handed me a pair of Nike trainers and socks. I swapped them with my shoes. Fortunately, they were at least two sizes larger. He put my shoes into the bag containing my jacket and trousers.

Finally, he produced two pairs of latex gloves from his coat pocket. Throwing one pair at me he said, "Put these on and sit behind the table." He tugged the other pair onto his hands.

After ten minutes, which felt like an eternity, we heard loud rapping at the door.

Bruno opened the door but didn't reveal himself, staying behind it. Johnson, wearing a short-sleeved sports shirt splattered with rain, came inside and peered through the gloom. As he spotted me through the torchlight, sitting facing him, his thin reedy voice, which I recognised from his court appearance, rang out.

"'Artley... is that you? You sure you're 'Artley? Who the fuck *are* you?"

Bruno appeared quickly behind him and, taking Johnson by surprise, expertly kneed him in the back of his legs, forcibly driving his face down into the concrete floor.

Within seconds, he had Johnson's hands cuffed behind him and had frog-marched him to one of the chairs facing me, yelling at him to sit down.

Johnson's facial expression revealed terror. He'd not expected this.

"What the fuck's going on? Where's 'Artley? 'E's supposed to do a deal wiv' me. Who are you?"

I'd rehearsed being face-to-face with the killer of my family more times than I cared to remember.

Now that time had come.

Bruno stood back in the shadows as I let my rage take over. I visualised Johnson pouring petrol through the letterbox of our cottage in Lymington and setting light to it whilst Lynne, Georgie and Emily lay sleeping upstairs.

Flashbacks of the funeral and the coffins, especially the tiny one bearing Emily being carried down the aisle of the crematorium, exploded into my mind.

I yelled at Johnson, "What kind of sick bastard are you? How could you have possibly set fire to a house with a young family sleeping in it?"

He'd gathered his composure and his cocky expression wound me up.

"Fuck off!" he shouted.

I stood up, pushed the table to one side and punched him hard in the stomach and, as he yelped and bent forward, I followed up with a hard bony fist on the side of his jaw. He spat out bloody phlegm onto the floor. I hit him again, this time with my other fist on the other side of his face. Fragments of an equally bloody tooth ricocheted off the rock-solid floor.

"Not so cocky now, are you, you sack of shit!"

I hit him a few more times around his head, which rolled from side to side with each blow like a ventriloquist's dummy.

Then I stopped.

I slumped down in my chair, exhausted by my efforts. Johnson sat opposite, hunched over, blood dripping from his nose and mouth. He started whining.

"It wasn't just me! 'Artley's the bloke you really want. Lemme go!" I nodded to Bruno to take over. He'd watched the proceedings, the merest hint of a smile creasing his face. Unseen by Johnson, he produced a brown bottle of clear liquid and a white cloth from his pocket. He undid the bottle and shook out its contents.

He came at Johnson from behind, put an arm around his neck, wrenching his head backwards, and with his other hand holding the cloth, he placed it over Johnson's nose and mouth. He held it in position whilst Johnson's mangled face registered first surprise, then fear as he slumped unconscious, almost falling off his chair.

Another train rumbled overhead and the walls of the archway quivered.

Bruno unlocked the handcuffs holding Johnson, turned off the torches, and threw them into his holdall. In the darkness, we hauled Johnson to the door.

Once outside, Bruno locked up and threw me the keys to the railway arch door as we dragged Johnson to the Toyota Avensis on the far side of the car park. He opened the boot, we fed Johnson in and slammed it shut.

We threw our bags on the back seat and Bruno pressed the ignition keys into my hand. He sat low down into the rear passenger seat as I got into the driver's seat.

I'd memorised the route we'd previously decided to take at our meeting with RP. He designed it so that road traffic CCTV cameras could pick us up.

I drove the one and three-quarter miles to Mill Street, close to Butlers Wharf, and turned right into Bermondsey Wall West, parallel with the River Thames. I parked and turned off the lights. We sat there for a short while to ensure no one had ventured out for a late night walk along the Embankment.

The rain had subsided slightly but the wind had picked up, whistling around the warehouses facing directly onto the river.

We both got out of the car. Bruno opened the boot and taped Johnson's hands together behind his back, whilst he remained unconscious. Between us, we hauled him onto his feet.

Bruno took a black, rusty anchor from the boot. It must have weighed around five kilos. He quickly tied it around Johnson's waist as I held him. Despite this weight attached, we were easily able to lift him over the four-foot wall and drop him into the murky Thames.

Due to the high tide, he splashed into the water quickly. It was over in less than two minutes.

I glanced over to my left and saw Tower Bridge lit up like a Christmas tree, its reflection shimmering in the water. Adrenaline rushed through my body. Johnson had forfeited his right to life for what he did. I'd dealt with one worthless lowlife.

I couldn't wait to tackle the next.

★

I took the driver's seat and Bruno tucked down out of sight in the rear passenger seats again. This time, I stuck to back streets favoured by cab drivers, where there were fewer CCTV cameras. Twenty minutes later, we arrived at a two-storey block of flats in Percival Street in Clerkenwell, north of the Thames.

We parked in a residents' parking place with poor street lighting. Almost before the wheels had stopped turning, Bruno grabbed his holdall, silently nodded to me, got out of the nearside rear passenger door, and swiftly made off.

I never saw him again.

Killing the engine, I picked up the bag with my clothes and shoes in it and locked the car. I crossed the road and made my way to flat number 14 on the first floor. I opened the door with a key on the same ring as the car keys.

Still wearing the latex gloves, I stumbled into the entrance in the darkness and made my way to the bedroom. Hartley lay on top of the bed out for the count, gently snoring, his eyes closed and his jaw slack.

I had an overwhelming urge to go the kitchen drawer, select the biggest knife and thrust it into Hartley's chest. I regretted that wasn't part of the plan.

Earlier that evening, Bruno had gained access to Hartley's flat and blagged his way in, taking Hartley by surprise using his seemingly well-practised chloroform routine. That's when he'd taken Hartley's clothes and trainers and stuffed them in his holdall.

I found a cupboard housing a central heating boiler, took off Hartley's 'borrowed' clothes and stuffed the damp jacket, trousers, baseball hat, trainers and the bottle of chloroform behind the boiler, making them difficult to spot.

I removed the paper overalls and socks and stuffed them into my bag. I planned to burn them once I returned home. I retrieved my own clothes from the plastic bag and put them on.

I hung the car keys back on the hook behind the front door. I put the railway arch keys in a sideboard drawer. Removing the latex gloves and placing them in my bag, I silently went out of the door, down the steps onto the street.

The rain had finally stopped and I walked for over an hour though the puddles to clear my head. Crossing a deserted London Bridge, I paused for a while and stared down at the Thames, glossy from the lights on the embankment.

I swear I saw Johnson's body floating downriver carried by the current. I knew it wasn't possible with a 5kg weight attached.

Nonetheless, I bawled, "Good riddance, you fucker!"

★

Now 1.30am, too late to talk to Alisha or RP, I hailed a cab near St Thomas's Street. The last thing I wanted was to have a conversation with the driver. I pretended to sleep. Arriving home twenty-five minutes later, I poured myself a large brandy, which I downed in one gulp.

Once I'd downed the second glass, my satisfaction with the plan slowly turned to remorse. Had I actually conspired to murder Leroy Johnson? I realised I'd have nightmares about it for a long time.

I prided myself that I could always instinctively separate right from wrong in life. But now, the needle on my moral compass had unswervingly swung in the direction of getting justice for Lynne, Georgie and Emily. I reasoned that if I hadn't dealt with Johnson, I'd have failed them.

I reminded myself of his callous and heartless actions. This, plus the calming affect of the brandy, brought a modicum of relief.

I couldn't sleep, my mind going over every detail of the evening's events. The sound of Johnson's body splashing into the Thames continuously replayed in my mind.

Next morning, I called RP on his office landline soon after nine o'clock. He said it was safer than using a mobile – less chance of being traced. He'd already heard from Bruno, who'd brought him up to speed. He asked me if the rest of the plan had gone as we'd agreed.

"Yes… yes, very well. Everything's been returned to its rightful owner. Thanks for your input."

"That's OK. Now leave it at least twenty-four hours. Then make the phone call."

I called Alisha at her office and gave her the same cryptic message.

"Good!" she grunted.

CHAPTER SIXTEEN

October 1999

The phone call RP had reminded me to make was to Crimestoppers. I thought it was a risk and remained sceptical. However, RP assured me that Crimestoppers' promise of anonymity had never been broken in over eleven years since it started.

"Think about it," he said. "Their reputation lives or dies on this single promise. If just one caller's name is discovered, that's it. No-one will trust them."

However, I couldn't help thinking it a bizarre thing for me to do. I'd just helped to murder a man. Now I planned to tell them about it.

I went to a payphone box a mile from home to make the call. Despite RP's assurance, I didn't want Crimestoppers to trace it.

I'd written down the key points I needed to get across and checked them again and again. I picked up the phone and returned it to the cradle at least half a dozen times.

Finally, I dialled the number and held on. The call handler, a volunteer called Sue, introduced herself with a kind, soft voice and listened without interruption whilst I read from my brief notes. I told her the precise location where we'd thrown Johnson over the river wall and gave Hartley's name as the likely suspect, together with his address.

She read back the notes she'd taken and asked me to confirm them.

"Did you witness the crime?"

"No, I overheard a conversation in a pub earlier tonight."

"Do you know the person you suspect threw this person into the river?"

"No, I don't."

"How do you know his address, then?"

"Oh… I… er… *used* to know him. I heard his name mentioned. I'm sure it's the same man."

I wanted to hang up.

Before I did, she said, "OK. I'll pass on a report to the Metropolitan Police. They'll want to consider what you've told me and decide what to do."

"Yes, OK."

"You know, this is a serious allegation you've made. If you have any more information to impart please call us again." She gave me a reference number. "Thank you for calling Crimestoppers."

It didn't feel like such a good idea phoning them after all. Could be the police would treat it as a hoax call and not take any action.

We'd have to wait and see.

★

The next few days dawned crisp, bright and sunny and the high temperature for the time of the year lifted my mood marginally.

I chastened myself continuously about my inadequate call to Crimestoppers. Every day, I avidly scanned the local and national newspapers to see if the press had picked up any news of our exploits.

Three days later, several papers ran a story following a statement from the Metropolitan Police. On page six of the *London Evening Standard*, I read the report with a mixture of excitement and trepidation.

BODY RECOVERED FROM THAMES

> *The Metropolitan Police announced yesterday that following a tip-off, police divers have recovered a body from the River Thames, downriver from Tower Bridge. They have named the man as 26-year-old Leroy Johnson. The circumstances appear suspicious and police are following up several lines of enquiry. If anybody has any further information or witnessed anything unusual in the vicinity of Bermondsey Wall West or Butlers' Wharf on or around Thursday 9th October 1999, please call Southwark Police Station in Borough High Street, London SE 1 on 0207 177666 or call Crimestoppers anonymously on 0800 555 111.*

I phoned RP and told him the news. "Good... that's good. Let's get together for a review tomorrow, the three of us. Can you make 10ish?"

★

RP, dressed in his usual immaculate style, sporting a bright yellow handkerchief flowing out of the top pocket of his navy-blue blazer, appeared in good spirits. He got down to business once Lucy had brought in the coffee and biscuits.

He took a mobile phone from his drawer.

"Exhibit number one," he announced, waving it in the air. "This is Hartley's. Bruno 'borrowed' it from Hartley's flat at the same time as the other items."

"Has it still got all his messages and voicemails on it?" I said.

"Too right. The police would find this useful. It's possible they may not be able to use this as evidence, but it'll point them in the right direction. Give them an excuse to search his flat, find the stuff we left there."

"How do we get the mobile to the police?" I said.

"I'll get one of my contacts to take it in, say they found it in a cafe close to Hartley's flat."

"And how will they know it's Hartley's?"

"It's standard procedure for them to check the serial number printed on the sim card tray, phone the service provider and get the name and address."

"That's neat," I said.

"It gets better. Any half-decent detective will check the name given to them by the phone company on the Police National Computer and discover Hartley's criminal past. Then they'll check his mobile and see the messages."

"Suppose the police don't?" I said.

"I'm confident they will but if not, we can play our ace card."

"Which is?"

"Greenland. He'd be the prosecution's star witness. He knows so much about Hartley. And, from what you've told me, he's shitting himself about being charged in connection with the arson attack. Contrary to popular belief, there is no honour amongst criminals, believe me. And the police could do a deal with him, unofficially, of course."

Alisha had remained quiet ever since we entered RP's

office. Although she'd approved of the plan to dispose of Johnson, I don't think she believed we'd actually carry it out. She broke her silence.

"What if Hartley comes up with an alibi for the Johnson murder?"

RP responded, "Well, that's neat too. Hartley would have been out cold for at least four or five hours. He won't remember a thing. All he can tell the police is that he spent the evening at home."

"Couldn't he pay someone to vouch for him?"

"Well, he could, but it would have to be a damn good alibi. I don't believe that with this evidence, he'll be able to wriggle out of either the arson or the Johnson murder. That's what we want, isn't it?"

RP poured more coffee as a police siren wailed, rushing up St James's Street.

Waiting for the noise to subside, I sipped my coffee and said, "The police press release said they were following up several lines of enquiry. But the longer the police take to get to his flat, surely the more time Hartley has to discover the clothes and chloroform bottle."

"Yes…?" RP motioned with his hand for me to continue.

"Well, if he finds them, won't that signal that he's been set up by us for the Johnson murder? He already knows about Alisha's involvement with Johnson… and Greenland."

RP, without hesitation, said, "You're right. That's why we need Hartley off the streets… quickly." He glanced at both of us in turn. "We don't want him doing anything silly, do we?"

"We certainly, don't," I said.

"I'll make sure the police have Hartley's mobile as soon as possible. I'll make a few calls later today; try to find out where the investigation's heading."

RP eyeballed me and said, "But, of course, there's someone else with a motive for killing Johnson, isn't there?"

"Who?"

"I expect the police will want to interview you, James."

"I bloody hope not!"

"Well, someone may have remembered your outburst at Winchester Crown Court after Johnson got off. You were understandably upset. It's possible the senior investigating officer on the case will want a chat. DI Flood wasn't it?"

"Er… yes. He appeared in court that day. He was as upset as me about Johnson getting off."

RP, slowly stroking his chin once more, said, "Being upset isn't a crime. Doesn't automatically follow you'd kill someone as a result. I think it might be a good idea to have an alibi in case things turn nasty. Alisha, I'm not sure you'll want to agree to this, but are you prepared to say that James spent the night at your flat?"

"You know me. I'd do anything to get Hartley banged up."

"Well you two should work on getting your stories absolutely straight. OK?"

We both nodded.

"Bloody hell, Roger, I'm not looking forward to being interviewed by Flood, of all people. He's a miserable sod."

"It may not come to that. I'm sure you'll be fine. Just make sure your alibi's foolproof. And remember, Hartley's clothes will be brimming with forensics, proving him to be Johnson's killer. You'll just have to keep your nerve."

I wasn't convinced I could.

"Right, let's leave it there then shall we? If I get any more information I'll let you know." RP stood and shook hands with each of us.

Hartley's arrest couldn't come soon enough.

★

Alisha and I walked up to Green Park and found a bench away from the many tree-lined paths, full of kids kicking the late autumn leaves in the bright sunlight.

We spent an hour rehearsing our alibis, especially the time I'd arrived in the evening and left the next morning. This implied that I'd slept with her, although we never had. It added substance to the alibi.

RP's influence had prompted me to ask Alisha about CCTV cameras, but she assured me there were none covering her flat in Canary Wharf.

Late the next morning, RP called me on my landline at home. He sounded excited.

"Right, there have been several interesting developments. I got Hartley's phone sent to the nearest police station to his flat yesterday. The conversations with Greenland and Johnson led to the police visiting Hartley. Problem is that he's gone AWOL. They got a search warrant and this morning, they took away a lot of stuff which I'm told is *of interest*. I'm hoping that means what I think it means."

RP's connections were proving invaluable.

"Great," I said. "At last something's happening."

"It is. The forensic service is testing the stuff as a matter of urgency. It'll take a few days, I'm afraid."

"Oh no! I hope they find the bastard quickly."

"I'm told they're treating this case as a priority. I'll be in touch if I hear anything else."

I tried to get inside Hartley's mind, imagining what his next move might be. I was turning into RP by the minute.

He called me at home that evening. I was working on the budgets for next year's business plans.

"Have you seen the nine o'clock news on TV?"

"No. I don't have the TV on. What's happened?"

"Greenland's been found stabbed to death in the early hours of this morning."

"What? Are you sure?"

"BBC News just reported it. Not many details yet. It'll be in the papers tomorrow. They haven't given any indications as to the perpetrator, but I can guess, can't you?"

★

Channel hopping every news bulletin for the next half-an-hour, I realised the implications of Greenland's demise. Our fallback plan of using him as a star prosecution witness had crashed.

I called Alisha to warn her she may be in danger. I planned to go over and stay with her if she felt vulnerable. I tried both her landline and mobile and got her messaging service each time. I waited ten minutes and called again — same message. A knot grew in my stomach. It was 10.30pm.

I remembered that RP had placed a tracking device on the mobile he'd given her. I called him, explained the situation and asked him to investigate. He checked in with one of his techies at his computer room, staffed around the clock, and called me back. He confirmed the stats showed the mobile's location as Piccadilly.

"But that's where she works, Roger. She wouldn't be there now, surely. And if she is, why isn't she answering?"

"Sorry, James. Can't answer that. Keep trying to contact her. If there's any change in the location, I'll call you."

I picked up my car keys from the table, ran out to the garage and leapt into my Mercedes. On a frosty, cloudless evening, a full moon lit up the sky. Emerging from the Blackwall Tunnel, I felt on edge. As well as concerned about Alisha's absence, I became aware of the glittering River Thames and the events that had taken place there several nights ago.

This happened every time I got close to the river. The adrenaline rushes I'd experienced then were now replaced by gnawing, anxious feelings that ate up my insides.

In light traffic, I arrived at her apartment within twenty minutes.

I parked outside her block, ran up the stairs two at a time to the second floor and pressed the buzzer. No reply. I rang again. Still no reply. I ran back down the stairs and gazed up at her window. It was in darkness.

I walked the half-mile back towards South Quay DLR station and checked a couple of restaurants and bars nearby that I knew she used.

No joy.

I walked back to her flat and decided to stay in my car until she returned. Another half-hour passed. I checked with RP the location of her mobile again – no change. I tried to convince myself that she must have gone out with a girlfriend and forgotten to tell me.

I continuously called her mobile and landline alternately.
Nothing.

Her repetitive message irritated me. I struck the steering wheel with the heels of my hands and shouted, "Bugger!"

A few minutes later, around 1am, I breathed a huge sigh of relief as I spotted Alisha in my rear view mirror. I recognised her confident gait. Now seventy or eighty yards away, she strolled slowly towards my car and the safety of her flat.

What happened next resembled a scene from a movie.

A tall, well-built, hooded figure emerged from the shadows, swiftly approached her from behind and thrust a canvas bag over her head. He put one hand over her covered mouth and dragged her backwards, as she kicked and struggled, towards a nearby car facing the opposite direction to mine. He opened the boot with a remote and bundled her in, slamming it shut. The whole scene lasted less than twenty seconds.

I lost precious time before I realised what was going on. Finally, I sprang out of my car and ran towards them, shouting at the top of my voice, "Let her go! Let her go!" I got close enough to gulp, inadvertently, a lungful of exhaust fumes as the tyres screeched, spinning the car away from me.

I immediately recognised the make, model and registration number. It was Hartley's car. The thought that Alisha now occupied the same place as Johnson's unconscious body a few days earlier flashed through my mind.

I sprinted back to my car, u-turned and roared off in pursuit. I took a guess which way Hartley would head. To my relief, I spotted his car turning left at Westferry Road onto Burdett Road, heading north. Surprisingly heavy traffic for this time of the morning held me back, but I finally got to within two cars of him. Despite constantly flashing my lights and sounding my horn, no one moved over. A couple of drivers actually gave me the finger in return.

Hartley, realising he was being followed, took unbelievable risks, overtaking at crossroads and once nearly mounting a pavement, trying to get past a car turning right. I shot a couple of red lights myself. Then a large supermarket truck making late-night deliveries pulled out of a store immediately in front of me and stalled his engine. He took ages to get it going again.

"Bugger! Bugger!" I yelled at the anonymous driver before I passed. I carried on heading north for a couple more miles, hoping Hartley hadn't turned off.

I thought I'd lost him, but then I spotted the car parked in a lay-by with the boot open, less than fifty yards in front of me. Out of the gloom, Alisha appeared, waving her arms and scampering away from the car in my direction. Hartley wasn't far behind her.

I stopped. I had to choose between getting out and challenging Hartley or rescuing Alisha. I chose the latter and swung open the passenger door from the inside. Hartley, seeing my car, stopped chasing her, turned and scrambled back into his driver's seat. He almost struck another car as he gunned his, rejoining the main road.

As Alisha jumped in, breathlessly she said, "Oh James… I'm so relieved to see you… how the bloody hell did you know I'd been abducted?"

"I'll tell you later. Let's get after the bastard."

Alisha took several deep breaths to calm herself as we chased after Hartley's car.

He drove like a maniac. I couldn't keep up and after a couple of miles, we gave up.

Driving back to her flat, Alisha spat out her anger.

"I can't believe I let him get me into the boot. I tried as hard as I could to get away. He was too strong for me." She closed her eyes at the memory.

"You must have been scared to death. How did you get out of the boot?"

"After he bundled me in, I managed to get the bag off my head, but I was still in complete darkness. I could barely breathe. I heard the rumble of tyres. He was taking me to God knows where. At first, I panicked. I hit the boot lid with my fists and kicked out at it, shouting at the top of my voice. I became hysterical but I realised I was wasting energy."

Just listening to Alisha's experience made me sweat. I suffered badly from claustrophobia.

"I pulled myself together, reasoned that the boot locking mechanism must be on the inside, if only I could find it in the pitch darkness. I lifted up the carpet and fumbled around the perimeter of the boot. Fortunately, I found a cable. I ran my fingers along it and traced it back to the locking mechanism."

"Good thinking."

"I pulled as hard as I could, praying the latch would give way. It didn't. I tried a dozen times but it wouldn't budge."

"How did you get it open?"

"Thank goodness, I'd kept hold of my handbag. When he attacked me from behind, I thought someone was trying to mug me. I instinctively hung on to it for dear life. I had a small pair of nail scissors inside. I scrabbled in the dark and finally found them. I felt for the latch with my fingers again and fiddled around for a good five minutes digging about, anxious not to make any noise.

"I couldn't believe it when suddenly, something clicked and the boot lid sprung open. It shot up before I could haul it down again. I'd never appreciated fresh air so much!"

"Thank God!"

"I hoped the driver hadn't noticed. But obviously he had. He slowed down, pulled over to the lay-by and stopped the car. Before I leapt out, I spat into the boot. I'd seen someone do this on *Crimewatch* once – important to leave my DNA."

Impressed by her ability to think like this under pressure, I reached across to the passenger seat and squeezed her thigh. She placed a hand on top of mine.

"I grabbed my handbag and ran as fast as I could away from

the car. I've never been so glad to see your Mercedes. How the hell did you know where I was?"

I told her how I'd witnessed the abduction taking place and followed them.

"Where do you think he planned to take me?" she said.

"I don't know, but the lay-by where you escaped from is close to Victoria Park, not far from Hackney Marsh. I dread to think what would have happened to you when he got you there." She gave a shudder.

"By the way, the tracker on your mobile shows it's in Piccadilly. Is that right?"

"Didn't I tell you? One of the girls at work is getting married. Her hen night consisted of a pub-crawl in the West End. In all the excitement, I left my mobile at work. Of all the times for me to do that!" She raised her eyes.

"And when did you realise it was Hartley who abducted you?"

"What? Oh no, it wasn't him. Definitely not. When he put the bag over my face, whoever it was said, 'Don't scream.' I'd have recognised Hartley's voice. It's so distinctive."

"But it's definitely Hartley's car. I've driven it, remember. He must be involved. Oh, of course! You don't know, do you?"

"Don't know what?"

"Greenland was found stabbed to death early yesterday morning."

Alisha, stunned, closed her eyes. "Oh, my God!" she said, as she put her hand to her mouth, and sank back deeper into the passenger seat.

★

As we reached her flat, I said, "Look, I'll stay with you tonight.

You've been through a lot. I'll call RP in the morning; see what he has to say."

Alisha, normally defiant and feisty, looked beaten.

I poured a couple of brandies, my go-to remedy in times of crises. I handed one to her after she'd flopped down on the sofa.

"Well, that was a fucking nightmare!" she said.

"Don't worry, Alisha. I'm not leaving you. I'll stay here for as long as you want me to. Why don't you take your brandy and go to bed? I'll doss down on the couch."

"Yes, I think I will."

Five minutes later, I put my head around her door to make sure she was OK. She sat on the bed with her arms wrapped around her legs, still holding the empty brandy glass in one hand. She had a vague expression on her face but, smiled as she said, "You're so good to me, James. Come here." She waggled her finger at me and as I leant closer to her face, she kissed me fully on the lips.

"Why don't you sleep in my bed tonight?"

She'd brushed her hair and her dark brown eyes locked onto mine as she continued smiling. I wasn't sure where this was leading, but I found myself drawn to her.

Since Lynne's death fifteen months earlier, I'd missed the intimacy of feeling naked, warm flesh nuzzling into me in bed. And the way her curves melted into mine – a perfect fit.

I knew this wasn't the right time or place, but as I glimpsed Alisha's toned shoulders and arms and the revealing transparent nightdress, I lost the battle…

★

When I woke, it took me a while to realise where I was. The sun streamed through the windows and I smelt coffee brewing. Sitting up in the bed, an overwhelming guilty feeling washed over me.

During the night, we'd become unbelievably aroused and excited as we abandoned our inhibitions and eagerly committed ourselves to sexual gratification. But the first pangs of guilt had kicked in when we'd finished.

Now the guilt turned into shame. What had I done?

I fought back my tears. I felt I'd let Lynne down.

Alisha entered the bedroom wearing her dressing gown. She carried a cup of coffee in each hand. I turned my face away from her.

"What's wrong, James?"

"Er… nothing. I'm fine."

"Oh, yeah? Come on, what's really the matter?" She put the cups down on the bedside table and placed an arm around my shoulder.

I tried to explain how I felt, but the words wouldn't come.

She sympathised. "I know how much you loved Lynne and how much she loved you. I can feel your pain. Really, I can. I feel pain too. Lynne was my best friend. More than a sister to me. I wouldn't do anything to upset her."

She stroked the back of my head, at the same time gazing into my eyes. "But last night, we both needed comforting, don't you see? In a funny kind of way, I think Lynne would have approved. We're both still grieving for her."

I looked away, breaking eye contact.

Alisha continued, "The fact is you met each other and fell in love. You were two sides of the same coin. But now, she's gone. Nothing will bring her back."

"Yes, I know, I know."

I slid off the bed and made for the bathroom, fighting back the tears once again.

*

Later that Saturday morning, after I'd showered and shaved with Alisha's lightweight woman's razor, I dressed and popped down to the newsagents to see if the papers had any more news on the Greenland murder.

The *Daily Mail* covered the story.

MAN FOUND STABBED IN VICTORIA PARK

In the early hours of yesterday morning, a man was found stabbed to death in a copse in Victoria Park close to Hackney Marsh. He has been named as Colin Greenland, aged 47 and a well-known drug dealer. Police are following up a number of leads in this direction. They haven't ruled out a possible connection with the apparent gangland killing of Leroy Johnson, aged 26, whose body was dragged from the River Thames near Tower Bridge five days ago. If anyone has any information on either of these incidents please call Crimestoppers 0800555111 or Southwark Police Station 0207177666.

The references to Victoria Park near Hackney Marsh, close to the location where Alisha had escaped from the boot of Hartley's car, sent a shiver down my spine. Now the Metropolitan police had linked these murders, presumably from the messages and conversations on Hartley's mobile, we needed them to tie in the arson attack and pin it on Hartley – except he'd gone missing.

I called RP at home from Alisha's landline, told him about the *Daily Mail* article and updated him on last night's events. He sounded genuinely concerned and relieved Alisha had survived her ordeal.

I asked him, "Do you think Alisha should go to the police, tell them about this abduction attempt and mention Hartley's car?"

After a moment's pause, he replied, "I don't think that's a good idea. It could look like Alisha's setting up Hartley. It's too obvious. On the other hand, it'll appear strange if she doesn't inform the police. Someone may have witnessed the incident and already reported it for all we know. I'd say get her to go to her local station, make a statement but don't mention the car's details."

I told Alisha RP's thoughts, to which she agreed.

I added, "You know, I think it would be a good idea if you moved into my place whilst Hartley's still at large. He obviously knows where you live and I wouldn't forgive myself if he sent someone else to abduct you."

"You're assuming he's behind it, are you?"

"Who else had a motive?"

"You're right. Well, if you don't mind?"

"Of course I don't mind."

"OK. I think you're right. I'll pack a case. Won't be long."

As she left the room I shouted after her, "I'll run you over to my place as soon as you're ready and then, if you like, I'll drop you off at the police station."

When we got to my house, I carried her bag and took it upstairs to the second bedroom. She followed.

"Look, Alisha, I know it sounds silly after last night, but I don't think I'm quite ready yet to… you know –"

"No... no... that's fine, James. I understand. I do." She sighed as she added, "This whole business is surreal."

I left her to sort out her things and when she finished, we drove over to the police station after lunch. I dropped her off, wished her luck, pecked her on the cheek and told her to call me when she'd finished.

The police station in Canary wharf was close to my BMW showroom and office. I decided to go in. Being a Saturday, the showroom was busy. I walked through, acknowledged a couple of my salesmen and went to my office.

With only eight weeks to go, there'd been a great deal of media attention to the possibility that at midnight on the last day of the twentieth century, the world's computers would crash. The media called it the Millennium Bug or the Y2K problem.

It was about how the programmers had written their codes. Many had taken a shortcut to save memory by only using the last two digits of the year. This had the effect that as the year rolled over into 2000, the computer system would think it was 1900. Many experts forecast an epic meltdown on the scale of Armageddon.

As if I didn't have enough on my plate.

Like every other business, we were setting up contingency plans in case this 'Doomsday' prophecy became reality. I went into the office and read the latest reports from our consultants who were working on the problem.

Two hours after dropping her off, Alisha called and I collected her from the police station. I asked how the interview went.

"Fine. I made a statement. I think it went OK. Pretty straightforward, actually."

CHAPTER SEVENTEEN

Late October 1999

The following morning, a loud knocking on my front door around 7am made me start. I'd only just got up and made coffee whilst still wearing my boxers and T-shirt. I threw on my dressing gown and answered the door.

Two burly men were standing on the threshold. I immediately recognised one as DI Flood.

"Mr Hamilton. Remember me?"

"How could I forget? Yes, of course I do."

"I've been transferred to the Met. I'm now a Detective Chief Inspector working for the Major Crime Team. This is Detective Sergeant Lyle." They both flashed their warrant cards as a matter of course. "May we come in?"

"Yes, of course."

RP's warning rang loudly in my ears.

I showed them into the sitting room. Drizzly rain patted against the windows. I waved an arm at two armchairs and offered them coffee. They both refused.

I recalled DCI Flood's gaunt and serious expression, exhibiting every inch the hard-bitten police officer. DS Lyle, younger, around thirtyish, wasn't in as good a shape as his boss, a slight paunch poking out of the top of his trousers as he sat down.

"Should I get dressed?"

The newly promoted Detective Chief Inspector replied in his usual brusque manner. A darkness shrouded him and he had an unerring knack of putting me on edge.

"That won't be necessary for now. We're investigating a possible link between two recent unexplained deaths in London with the arson attack on your family in August 1998. As you know, I was the SIO on that case. The powers-that-be decided I should follow up these developments. It's possible you may be able to help us with our enquiries."

I wasn't overly excited that Flood was still on my case. But at last the police had made the connections we wanted.

"If I can be of any help, of course I'll give you any information I can."

DCI Flood glanced down at his notebook and flicked back a few pages before saying, "Good. I suspect it's a bit painful, but can you tell me everything you know about the arson attack on your cottage in Lymington?"

Trying not to sound too defensive, I fought back the temptation to react strongly.

"I've been through all this with you before. As I recall, you implied then that, somehow, I might have been involved. You've never confirmed otherwise, incidentally."

"Just answer my questions, Mr Hamilton. It's all new to DS Lyle." He stared at me, forcing me to blink first, clearly laying down a challenge.

Trying to recall precisely what I'd said previously proved difficult. At the time, I couldn't function properly in the midst of disbelief, then grief and anger.

"And explain to us again why, for the first time ever, you didn't accompany your family down to the cottage on that Thursday evening?"

"How many times have you asked me that? Check the notes you made at the time."

"Oh, I have. I want to hear your reason again. Maybe it's changed?"

I told him about the important business meeting, which, as I repeated it, now sounded like a lame excuse.

When I finished, Flood said, "When did you realise your wife was having an affair at the same time you were seeing her?"

The question took me completely by surprise. How the hell did he know about that? I assumed the police had found something when they searched Hartley's flat. Or maybe Hartley had confided in someone else other than Greenland.

"What? I don't know what you're talking about. I've never heard anything so crazy! We were very happy. Ask anyone."

I didn't even convince myself. The back of my neck grew sticky with sweat.

Whilst DS Lyle scribbled something in his notebook, Flood pressed on.

Inspecting his notes again, he said, "How did you feel about Leroy Johnson's acquittal on a technicality despite the overwhelming DNA evidence against him?" He'd touched a raw nerve, no doubt intentionally. I found it impossible not to rise to the bait.

I yelled, "You know damn well how I felt. You were in the court when that dumb apology for a judge let him go. You'll recall that, apparently, Johnson's human rights trumped mine."

"That was unfortunate, yes."

"*Unfortunate?* Is that the best you can do? How the bloody hell would *you* feel? You've not been in that position. Nor, I suspect, has he!" I nodded aggressively in the direction of DS

Lyle. "I wish to God I'd never been in that position either, but through no fault of mine, I was."

As soon as I'd said it, I recollected Flood's wife being the victim of a fatal revenge hit and run a few years previously by a criminal gang. She'd died after spending months in a coma. They'd never found the perpetrators.

Flood's face showed not a shred of emotion as he replied, "It's not *our* feelings we're concerned about. I can see you're still incensed. I need to know where that anger would lead you."

I recognised his now familiar interviewing techniques: asking intensely provocative questions designed to goad me into an emotional response and then changing the subject back and forth frequently.

I spat out the words, "That's the whole point. It hasn't led me *anywhere*. I'm just trying to get on with my life."

"Did you know that Leroy Johnson was found, murdered, in the River Thames a few days ago?"

"Yes, I do read the papers, you know."

"Can you tell me where you were between the hours of 10pm and 2am on Thursday 9th of October?"

"You're not *seriously* suggesting I had anything to do with that, are you?"

"Just tell me where you were."

I gave him the alibi I'd rehearsed with Alisha. The DS carefully made a note.

Flood continued, "You may also have read recently that another person, Colin Greenland, was discovered in Victoria Park stabbed to death. He appears to have had connections with Johnson and your wife's lover, a certain John Hartley. Do you know Colin Greenland?"

"I've absolutely no idea what you're talking about. And no,

I don't know a... whatever his name is... Greenland. And how dare you insinuate that my wife had an affair. I suggest that unless you have hard evidence, you shut up!"

For a fraction of a second, I'd caught him off-guard.

Eventually, he said, "I think you should calm down, Mr Hamilton. I'm simply attempting to put all the pieces together here." Scanning his notebook once more, he said, "Ah, yes. There's another link between you and John Hartley, isn't there? He used to work for you. Is that correct?"

"Yes, he did. He left my business years ago. I've not seen him since."

"Well, the way I see it, there appears to be a definite link between Johnson, Greenland, you and Hartley. Someone's murdered Johnson and Greenland. The only way to get to the bottom of this is to talk to you and John Hartley. Unfortunately, he's gone missing. Are we likely to find him murdered too?"

"What am I supposed to say to that? That's an outrageous thing to say. I'm not even going to answer you."

Flood sat back in the sofa. Closing his notebook, he said, "OK. Let me tell you where we are. It appears to me that you undoubtedly have strong motives to cause harm to Johnson, Greenland... *and Hartley.*"

"Don't be ridiculous!"

"I don't think I'm being ridiculous. Your motives are especially strong in wanting to harm Leroy Johnson. I'd like you to get dressed and come down to the police station. We'll need to check out your alibis and pursue other lines of enquiry with you under caution."

"This is crazy!"

"I'm arresting you on suspicion of the murder of Leroy Johnson. You do not have to say anything but it may harm your defence if you do not mention, when questioned, something which you later rely on in court. Anything you do say may be given in evidence."

As he finished the caution, Alisha walked into the room.

Glancing at the detectives, she said, "What's going on, James? I heard voices and – "

"Do you believe this? They're arresting me on suspicion of murder! They want me to go down to the station for further interrogation."

"What? That's ludicrous!"

"I know, I know."

Flood frowned and stared at Alisha trying to work out our precise relationship. I'd just given her name as my alibi.

Before he could say anything, I said, "Alisha's a good friend of mine. She was a *very* good friend of my wife's too."

★

DS Lyle drove through the early morning rush hour traffic with the windscreen wipers clearing the spitting rain. Flood occupied the passenger seat and I sat in the rear. I broke the silence and spoke to the back of Flood's head. "Can I phone someone?"

He half-turned to me and said, "You have the right to make one phone call and to have a solicitor present at the interview. You can make the call once we get to the station."

The rest of the journey continued in silence.

I mentally went through the plan we'd hatched with RP. Most of it had worked, but Greenland's murder, Alisha's abduction and Hartley's disappearance were things we couldn't possibly have foreseen.

And I hadn't anticipated my arrest on suspicion of murder. Our plan had turned into a nightmare.

When we got to Southwark Police Station, the custody officer, a bulky veteran with greying hair and a square jaw, took over. He was ideally suited to the role of banging up offenders, positively enjoying the process.

DS Lyle gave him details of my arrest. Then a PC searched me, took my mobile phone, and placed it in a brown envelope. I signed a receipt thrust in front of me.

The custody officer said he needed to take a DNA swab, my fingerprints, a blood sample and a photo.

"Why the hell do you want all that? This is ridiculous."

He sighed and said, "We can do this with or without your help. It's the law."

I had no choice. "When I'm released without charge, make sure my DNA samples are destroyed. *It's the law.*"

He grunted and muttered, "Smart arse," under his breath.

The constable said, "You have the right to consult a solicitor and to make one phone call to let someone know your whereabouts."

I called RP. Alisha had already contacted him after I'd been taken away. He'd expected my call.

"Well I did warn you about the possibility. Be keen to know what evidence they have, though. Could be the search of Hartley's flat revealed something other than the obvious."

Not the most helpful thing to say, I thought.

"Roger, look, how long can they keep me here?"

"Twenty-four hours. A police superintendant can authorise a further twelve, based on the evidence. They'll have to go to court to get an extension. After that, they'll have to charge you or release you. You need to sit tight for the next day and a half. You'll be fine."

I mentioned Flood's view on my motive for wanting Johnson murdered.

"Christ, if they banged up everyone who had a motive we'd have to build thirty more prisons!"

He calmed down and said, "I'll get my lawyer, Simon Brotherton, down to you right away. He's bloody brilliant. Expensive, but the best in the business."

When I'd finished, another uniformed constable led me down the corridor to a stark interview room with utilitarian grey-green painted walls. The only furniture was a wooden table with an audiocassette recorder on top of it and two chairs either side. Neon strip lighting reflected off every surface. A whiff of stale air caught in my throat.

The PC returned and I told him my solicitor would arrive shortly. He said, "When he arrives, we'll explain the circumstances of your arrest and then you'll be allowed time to brief him. After that, the detectives will want to get started." He slammed the door shut.

Mulling over the day's events, I sensed someone observing me. Probably my paranoia kicking in again.

About an hour and a half later, the door opened again and Simon Brotherton entered. Aged sixtyish with balding grey hair and a large girth, he wore a pinstriped suit and stylish glasses shielding bright, darting eyes. He handed me his card and took out a large notebook from his black leather attaché case.

He said in a refined, measured tone, "I've spoken to RP and he's filled me in on the background to you ending up here. He's told me *everything*." He stared at me for a moment. There could be no mistaking what he meant.

"OK, let's go over the details from *your* point of view."

We spent half-an-hour together, with Simon asking question after question. He made copious notes, which he added to those he'd already made during his chat with RP.

When Simon was satisfied with my answers, he poked his head outside the room and said something to the PC standing outside. A few minutes later DCI Flood and DS Lyle entered the room and sat opposite us.

The detective sergeant unwrapped a pack of tapes. He loaded two of them into the cassette recorder. He switched it on and recorded our names, the date and time. Flood faced me and said, "I would remind you that you are being interviewed under caution."

The interrogation begun with detailed questioning of my knowledge of Hartley. I repeated that he'd once worked for me. Flood mentioned the embezzlement but didn't say how they'd discovered it. We'd never made it public knowledge.

Flood said, "It's a lot of money he got away with. Why didn't you pursue a criminal case against him?"

"I thought that trying to trace Hartley, getting the evidence and going to court would be exhausting and frustrating. I considered my time would be better spent developing the business. So did my other shareholder, who is also my business partner."

"You weren't tempted to take retribution then? Especially if you discovered his affair with your future wife?"

Simon butted in. "You don't need to answer that, James."

"No comment," I said.

Flood pressed on.

"Do you know anything about Hartley's claim to being Emily's father?"

"No, of course I don't. That's rubbish."

"You're sure?"

"Yes."

"Because, if I can prove you knew about the affair and his claim, together with the embezzlement, you'd be highly motivated to want to harm your family and especially Hartley, wouldn't you?"

He kept up this interrogation, often rephrasing the questions, trying to catch me out. I repeatedly told him I had no idea about any of this nonsense. Simon challenged him on more than one occasion to provide hard evidence.

Flood responded, "We're close. Once it's confirmed, we'll present it to you, be sure of that."

Simon butted in again. "You've made your point. My client has told you on several occasions that he had no knowledge of the affair or Hartley's claim."

Flood ignored him. He leaned forward, putting his sneering face close to mine, said, "Do you know where Hartley is?"

"Of course I don't! How many more times must I tell you! I haven't seen him in years, not since he left my business."

Flood changed the subject abruptly yet again, deliberately upsetting the rhythm of the interview. "Let's go through your alibis for the Johnson murder once more, shall we?"

Simon interjected again. "I should have thought by now, you'd have this aspect sorted. Either you accept my client's alibis or you don't. From what I've heard so far, all you've got is a cloud of suspicion. There's precious little other evidence being offered to substantiate the arrest of my client other than motivation. And as you know well enough, motivation to commit a crime is not evidence."

I wanted to say, 'Good point, Simon' but thought better of it.

Flood responded. "I want to be absolutely sure in my mind that your client's alibi for his whereabouts when Leroy Johnson was murdered still stacks up now he's being interviewed under caution."

Flood turned to me. "Well?"

I trotted out the alibi once again.

"I see. And where were you at the time of Greenland's demise?"

I sensed a trap. I said, "I've already told you. I don't know a Greenland."

Flicking over a page of his notes, he said, "Where were you between 10pm and midnight on the 12th October?" I had a job to remember.

Finally, I recalled I'd also spent that evening at Alisha's flat. Given what Flood might have deduced about my relationship with Alisha, I couldn't blame him for thinking there may be collusion between us. But it happened to be the truth.

"Are you in a relationship with her? Is she your girlfriend?"

"Well, no… not exactly. I told you before; she was a very close friend of my wife. She's helped me come to terms with my loss."

"Close enough to be staying at your house?"

"It was just for the night. Spending time with my late wife's best friend isn't a crime, is it?"

"No, but under the circumstances, your alibi can hardly be classed as impartial, can it?"

DS Lyle and Flood nodded to each other and Flood declared the interview over. Turning off the cassette recorder, he said, "That's it for now. We're going to check on the progress of the forensic tests we're expecting. Back shortly."

When they'd left the room, Simon leant forward and said, "They're struggling here to find any hard evidence against you. They're relying heavily on the fact you have strong motives for wanting Johnson and Greenland out of the way. Suggesting you had anything to do with Hartley being missing is ludicrous. As far as I can see, they have nothing else."

"I hope you're right." Simon must have noticed the apprehension in my eyes.

He shook his head wearily. "I've seen all this before. If the police don't have enough evidence, they pile on as much pressure as they can, hoping to get an admission of guilt. It's the easier option for them."

Half an hour later, the detectives returned to the interview room. Flood said, "We believe we're getting closer to obtaining the evidence we require to charge you with the murder of Leroy Johnson —"

I spluttered, "You… you must be joking —"

"I'll get a warrant to search your house as part of that process."

"You've already searched it once, straight after the arson attack," I yelled.

"I know, but that was over a year ago. We'd like to take another look. Oh, and I'm assured the forensic results should be available soon."

"Good," Simon responded. "Then on that basis I assume my client will be allowed police bail?"

"Not at this time," Flood said. "It would be very remiss of me to release your client so that he can agree his alibis with his *girlfriend*, don't you think?" A smirk creased his pocked face. I held back the temptation to smash my fist into it.

He continued, "You'll be detained here until we complete our enquiries. Unless there's something you'd like to get off your chest?"

I shook my head in disbelief as Simon hit back. "Well, I hope your enquiries are concluded swiftly. You don't need me to remind you of your time constraints. And you'll need to produce a lot more evidence if you wish to retain my client any longer than twenty-four hours."

My confidence in him grew. But RP would never employ an amateur.

When they left the interview room, I turned to Simon.

"God, he pisses me off!"

"I'm sure that's his intention. I'll come back tomorrow morning. We'll see what further evidence they've dug up."

The uniformed constable led me back to the custody sergeant, who referred to a clipboard on his desk, ticked a box and said to the constable, "Cell Three."

Before going to the cells, the PC told me to take off and hand over my shoes and my belt. There didn't seem any point in arguing.

The windowless, brightly lit cell measured no more than eight feet by six feet with a stark stainless-steel toilet and sink. A single blanket lay on top of a low secured bench and a plastic-covered mattress.

As the door clunked behind me, the sound reverberating inside the confines of the cell, my claustrophobia kicked in big time. I breathed in slowly and deliberately several times, despite the air being far from fresh. I felt like a criminal.

I convinced myself this was still part of the game Flood was playing, upping the tension, giving me time to reflect and possibly confess.

I fought my irrational terror of confinement by concentrating on every aspect of Johnson's murder. But all it did was raise more questions.

What did Flood mean when he mentioned getting closer to having evidence against me for Johnson's murder? Did someone witness us dumping his body in the Thames? Did someone see us go in and out of the railway arches? Or was it a bluff?

Clever bugger, Flood. Expert at applying pressure.

As my concentration lapsed, the thought of being banged up in this confined space for twenty years or more drove me nuts. I kicked out at the white-tiled wall with the soles of my feet until they throbbed. Then I beat it with the heel of my clenched fists until they ached. Exhausted, I slumped down on the mattress, my stomach churning, fearing my life may be over.

During the night, the duty PC slid the spy hole back in the door every hour. Occasionally I heard a commotion outside my cell. New residents yelled obscenities. It didn't make much difference. My anxiety and general feeling of foreboding made sleeping impossible anyway.

What the hell was I doing in here?

Apart from being offered breakfast, which I refused — I'd have thrown it up immediately — I had no contact with any police officers or the detectives until mid-morning the following day. I'd been held for just under twenty-four hours.

A PC escorted me back to the interview room. Simon had arrived earlier.

"Any more developments, Simon?"

"No. Roger's been briefed. He's up to speed. We've got to wait to see what further evidence the police have dug up."

Flood entered the room. He didn't look happy.

"We've checked out your alibis. They *appear* to be genuine." His facial expression implied it pained him to say so.

"We've still got work to do. The forensic team are taking more time than we'd like. We're still obtaining evidence. You are free to leave on conditional police bail. We'll need to speak to you again."

I resisted saying 'I told you so'. I just wanted to get out of there.

"What are the conditions?" Simon enquired.

You'll need to check in with us at Southwark Police Station every morning at 10am until further notice. In addition, we'll need your passport. Bring it to the station tomorrow morning."

"Is that it? No other restrictions?"

"No, not at the moment."

After collecting my mobile, belt and shoes, we left. Outside the police station, charcoal-coloured clouds scudded across the sky. It had stopped raining and there were large puddles everywhere. The cars speeding up and down Borough High Street swished more rainwater onto the pavement. I breathed in fresh, moist air lustily, expelling the fetid version I'd sampled earlier.

I hugged Simon enthusiastically. "Thanks a lot. I'm grateful for your help."

"That's OK. Listen, we're not out of the woods yet. I'd like to know if a search of your home reveals anything. Call me if or when Flood gets in touch."

I felt dirty. When I arrived home, I immediately stripped off and took a shower. I spent half-an-hour under it, scrubbing away the clinging odour of the prison cell. I was amazed at how good I felt after a squirt of deodorant and a change into fresh clothes.

I called Alisha at her office. She was delighted to hear that I'd been released. I arranged to meet her when she finished work.

Over a bottle of *Merlot* and linguini and meatballs at my house, she told me Flood had relentlessly interrogated her about my alibis, particularly for the night of Johnson's murder.

"He pointed out the seriousness of perverting the course of justice if I didn't tell him the truth. Pompous bastard." She spat out the last two words. "He wanted to know which TV programmes we'd watched and what time they were on."

"He asked me the same question. What did you say?"

"I told him, we watched *Who Wants To Be A Millionaire?* Do you remember? RP insisted we spent time on getting that accurate."

"Yes, I do."

"Did he ask you anything else?"

"Yes, about how much one of the contestants had won."

"What did you say?"

"I told him that despite sharing a bottle of wine with you, I remembered that a school teacher won two hundred and fifty grand. He'd used up all his lifelines but guessed correctly the name of the county cricket team who played at Chester-le-Street. The answer was Durham."

"Good. I said the same. I supposed he also asked you which wine we'd drunk?"

"Oh, I told him. A bottle of *Montipulciano*."

"Right again. Excellent."

Although we got our stories spot on about our whereabouts at the time of the Johnson murder, a couple of things she told me she'd also said at the interview disturbed me.

"Oh, James, I don't know whether I've done the right thing. He asked me whether I ever had a relationship with Johnson. I didn't want to lie. And that phone call between Hartley and Greenland referred to it anyway."

"What did you say?"

"I said I saw him from time to time. Not so much a relationship, just a few dates, that's all. It didn't help when those detectives saw me at your house. "

I told her not to worry and that she'd done the right thing. "There isn't a law against who you see or don't see, is there?"

"No, I suppose not." She didn't sound convinced.

"He also asked me if I knew about Lynne's affair with Hartley. He boxed me into a corner. I admitted that I did know. But I stressed it happened years ago and he disappeared shortly after you appeared on the scene."

"Good. You said the right thing."

"He asked whether you knew about it. I told him I'd never mentioned it but I couldn't vouch for Lynne. I'm not sure he believed me."

Our plan appeared to be creaking under the pressure DCI Flood exerted.

CHAPTER EIGHTEEN

November 1999

I'd become an unwilling minor celebrity. There'd been a small piece in the London papers about a forty-three-year-old man being arrested on suspicion of murdering Leroy Johnson, who'd been discovered drowned in suspicious circumstances in the River Thames.

I thought it best if I stayed away from work. Although my name hadn't been released, most of my senior executives were aware of Johnson's trial debacle and my connection to him. I couldn't face the allusions or inferences that were sure to be made.

I kept in touch regularly, though. Pat couldn't believe I'd been arrested and released on bail. She told me not to worry. "Everything's under control, James. Peter's doing a great job and the business is going well."

I desperately wanted to talk to RP, but he'd flown up to Scotland for a couple of days, investigating another case. He'd told me he'd be happy to talk on the phone, but I needed to spend time with him face-to-face.

The following evening, a thirty-second breaking news item on my local London TV station had me leaping out of my chair. They reported a car fire on wasteland close to the port of Dover. It had only made the news because this was the fifth such car torching in the area within the past fortnight.

When they mentioned a Toyota Avensis, I shouted at Alisha, who was making coffee in the kitchen. By the time she responded, the newsreader had moved on, reporting on the state of the rubbish collections in Lewisham.

It had to be Hartley's car. If so, the forensic evidence from both Johnson and Alisha would probably have been destroyed.

I relayed this thought to Alisha.

"That's a bugger!"

"You're dead right it is. We'll have to hope traces of Johnson's DNA survived."

"But why would Hartley burn his car and go on the run? In a way, that's good for us isn't it?"

"Only if he did it, yes. It's possible he's panicked. Maybe he read about Johnson and Greenland's deaths in the papers and realised he's been set up."

Alisha slumped down into the sofa and sighed.

"How the fuck is this going to end?"

★

Next morning, I left a message with Lucy, RP's secretary, who confirmed he'd be back in the office at lunchtime. He'd call me then.

At 3pm, my landline rang. An excited RP spoke rapidly.

"James. I got back a bit early, thought I'd make a few calls to my contacts before I called you. Have you heard? The police have just found Hartley alive and well. They caught him boarding a cross-channel ferry from Dover. The police had put out an All Ports warning and an eagle-eyed passport controller recognised him."

"That's a bloody relief."

"Even better, they've arrested him on suspicion of the murder of your family."

I fell onto my chair and steadied myself by gripping the arm. I could hardly speak.

"Hello? James, are you still there?"

"Yes… yes… of course. That's fantastic news. When can we come and see you? There's much to talk about."

"Let me make a few more calls first. I'd like Simon Brotherton here too. Why don't we meet up lunchtime tomorrow? I'll spend the rest of the day assessing where we are, OK?"

★

The next day, I drove from Blackfriars to Southwark Police Station with Alisha and parked in a side road. She stayed in the car whilst I reported in precisely on time at 10am. I was paranoid about missing the appointment. I didn't want to be re-arrested for breaking the conditions of my bail.

We decided to leave the car parked and walk through Borough Market and on to the Thames Embankment, heading for RP's office. The sun shone brightly through the freezing air and our breaths turned to vapour as we spoke.

The smell of fruit and vegetables fought for prominence over the hot fast-food stalls purveying everything from steaming paella to German sausages and hot roasted chestnuts. We grabbed a coffee and sat with our coats tightly wrapped around us.

I said, "It's great news about Hartley's arrest for the arson attack, but one thing worries me. There's been no mention of him being accused of Johnson's murder. And Flood's hell-bent on charging me."

"Let's take it a step at a time. James. Hartley's arrest is progress isn't it?"

"I suppose it is. It worries me, that's all."

We got to RP's office around lunchtime as agreed. It felt like a second home to me. I could find my way there blindfolded.

Simon Brotherton had already arrived. Papers cluttered RP's usually immaculate desk.

"James, Alisha, come in. Sorry to hear about your arrest, James." RP stood and shook hands warmly with us both in turn and introduced Alisha to Simon.

"And Alisha, I hear the detectives have been giving you a hard time."

"Nothing I can't handle," she said, tossing her head.

RP's ever-elegant PA brought in the, by now, familiar tea set.

"Thanks, Lucy. Please make sure we're not disturbed, OK? We're going to be some time."

As he poured the tea, he said, "Simon and I have been studying our position. We're trying to assess the strength of the police's case against you, James and seeing what we have to do to convince them that Hartley's their man for all five murders: your wife and children, Greenland and Johnson."

The mention of *five* murders brought home the extent of our predicament. I had no idea RP's plan would end up like this. I reserved telling him until after I'd heard what he had to say.

RP continued, "All we know for certain is that Hartley's been arrested for the fatal arson attack, but not yet charged. We don't know specifically what the police have discovered about Johnson's murder. I'm still working on that."

"I told Alisha, Flood's looking at me for that," I said.

"I know. Let's start with your family, James. What worries me and Simon is that the police are implying that you discovered Lynne's affair with Hartley and his claim to being Emily's father. Therefore, you'd have been motivated enough to eliminate them."

"That's absolute balls! I had no idea! And there's no proof that I *wasn't* her father."

"I know. I'm playing devil's advocate. Stop me, Simon, if you don't agree."

Simon nodded and said, "If you look at it from a police point of view, it's a definite runner. There are precedents."

"But James wasn't there," Alisha said. "We know Johnson did it. That means James must have hired him, which is crazy, isn't it?"

RP responded, "Well, James's alibi is that he spent the night at home alone. Why couldn't James have hired Johnson? The police have already questioned why he didn't go down to Lymington with the family for the first time ever. It's entirely plausible."

We sat in silence for a moment, which Simon broke.

"The weakness in the police's position is the lack of hard evidence. However, I agree with Roger. There could be a case to answer." I shook my head in disbelief.

RP took up the argument again. "Now let's look at Hartley. He has a strong motive too. Plus, he demonstrates the classic symptoms of a sociopath, swinging from being utterly charming to callously controlling. And we know from what Greenland said, he was absolutely furious with Lynne for marrying you and you both bringing up *his* baby daughter whilst he rotted in Belmarsh prison."

I shot RP a disparaging glance. He countered by holding up both his palms facing me and said, "I know it's something you don't want to hear, James, but let's say, for the moment, it's a reasonable argument."

Alisha said, "But surely Hartley wouldn't murder his own child?"

Simon replied. "It's happened before. I've dealt with cases where men like Hartley can't stand the thought of losing their child to another man. The fact is, when he went to jail he lost control of Lynne. He couldn't accept 'control' had passed to someone else. And he blamed her. That's why he set up the arson attack. Sociopaths never think it's their fault."

"Obviously not," I spat out.

He continued, "As far as evidence is concerned we know the police have got the mobile messages connecting Johnson with Hartley. Not sure it'll be admitted in court, though. The defence would argue the police obtained the information without the defendant's permission. That would infringe his human rights."

"That sounds too bloody familiar!" I shouted, recalling the judge's comments when he acquitted Johnson.

Simon ignored my outburst and said, "And remember, Alisha, when questioned by Flood, told him she knew about Hartley's affair with Lynne. But didn't know if James knew or not."

I fumed, "But I didn't know anything about it until this week, for God's sake!"

Simon nodded and said, "I believe you. And it'll be the police's job to prove that you did know before the arson attack. Most of the other stuff they've got is circumstantial. That's not to say the court won't accept it. Circumstantial evidence is like an electric cable; full of different leads but in the end they all connect to the same point.

"It's my view the case against Hartley for the arson attack

is good, James, but it's by no means perfect. It rests on whether the police can prove you knew about the affair."

"Well, hang on a minute," I said. "Hartley's been arrested for the arson attack, hasn't he? And Flood and his team aggressively questioned me at the time. If they thought I had anything to do with it they'd have arrested me, wouldn't they?"

RP came straight back. "Yes, James. But we know Hartley's a particularly plausible liar and con man. He'll say anything to avoid being charged."

I shook my head again.

RP continued. "Let's look at the Greenland murder. You and Hartley both had motives for wanting him despatched. If the police can prove that Alisha mentioned to you Greenland's role in setting up the meeting between Hartley and Johnson, you'd know he'd played a part in the arson attack."

"But I've only ever seen him twice. And I told the police I was at Alisha's flat at the time of his murder and she confirmed it."

RP responded. "But you could have hired someone else to stab him and dump him in Victoria Park, couldn't you?"

"This is getting bloody ridiculous!" I snapped.

RP ignored me and continued, "On the other hand, we know Hartley shared with Greenland his deepest thoughts about his relationship with Lynne. Maybe he regretted it, got worried about Greenland. Didn't want him going to the police. Especially after your visit."

Simon turned to me and said, "And as far as we know, there's no other evidence to implicate you. Flood would have you back to the station in a heartbeat if he did."

Alisha, who'd been hanging on every word Simon uttered said, "Couldn't Hartley have used someone else to carry out his dirty work, just like he did with Lynne?"

RP replied. "That's right. I think that's the most likely explanation. The SOCOs will have crawled all over Greenland's flat. We'll have to wait and see what they come up with. Let's hope you didn't leave any evidence of your visit, James."

Simon added, shaking his head, "It's a real shame about what happened to Greenland. He'd have been the prosecution's perfect witness."

RP said, "I agree. He'd have made all the difference. Anyway, I don't know about you guys, but I'm hungry. I'll get sandwiches and a fresh pot of tea sent in and then we'll look at the Johnson murder."

★

We left RP's office at various times to use the washroom, check our mobiles and stretch our legs. We tackled the sandwiches unenthusiastically; none of us had much of an appetite, except RP.

Between bites, he spent most of the break with his phone crooked between his neck and shoulder scribbling notes.

Returning to his desk, still chewing his last bite, he said, "I've just heard from one of my contacts. The early signs are that any forensic trace evidence left in the boot of Hartley's car has been destroyed."

"Bugger! That's not helping, is it?" I said.

"No, it isn't. But if the police can prove *he* torched the car, they could argue he did it to destroy the evidence."

A frown creased his forehead. "You know, it's still bugging me who drove Hartley's car when you were abducted, Alisha."

"Me too," she said.

"We've got nowhere on that," RP continued. He hated not having an answer for everything.

"And as far as the Johnson murder is concerned, I've heard the police have found the stuff you planted at Hartley's flat. They're waiting for the results from the forensic team."

"Is that going to be enough?" Alisha said.

Simon, who'd been making notes, said, "Taken with the phone messages proving that Johnson was blackmailing him, I'd say the police would have to look at Hartley very seriously. But Flood may consider that you, James had a far stronger motive. After all, Johnson's the actual guy who destroyed your family."

I moaned, "Oh! Wonderful."

Ignoring my sarcasm, Simon continued, "And there's another point; we only have Alisha's witness statement to corroborate your alibi. If it got to the point where the police charged you with Johnson's murder and it went to trial, counsel would robustly cross-examine you, Alisha, given what they will know about your relationship with James. I'm sure you're both aware that perjury is a serious crime."

Alisha nodded and said, "Flood made the same point when he interviewed me. Don't worry; I'm sure I'll cope."

We'd come to rely a great deal on Alisha.

"I'm sure you will," RP said. "I'm confident it won't come to that."

I couldn't share his assurance. I began to doubt his infallibility.

He continued. "Of course, the big unknown here is the conversation Flood's having with Hartley as we speak."

He checked his notes yet again. "And from what Simon's told me, Flood appears determined to find hard evidence, especially against you, James."

"I know. That guy really winds me up!"

"I'm hoping you didn't leave any clues at Hartley's flat. We can't deny your motivation and your actions at the Johnson trial. All perfectly understandable, but added to any forensic evidence they come up with, that could prove fatal."

Simon spoke again. "And the police have already arrested you for this specific offence."

I glared at both of them in turn. "In other words, it's looking fucking awful for me. Is that what you're saying? I might as well hand myself in and confess to all the murders!"

"Don't be silly, James!" Alisha laid a hand on my arm.

RP was stuck for an answer. I'd never seen that before.

Eventually, he said, "OK, I'll try to get more information about the evidence they have on you. At least Hartley's under arrest for the arson attack. We've got to hope that Flood can pin Johnson's murder on Hartley too."

I stood and shouted, "So that's it, is it? My life depends on the *hope* that that cynical bastard, Flood, buys our plan."

Alisha tugged at my sleeve, trying to get me to sit down. I pushed her aside and walked around the room.

Simon remained seated, but turned round in his chair and addressed me directly. "Actually, it's not like that. The police will have to present a file to the CPS. There are a few hoops they've go to go through. Then they'll decide whether there's enough evidence to prosecute. It's extremely thorough."

"Simon's correct," RP said. "And the CPS is paranoid these days about what the public think. They won't want to waste money on a trial if there isn't a realistic chance of a guilty verdict."

I stood with my back to them, gazing down St James's Street, watching the endless trail of headlights heading for Piccadilly in the fast-fading light.

RP said, "I'll see if I can find out how Hartley's interview with Flood is progressing. I can't promise anything. We'll have to wait for the police to make the next move."

I felt like the first prize in an arm-wrestling match between RP and DCI Flood.

★

When I got home at 5.30pm, the red light on my answer phone flashed continuously. My gut wrenched when I played back the only message. Flood wanted to see me urgently. He said it couldn't wait until the next morning, when I was due to sign in as a condition of my bail.

I called him back immediately, hoping there had been positive developments in my favour.

There weren't.

CHAPTER NINETEEN

November 1999

The phone magnified Flood's brusque tone.

"I've more questions for you. You need to get down here as soon as possible. You should bring your solicitor with you."

My insides churned. I called Simon, who said he'd be at the police station within the hour.

The Christmas lights had been switched on in central London. They got earlier every year. Westminster City Council had made a special effort because of the Millennium celebrations. As the traffic would be more of a nightmare than usual, I took a minicab for the six-mile trip from my home in Blackheath to North Greenwich tube station and boarded the recently opened rapid Jubilee line to Southwark. A short walk later, I arrived at the police station at 6.30pm.

A PC escorted me to the same interview room. Simon joined me shortly afterwards.

Flood and the monosyllabic DS Lyle swaggered into the room, the latter clutching a large file, which he dumped on the desk.

Flood said, "We have more questions we'd like you to answer, *mainly* in connection with the murder of Leroy Johnson."

Why 'mainly', I thought? Did he have something else on me?

I guessed it might be as a result of his interrogation of Hartley in a similar interview room in the same building.

"We're applying to Tower Bridge Magistrates' Court at 10am tomorrow for an extension of the time we can detain you."

"On what grounds?" Simon shot back.

"We believe we can convince the magistrates we need more time for further questioning that will yield additional evidence. Also, we'll have the forensic reports available soon. You will, of course, be given the opportunity to make representation against this detention."

Simon responded. "We most certainly will object."

"Your client will be detained tonight and we'll see what the magistrates have to say in the morning." He left the room with the DS in his wake.

That was it. Interview over. If Flood wanted to unnerve me, he'd succeeded – yet again.

Simon and I held a quick debrief before a PC escorted me to the cells once again. Simon felt sure Flood had applied to the magistrates' court for an extension of time for Hartley too.

Neat.

Flood would have us both in the same building for a further three days' questioning. The forensic details would be flying in thick and fast; time enough to put a case to the CPS against *either* of us.

★

The thought of two more nights in the cells didn't thrill me. And I wasn't looking forward to three more days answering questions either. Flood's cynical goading and contemptuous manner was out of order and there was litttle I could do about it.

I focussed on the fact that at least, with Alisha, RP and Bruno's help, I'd dealt with Johnson. They'd helped ensure partial justice for Lynne, Georgie and Emily. Whatever happened to me, it represented a result... of sorts.

Lying on the blue plastic covering of the firm mattress, amongst countless other thoughts, I replayed in my mind a conversation I'd had with Alisha previously.

I'd said, "The more I think about Hartley's ludicrous claim to being Emily's father, the more I hate him. If it's true, what sick father would pay someone to burn down the cottage where *his* daughter slept?"

"I know," she said. "I don't understand. Some men are born evil."

Shaking my head, I responded. "The man's deranged."

The following morning, a squad car, driven by a uniformed police officer, accompanied by another sitting next to me in the rear passenger seats, delivered me to the magistrates' court in Tooley Street, a short distance from Southwark Police Station. Simon had already arrived.

I got the distinct impression my detention was already a done deal. The chief magistrate listened to both arguments intently, but asked few questions.

Simon put up a stirring argument, saying the police had already had enough time to decide whether to charge me or release me, but I sensed even he didn't believe he'd win them over.

After briefly conferring with his colleagues, the chief magistrate granted the police the extra time.

Back at the interview room, Flood and Lyle spent the rest of the day going over much the same ground we'd covered earlier, obviously trying to spot any discrepancies. Simon's exasperation reached boiling point.

"Do we really have to go over this same stuff again?"

"Let us do our job and you can concentrate on yours."

I knew it was pointless. Simon had told me he'd known detectives go over the same questions six or seven times. "Even the most skilled liars slip up under such intense interrogation," he'd said.

Flood turned his attention back to me and said, "You might like to know that we're interviewing John Hartley in the next room. We're discovering a great deal more about his relationship with your family. He's also informed us about his links with Leroy Johnson and Colin Greenland. Hartley claims he's been set up by you and your *girlfriend* for Johnson's murder. What do you say to that?"

My pulse quickened.

Desperately trying to remain calm, but failing, I said, "He would say that wouldn't he? I've never heard of anything quite so laughable. I think you should be charging *him* for all the murders."

Simon patted my arm as a way to make me shut up, and turning to Flood said, "I assume he's got evidence of this… allegation?"

"We're putting a case together to see if it fits. Actually, one thing he said is puzzling us. On the night of Johnson's murder, Hartley told us he'd spent it watching TV at home. He claims someone knocked at his door and the visitor stepped inside, forcibly held him and covered his face with a rag smothered in chloroform. He says he passed out and can't remember anything until the next morning."

Simon queried, "So?"

"The autopsy on Johnson showed chloroform burns on his face. Looks like he received the same treatment."

We'd been rumbled. My confidence in Roger Pendleton

and Simon Brotherton plummeted. I resigned myself to a twenty-year prison term, minimum.

Simon interrupted again, "What's any of this got to do with my client?"

"You can't go online or into a pharmacy and buy chloroform, just like that. You need a prescription. Doctors aren't keen to supply one. We wondered how the perpetrator got it. Then I remembered; your *girlfriend* works for a pharmaceutical company doesn't she? Maybe she got hold of it for you."

Simon interjected. "You're stretching a point aren't you? You'll need to prove a complete evidence trail to make that stick."

"That we intend to do, be sure of that." Flood looked pleased with himself.

He didn't realise how close he'd got to the truth.

When we'd discussed our plans, Alisha had said that the chloroform should be used sparingly.

She'd warned, "If the cloth is held over their nose and mouth for too long, it'll produce blisters and red blotches lasting several days."

I also remembered that once Hartley lost consciousness, Bruno had injected him with Rohypnol. I'd asked him about it in the car on the way back to Hartley's flat after dumping Johnson in the Thames.

"Isn't that the date rape drug?"

"Yeah."

"Isn't it a tablet dropped in people's drinks?"

"Yeah. You have to crush the tablets, make a powder and mix it with a saline solution. Then you can inject it."

"And how long will the effects last?"

"Chloroform only lasts a couple of hours, max. I hit him

with enough Rohypnol to drop him into a coma for about six to eight hours."

He went on to explain that one of the side effects was that the user had zero recollection of anything that may have happened to them in that time. It was also untraceable in blood, urine and saliva after twenty-four to forty-eight hours.

A highly effective drug for anyone with criminal intent.

★

Lying on the bed in my cell that second night, I realised my resolve the previous evening not to let Flood get to me was proving a severe challenge.

Next morning, my body felt like a wrung-out dishcloth. I'd had little sleep and my eyes stung every time I blinked. Usually a dose of ice-cold water splashed on my face would kick-start me into action, but not this time. I willed myself to get through the next two days, no matter how uncomfortable it became.

Simon said to Flood when he entered the room, "I'm sure you don't need me to remind you that you'll either have to charge my client or release him by 7pm tomorrow."

"Yes, we're quite aware of that. We've already spoken to the CPS and we'll be adding to the file during the day and seeking pre-charge advice later. Now, let's put Johnson to one side for a moment. I want to talk to you about Colin Greenland."

"I've already told you, I've never heard of him."

"Let me remind you that Colin Greenland and Hartley spent a great deal of time together on remand. They remained in touch when they were released. And we have evidence connecting both of them to Leroy Johnson."

Simon interjected. "And your point is?"

"My *point* is, from the evidence we have, it appears Greenland introduced Hartley to Johnson. It's highly likely but not yet certain that it was Hartley who paid him to burn down your cottage. We're not at the stage to charge him… yet. Hartley emphatically denies this, of course, but if he did pay Johnson, this means Greenland was part of a conspiracy to murder the Hamilton family."

"Meaning?"

"Meaning your client would have a motive for killing Greenland."

I dropped my head towards my knees and shook it vigorously. "I can't believe what you're saying!"

"You'll need more than just a motive," Simon added.

"Oh, yes. I know."

Flood turned to me and said, "For the week before Greenland's murder, we trawled through CCTV footage taken outside the precinct where Greenland lived. We ran your mug shot through the system and found a remarkable likeness to one of the people in the footage just two days before Greenland's death. We also showed your photo to the shopkeepers in the precinct and one claims to have seen you visiting Greenland's flat. Can you explain that?"

I'd loitered outside the shopping precinct for an hour before going up to the flat to ensure he didn't have any visitors. How could I be so thick?

Despite feeling a physical adrenaline rush pass through me, I bluffed as positively as I could, "Your eyewitness is mistaken. I've no idea who Greenland is or where he lives."

"So you won't mind taking part in an identity parade?"

Too true I'd mind, but before I could respond, Simon came to my rescue.

"As far as CCTV is concerned, even if there is a likeness to my client, it proves nothing. He's entitled to shop wherever he wants. And you will know that eyewitness testimony is notoriously unsafe."

"Well, let's cross that bridge later, shall we?"

A detective knocked and entered the room and without a word passed a note to DS Lyle, who read it and passed it over to Flood.

After scanning it, he stared at me and said, "Now let's talk about the arson attack. We've turned up another piece of evidence we believe to be of great significance."

I disliked Flood more and more, despite feeling sad at what had happened to his wife every time I saw him.

I didn't think my already elevated pulse rate could increase much further, but it did.

"I wanted to discover whether Hartley's claim to be Emily's father had any substance. I thought your *cheating* wife might have wanted to know for sure as well."

Flood licked his thin lips as he continued his offensive provocation. He knew which of my buttons to push.

"We browsed through every one of the London-based DNA paternity websites and contacted them. A clinic in Hammersmith confirmed that your wife had indeed sent off a sample of your DNA and Emily's for comparison. Emily was about six months old."

"You're joking?"

Flood relished unsettling me.

"I've had the result for a week, but to make absolutely sure there'd be no doubt about it, we checked the DNA samples taken from Hartley and compared them to a sample from Emily's clothes, which we found at your house. The results have just come in. Would you like to know what they say?"

We stared at each other, unblinking. What a bastard. I couldn't speak.

Eventually he said, "These results prove conclusively that John Hartley *was* Emily's biological father."

A combination of this revelation and Flood's sneering face made me react badly. I stood and attempted to go around the desk to attack him. Simon physically restrained me, pulling me back into my seat.

"You're lying! You're just winding me up!" I bellowed.

Flood stood and held his ground.

"Sit down!" he commanded.

Simon pulled me back into the chair. Flood sat down too and leant towards me.

"Bit of a temper you've got there, haven't you?"

"I don't think you need to antagonise my client, detective."

Flood ignored Simon's comment. "Did you and your wife ever discuss this?"

"Of course we didn't!"

"When did you find out about it?"

"I didn't find out. I know I can't prove it but you've got to believe me."

"If you *had* discovered this, it would add considerably to your motivation for murdering your 'family', wouldn't it? It's the missing link I've been looking for."

"What do you mean, missing link?" Simon asked.

"After the fire, it concerned me that your client, for the first time ever, didn't go down to the cottage with them. He said he had a business appointment. Then he said that shortly before the fire he'd dumped Lynne's computer. Probably buried under six feet of rubbish and mud in a landfill site by now. Is that because there's evidence of the paternity test on it? Or something else showing that your client had a motive?"

"That suggests my client hired Johnson. We all know he did it. You're trying to join up dots you don't have."

"We believe we've linked them sufficiently well to make a case."

I shouted, "You've totally lost it! If, as you stupidly suggest, I murdered my family, why the hell would I murder Johnson and Greenland? It doesn't make sense."

Flood, clasping his hands together and placing them on the table, said, "I've been thinking about that. Hartley's the one who caused you the most pain, hasn't he? First, he had an affair with your wife, made her pregnant and then embezzled a considerable sum of money from you. It would be a neat solution for you to murder Johnson and Greenland, both involved in the arson attack, and frame Hartley for their murders. That would cover your tracks, wouldn't it?"

Before I could yell at Flood again, Simon sarcastically said, "I think you've been reading too many crime novels. What you're suggesting is pure hypothesis. And you're desperately short on evidence."

Flood sneered, "Not as short as you may think." He referred to his notes yet again, whilst swivelling annoyingly in his chair. His smugness went up a notch.

"Something else has turned up. Following a search at your house, we found a hand-written note addressed to you from your wife in a desk drawer. Would you like me to read it?"

He didn't wait for a reply.

> *"Darling James, I'm so sorry we fell out so badly last night. I hate it when you're cross with me. Please believe me when I say that what I did was for the best for Emily. I'll never take you for granted again. I love you so much. Please forgive me.*
>
> *Love Lynne ☺ xxxxxx"*

Simon asked, "So?"

"I believe this note refers to Lynne Hamilton contacting the paternity agency and discovering that Hartley was Emily's father. It suggests that either your client had found out about it or she'd told him." He waved the note in the air. "This confirms they'd had a row about it. There's the motivation."

He couldn't have been further from the truth.

We'd only ever had one major disagreement in our short married life. It was over something so trivial, we laughed about it afterwards. Flood's assumption placed the note entirely out of context.

After Emily's birth, Lynne's obsessive preoccupation with the baby's well-being countered the joy of having her. She'd check on her several times a night, whether Emily was crying or not. She fussed over her constantly to the exclusion of everyone else. We'd already had to deal with Georgie. Now I knew how he suffered: excluded and envious.

Matters came to head one evening when, for the umpteenth time, she broke off an amorous exchange to check on Emily's cot.

We had a blazing row and both of us said things we'd rather not have said. However, it cleared the air and I apologised. I assumed this was normal behaviour for a woman with a young baby; it's something I'd have to get used to. She apologised too; said all she wanted was for us to be one happy family.

I told Flood the true reason for the note and that he'd jumped to an erroneous conclusion.

"I don't believe you."

Simon asked, "Is there a date on the note?"

Flood glanced at it, turned it over and said, "No."

"So it could have been written anytime. If it had been dated close to the date of the arson attack, it would *possibly* have had more relevance to your assumption. As it is, I think my client's version is likely to be more accurate."

"We'll let the CPS decide on that."

Flood closed his notebook. DS Lyle said, "Interview terminated at 12.45pm," and turned off the cassette recorder. They both stood and Flood said, "That's all for now. We'll spend the afternoon preparing our case."

Simon and I stayed in the interview room to discuss my situation.

I'd never felt less sure about getting away with our plan. I faced a skilful detective who appeared hell-bent on building a case against me, and a smooth-talking con man *par excellence* in Hartley.

My confidence in Roger Pendleton and Simon Brotherton plummeted.

Still reeling from what I'd just heard, I asked Simon what he thought about the case against me now.

"Before I answer that, tell me truthfully, when did you first know about Emily being Hartley's daughter?"

"I can't believe you're asking me that. I didn't know… not until now, I swear."

"You had no idea Lynne had sent off for a paternity test?"

"No, of course I didn't."

"But she'd have had to get you to sign a consent form, send off a cheek swab, a used tissue or something. You're saying she never told you, which means she must have sent off a sample without you knowing and forged your signature."

"I can't believe she'd have done that… but she must have."

"If the police can prove you did know, that's bad news. Having said that, they'll also have to prove you paid Johnson. They've said nothing about that. And don't forget, Hartley's going through the same interrogation. We've got to hope Flood thinks Hartley's a stronger candidate."

I slumped forward in my chair.

"God, I hope so."

Simon paused, then continued. "At least it's encouraging that there appears to be a lack of hard evidence against you, especially for the Johnson and Greenland murders. They'd have challenged you by now if, say, they had evidence of you dumping Johnson's body."

I looked nervously at the cassette recorder. Simon noticed and said, "Don't worry about that. You have the right to speak with your solicitor in private. Even if they were secretly taping this conversation they wouldn't be able to use it."

"I hope not."

"Anyway, with the Greenland case, I shouldn't worry too much about the eyewitness evidence. It's difficult for anyone to be one hundred percent sure and beyond reasonable doubt. That's why judges are now legally bound to warn juries about not giving too much credence to it. Flood's chucking everything he can at you, hoping some of it'll stick."

I asked Simon about Flood's chloroform presumption. Although he'd identified a potential link to Alisha and her job, I hoped there wasn't a spurious trail leading from her to the back of Hartley's boiler room, where the bottle of chloroform had ended up.

"Flood's got a valid point. It's not going to help," Simon warned. Thanks a lot, I thought.

★

He went back to his office, telling me he'd be on standby for the rest of the day if I needed him. A PC escorted me back to my cell.

My head still ached, not helped by thinking how on earth did I become a suspected serial killer.

I found it impossible to come to terms with the fact that I wasn't Emily's father. For God's sake, my name was on her birth certificate.

Christ, I'd even cut her umbilical cord. Fatherhood had made me. Hartley had taken that away.

I agonised over why Lynne had carried out the paternity test without my knowledge. I could only guess that she had tortured herself over whether I might discover the truth. Or that Emily would when she grew older.

If the results proved I was the father, no problem. She might even have told me. But she lived with her secret. I wanted to ask Alisha whether Lynne had ever told her about the paternity test result.

I knew I wouldn't cope well spending twenty years plus in a prison cell. Just the thought of it brought me out in a sweat and my claustrophobia kicked in hard.

However, I still had a life to live. I was nearly forty-four years old. I had no financial worries and possibly a future with Alisha.

I could contest these issues all day; it wouldn't make any difference… my immediate fate lay with the CPS.

★

At lunchtime the next day, a uniformed PC led me back to the interview room. Simon arrived shortly afterwards. He'd spent the previous afternoon updating RP and Alisha.

Flood, whose expression remained deadpan, entered the room with DS Lyle in his wake.

"As you know, we passed our files over to the CPS for pre-charge advice. They've decided we should not charge you… at the moment. This advice may change if further evidence comes to light. You are free to go."

Simon responded first. "Are you charging Hartley?"

"I can't tell you that."

"Why not?" I shouted. "I think I have the *right* to know."

"I suspect you'll hear in due course."

I wanted to pursue the point, but Simon tugged at my arm again in an effort to shut me up and get out of the police station as soon as possible.

Once outside and mightily relieved, I hugged Simon again. He offered to run me back home to Blackheath.

I called Alisha on my mobile from his car. Even with Hartley in custody, she said she preferred to remain at my house. She sounded ecstatic and couldn't wait for me to arrive.

Still not believing Flood hadn't charged me, I asked Simon, as he drove, why he thought not.

"It's always difficult to answer that when two suspects are taken in for questioning. Obviously, the police believe they have more evidence against Hartley than against you. It's as simple as that. And we won't know what that evidence is unless Hartley's charged and he goes on trial."

"That'll take months."

"It'll soon pass. I'm guessing the police found Hartley's clothes and trainers and the results from the forensic team sealed his fate for the Johnson murder. They must have believed Alisha's alibis for your whereabouts too. That's so important. She deserves a medal."

"She certainly does."

As he pulled up at some traffic lights, Simon turned to me and said, "And regarding Greenland, I don't think Flood really thought you were involved. All he has is the blurry CCTV stuff and the eyewitness."

"Yes, but I'll be happier knowing Hartley's been charged."

"Well, as far as the arson attack, it's clear to me Flood's not dug up enough stuff to discover precisely *when* you knew about Lynne's affair. As I said to you before, James, it was always going to be a close decision."

"I'd love to have been a fly on the wall at Flood's interviews with Hartley."

"Me too. I'm convinced Flood'll charge him with the arson attack. Then we'll have to wait to fill in the blanks."

As we pulled into the driveway, Alisha's face appeared at the window. Even before I got to the front door, she'd opened it. She threw herself at me, almost knocking me over.

"Oh, James! It's so good to see you!"

I revelled under a long, hot shower and changed my clothes. Alisha had made my favourite curry, chicken and sweetcorn, and we spent the evening eating and drinking a bottle of chilled *Lanson* champagne. It felt good to be back in the comfort of my home.

She pumped me for every detail concerning Flood's inquisition. She pursed her lips together and frowned when I explained his theory about the chloroform.

"I can see his thinking," she said. "I could have easily got some if RP had asked me. A close shave, eh?"

"Yeah. Remember my visit to Greenland? When he told me about Hartley believing Emily to be his? Did Lynne ever mention it?"

"Er… no. The first I heard about it is when you told RP and me after your chat with Greenland."

She fidgeted with her glass before taking a sip. I didn't find her answer convincing.

"Are you sure, Alisha?"

"Yes. Of course I am."

"So Lynne never knew Hartley felt this way?"

"No."

"And she didn't try to find out Emily's true father?"

She fidgeted with her glass again.

"I don't know where you got that idea from."

As she said it, she turned her head away from me. A dead giveaway.

"You knew, didn't you? Don't lie to me!" I raised my voice.

"James... I'm in a difficult situation." She took another sip of wine.

"I promised Lynne I'd never tell anyone."

"So you *did* know?" I wanted to pick her up and shake the truth out of her.

She put down the glass of champagne slowly and deliberately on the table, buying time before she answered.

"Yes... I did know." She avoided my eyes and stared up at the ceiling.

"Christ, Alisha!"

She at last made eye contact and sighed.

"Look, this is not easy, OK? Lynne told me that, before Hartley disappeared, he'd claimed the baby was his. Apparently he had always been obsessed about becoming a father. She was adamant he wasn't, but later, she had doubts. Although horrified at the prospect, she realised it was a possibility."

"Is that why she had the test?"

"Yes. I asked her whether she thought it a wise thing to do. But she said she *had* to know. If Emily were Hartley's she said she'd have to protect her from ever finding out. She prayed for the right result."

"I bet she did!"

"She hated knowing the truth. It truly bugged her. Even when Hartley disappeared out of her life for two years when he went to prison. She thought he'd given up on her."

"Why the hell didn't you tell me?"

"I didn't tell you because you were so happy being a father. I didn't think you'd ever find out. And if you did, I'm sure you wouldn't have *wanted* to know. I thought I did it for the best. I'm sorry."

"So you lied to me and RP when you said you had no idea Hartley had claimed he was Emily's father?"

"Yes... I've already told you why. I'm sorry."

"I can't believe you'd not tell me something like this." I stood up from the table, walked to the window, stared out at the darkness of the garden, balling my fists, fighting to keep my temper under control.

Alisha remained seated. She spoke to my back.

"Well, for all I know, perhaps you *did* know about it."

I turned on her sharply. "God, you sound just like Flood."

"Well, you told me that's what he thought. What would you have done if you *had* known? Would you have been upset enough to do something foolish?"

She remained seated at the table as I leaned over her and said, "I can't believe you're suggesting I'd murder my family."

Her eyes blazed back at mine. "I don't know what to believe any more."

"Oh, thanks for your support. Anything else I should know?" I moved closer, my face now inches away from hers.

She held her ground and glowered. "No... there's nothing else."

"You really should have told me, you know. I've had

enough of this." I turned away and stomped to my study, slamming the living room door behind me.

She shouted out after me, "So have I!"

Later, I saw her carrying a suitcase as she headed out to her car and then drive away.

CHAPTER TWENTY

Early November 1999 – August 2000

The next day, despite my concern about going into the office, I met up with Peter. We were still nervous about the Millennium Bug issue and after discussing it with a software consultant, we finalised our contingency plans. I appreciated the opportunity to forget the events of the last few days.

On the way home, I picked up a late edition of the *London Evening Standard* and threw it onto the back seat of my Mercedes. After parking in the drive, I retrieved the paper and entered the house.

I poured a glass of *Merlot* and settled down to read the paper before preparing dinner.

On page five, I read the headline I'd dreamt about for so long.

LONDONER CHARGED WITH FIVE MURDERS

At Tower Bridge Magistrates' Court earlier today, a 50-year-old man was charged with the murder of five people in three separate incidents.

John William Hartley of Percival Street, Clerkenwell, spoke only to give his name, address and date of birth.

> He is accused of conspiring with another to murder Lynne Hamilton, her son and her baby daughter in an arson attack. The incident took place in Lymington, Hampshire on 3rd August 1998.
>
> He is also accused of the murder of Leroy Johnson, whose body was discovered, drowned, in the River Thames near Tower Bridge, on or around 9th October 1999.
>
> He is also accused of conspiring with another to murder Colin Greenland, whose body was discovered stabbed to death in Victoria Park near Hackney Marshes on 12th October 1999.
>
> Hartley was remanded in custody and is due to appear at The Old Bailey on January 17th 2000 for a plea and case management hearing.

I read the piece several times as feelings of elation and relief coursed through my body.

"Yesss!" I shouted, punching a hand in the air. I almost knocked over my wine glass. I felt I'd just scored the winning goal at Wembley.

I called RP and read him the press report. His calmness countered my excitement. I sensed his pleasure though, despite the plan threatening to unravel on several occasions.

He warned me the tabloid press would pounce on this. "This case has all the ingredients of a melodrama. They'll suck every last juicy detail out of it. Mind you, until the court case, their reporting will have to be restrained."

"I think I'll do what I did before, Roger. Just not read it or get involved."

"Very wise."

Next, I called Alisha at home. Although still pissed off with her, I felt she ought to know the facts.

We exchanged half-hearted 'Hi's' and I asked, "Have you seen tonight's *Evening Standard*?"

"No, I've only just got in," she replied in a monotone voice.

I read out the press report. "This is a result, isn't it?" she said.

"Yes, it is, but we thought that when Johnson was charged. Remember?"

"Well, let's hope we don't get a feeble judge this time."

After an awkward silence, I said, "Listen, I think we should talk."

"There's nothing else to say, is there?"

"Don't be like that. I want to know if you really meant what you said last night. I'll pop over to your place now, OK?"

"If you must."

I felt uneasy about Alisha and me not being on the same side. It wouldn't do either of us any good. We both knew too much about each other.

Although her comment that I may have had something to do with the arson attack upset me, I realised how important to my life she'd become. We'd fused together, sharing our grief and anger whilst working hard to get justice. This dark secret bound us. And she'd been fantastic, helping me handle my grief.

But holding back her knowledge of Lynne's search for a paternity test was unforgivable. It bugged me. I didn't know what I truly felt for her anymore. I needed to clarify the situation.

As she opened the door to her flat, she said, "Hi," without even offering an air kiss.

"Glass of wine, cup of coffee?"

"Coffee's fine." I wanted to maintain a clear head.

As she put her cup on the table, I came straight to the point.

"Alisha, what did you mean when you implied that if I'd known about Hartley and Emily, I might have done something silly?"

"You've changed, James. I've seen it first hand; how angry you got when, first Johnson got off and then when the truth came out about little Emily's parentage. I felt you'd stop at nothing to get revenge. You became irrational."

"Don't you think I bloody well had every right to be? Hartley destroyed my life. Once I found out about what he'd done, of course I wanted my revenge. But I'd never in a million years want to hurt Lynne, Georgie and especially Emily."

She stared at me.

"Alisha, you've got to believe me. I didn't know anything about Hartley and Lynne until Greenland told me, I swear. It shocked me more than I can say. And as for Johnson, of course I was bloody upset about him getting off. Who wouldn't be?"

"It upset me, too. That's why I agreed to help you."

"Yes, you did. So we're in this together, aren't we?"

"Yes, we are."

"The thing is, it's no good us falling out."

She took a sip of coffee and said, "I know. Listen, it really concerned me when you said Flood insinuated you were involved in the arson attack. I thought you were just like all the other chauvinist pigs I've known. What is it with men? They *must* be in control, win *every* contest."

"Do you really think I'm like that? Do you?"

She couldn't face me, just fiddled with her cup.

After another short silence, I said, "Look, I can't say anymore. I'm fed up with defending myself. You either believe me or you don't."

I turned to look out of the window and said, "So… where do we go from here?"

"It's up to you."

I turned back to face her. "Well, let's at least remain friends, OK?"

"OK. Look, I'm sorry, James. You know me. I can't help it. I have to say what I think."

"You certainly do."

We carried on talking. She reminded me how happy Lynne had been when we married. She'd told Alisha that meeting me had been by far the most wonderful thing that had ever happened to her.

"I *know* Lynne desperately wanted you to be Emily's father. She was unbelievably distraught when she found out you weren't. I was upset too. And didn't want to burst your bubble."

I believed her.

★

RP's assessment of the media proved correct; the tabloids devoted whole pages to the saga over the next couple of days. My curiosity got the better of me and I read a few of the articles.

The reports were understandably sympathetic for my loss. I don't know how they'd got the photos they'd published. One, a favourite of mine, showed the four of us smiling contentedly on a beach with Lynne holding Emily in her arms. A couple more showed just Lynne with her stunning trademark smile – the one that first hooked me. I stared at the photos for ages, my mind drifting over the gloriously happy times we'd spent together.

I know I should have felt angry with her, but she now appeared to me as a vulnerable, tragic figure. As well as suffering long-term abuse and emotional damage from the men in her life, she also carried the burden of knowing the truth about Emily's father and the guilt about not telling me. I felt sorry for her. I still loved her.

There were also unflattering photos of Hartley, Greenland and Johnson, presumably taken when they were in prison.

Sorrow was the last emotion I sensed for them.

★

Life slowly began to get back to normal. I spent more time in my business. At least, I felt confident and assured there.

I kept in touch with Alisha, calling her once a week and having the occasional dinner. Neither of us brought up the issue that led to us falling out; we both tucked it away to the back of our minds.

In January, we learnt that Hartley had pleaded not guilty to all five murders and the date of the trial had been set for Monday, September 15th 2000.

We had nearly nine months to wait before we could, hopefully, celebrate getting justice for my family. I recalled this familiar vacuum of unfinished business had also existed just before Johnson's trial.

Back then, deeply shocked and confused, with mixed feelings of anger, grief and sorrow, I became an emotional wreck. Alisha had seen me through.

I wished I could speed up the process, but I had no control over the matter. The CPS needed time to build a cast-iron case, robust enough to ensure a successful outcome for the Crown against Hartley.

I still harboured a gnawing concern about him getting off on a spurious technicality. I'd read somewhere that lightning has struck in the same place twice.

I fell back on my usual remedies of working hard and going on long runs. Both failed to lift the cloud of apprehension hanging over me as the trial date got nearer.

The World's IT population, including Peter and I, held collective breaths and crossed fingers as midnight approached on December 31st 1999.

Fortunately, the Millennium Bug proved to be benign — one less problem to worry about.

★

By the end of July, six weeks before Hartley's trial, the media built up a head of steam speculating about our back stories. The intensity became so great that Alisha and I discussed getting away for a week or two, somewhere quiet, sunny and relaxing. We'd both agreed, no strings. Separate bedrooms.

Shortly after Hartley had been charged, the police returned my passport and I no longer had to report to them daily. I was free to go where I wanted.

One of my golf club mates owned a villa in Grenada in the Caribbean. We rented it from him.

I dreaded the second anniversary of the murder of my family on 3rd August. Another reason why we didn't want to be in London.

Going away with Alisha would be a good test of our true feelings for each other. I still hadn't worked out what mine were.

The glossy travel brochures described Grenada as the prettiest island in the Caribbean; they weren't wrong. White sandy beaches, turquoise sea and purple Bougainvillea flowers climbing almost every building supported their view. The breeze carried a heady mix of nutmeg, cinnamon and ginger, completing the exotic effect.

The villa sat right on the beach. Each night we listened to the waves gently lapping the shore accompanied by the clinking of the halyards against the masts of the dozen yachts moored in the bay.

Drinking *Carib* beers and rum punches with lunch and having dinner *al fresco,* prepared by a visiting cook, proved to be the ultimate in relaxation. However, thoughts of the impending trial hovered in the background.

We rarely left the villa. We lazed on the beach under the parasol, read, swam and sometimes took out a rowing boat into the calm Caribbean Sea.

We sometimes kissed but hugged a great deal, not in a sexual way, more like brother and sister.

On the anniversary of the fatal attack, we decided to hold a vigil on the beach in front of the beach house. After dinner, we lit three candles in memory of Lynne, Georgie and Emily. We remained silent for ages, holding hands and concentrating on our respective memories. We devoted the rest of the evening to comparing our time with Lynne. Sometimes we laughed, sometimes we cried.

She remained an integral part of us.

Alisha was the only person in the world with whom I could share this cathartic experience.

CHAPTER TWENTY-ONE

September 2000

Two weeks after we returned to London, the trial of John William Hartley began at the Old Bailey. As the start date grew nearer, the ethereal experience of Grenada dissipated. The spectre of a repeat of Johnson's acquittal stuck stubbornly in my mind.

Media interest in the case grew even more frenetic. One newspaper described it as being potentially one of the most dramatic trials of the last few years.

I wouldn't miss a day. Alisha had received a letter from the CPS requiring her appearance as a witness for the prosecution. RP had warned her about this being a possibility, since we knew the police held information linking her to Lynne, Johnson, Greenland and Hartley. I hoped she'd cope well, but typically, she had no doubts.

Although she could attend court and sit in the visitors' gallery *after* her evidence had been heard, RP had advised that it wasn't a good idea.

"The less contact you are seen to have, the better. We don't want the defence to use your relationship with James as fodder for a set-up."

The CPS had set aside four weeks for the trial. I arranged for two drivers from my business to be on hand for the entire case, one to act as my 'minder', protecting me from the media scrum.

On the first day of the trial, newspaper reporters, photographers and TV cameramen surrounded the entrance to the Old Bailey. As my car drew up outside the court, they engulfed us. My minder helped me negotiate my way into the building. This happened every day of the trial.

Court 16 bore an uncanny resemblance to the courtroom in Winchester Crown Court where the judge had screwed up Johnson's trial. I looked down on proceedings with a clear view of the dock, the jury, the bench and the barristers from the packed visitors' gallery.

Hartley sat in the dock flanked by two security men. I had a good view of him from the front row. He'd have to turn his head up to the gallery to see me. The judge, Mr Justice Winter, sat high on his bench, overseeing the well of barristers and clerks.

The jury, comprising eight women and four men, looked sombre, their eyes flicking from Hartley to the barristers and to the judge.

Dressed smartly with a white open-necked shirt beneath a black jacket, Hartley appeared thinner, especially so in the face. The last time I'd seen him was when he lay comatose, drugged-up with chloroform and Rohypnol, on his bed when I returned his clothes after dumping Johnson. He wore a hard-done-by expression as if questioning the travesty of being in the dock on trial for five murders.

Seeing him in the flesh brought home to me how much he'd affected my life. The fact he was Emily's father filled me with revulsion.

I worried I might have another meltdown in the courtroom. Not a good idea. I didn't want the judge barring me from the proceedings. I bit my lip until it almost bled.

The court clerk read out the charges: conspiracy to murder with another, Lynne, Georgie and Emily; conspiracy to murder with another, Colin Bruce Greenland and the murder of Leroy Gibson Johnson.

Simon Brotherton had previously confirmed that the sentences for conspiracy to murder and murder are the same.

I'd been counting the days to the trial, anxious to hear the evidence against Hartley. It would surely, finally reveal why the CPS had charged him and not me, especially for the Johnson murder.

The chief prosecutor, Michael Winn QC, a diminutive, handsome man in his late forties, put forward a powerful argument linking all three charges.

I'd googled him. He enjoyed a reputation for successful prosecutions in high-profile murder cases. I hoped he'd enhance it by the time this trial ended.

Mr Winn's opening speech outlined the deadly path Hartley had taken, first seeking revenge for his rejection by Lynne and covering his tracks by murdering his accomplices, one of whom blackmailed him and the other because he knew too much.

He described the events strictly in chronological order, placing great emphasis on the reason for Hartley being in the dock – his failed, obsessive affair with Lynne.

"This case is the climax to a dramatic and tragic tale of obsession and revenge. The prosecution will provide evidence to support the fact that the defendant couldn't handle the rejection by his mistress, Lynne Hamilton, despite his best efforts to persuade her to run away with him and set up home together with his daughter. Instead, she met and married someone else. *They* were bringing up the child together without him.

"The prosecution will prove that the defendant is manipulative and controlling and when Lynne Hamilton finally found the courage to stand up to him, he lost that control. He found that absolutely unacceptable."

He paused, giving the jury enough time to absorb his point.

"We'll provide further evidence to suggest that the defendant employed a hit man, Leroy Johnson, to set fire to the cottage in Lymington, where the defendant's ex-mistress, her son and two-year-old daughter were sleeping. Overwhelming evidence supports the fact that Johnson committed this cold-hearted and pre-meditated act on Hartley's orders.

"When Johnson tried to blackmail the defendant by threatening to go to the police unless he paid more cash, the defendant murdered him.

"And we'll provide additional evidence to suggest that when the defendant thought that Colin Greenland, to whom he admitted his intentions and who had put the defendant and Johnson in touch, might also go to the police regarding the arson attack, the defendant paid another hit man to have Greenland eliminated too."

This confirmed our thoughts. One more piece of the jigsaw clicked into place.

Impressed with this opening salvo, I recalled feeling the same way at Johnson's trial. However, that hadn't turned out exactly as I'd expected.

Mr Winn, keen to establish Hartley's obsession with Lynne, asked the court official to hand to the jury a dozen thick packs of documents, which he passed to each member.

When they all had a copy, Mr Winn said, "The document before you is a record of phone calls made by the defendant between 6th July and 1st August 1998, just two nights before the arson. The defendant's mobile phone supplier has provided this information.

"A highlighter marks the dates. Can you all see them?"

Every member of the jury nodded. Mr Winn put on his reading glasses and examined his copy of the document.

"These records show that in that period, Hartley rang Lynne Hamilton's mobile number no fewer than seven hundred times, an average of *fifteen* times a day. Towards the end of this period, the calls were more frequent, up to *twenty* times a day."

He paused again whilst the jury flicked through the document.

Then he said, "Now I'm going to play a recording of some of the messages he left during this period."

Hartley's booming voice came through loud and clear on the tape, the messages becoming increasingly threatening as the day of the arson attack loomed.

He referred to me in his messages as a wanker, a tosser or a flash bastard.

He continually implored Lynne to run away with him. He said he had the right to bring up *his* baby — "Don't let that prick Hamilton anywhere near her!"

His rage and anger increased with every message, causing him to lose control a few times. I visualised his spittle showering his mobile phone.

The jury were played the final message that I believed would surely seal his fate.

"If you refuse to come away with me, Lynne, believe me, you'll be sorry. No one else is going to bring up *my* baby. You'll all suffer, I'm not kidding."

The court official turned off the audio cassette player and Mr Winn maintained a dramatic silence, enabling the jury to absorb the implications.

I realised the full extent of the torment Lynne must have endured. Why didn't she tell me? Probably thought if she did, she'd lose me. If only I had known, I'm sure I could have done something about it.

I remembered too, that the intense fire had destroyed her mobile phone with the incriminating messages on it. Otherwise, the police might have arrested Hartley sooner.

Mr Winn moved on to the murder of Leroy Johnson. He played the mobile messages between Greenland and Hartley and between Johnson and Hartley. They clearly signalled Johnson's intent to blackmail Hartley for the arson attack.

The judge had previously agreed the messages could be admitted as evidence.

In the final message played to the court, Hartley said to Greenland, "He's (Johnson) blackmailing me over that arson business." A few members of the jury made a note.

Then he played the taped conversation between Hartley and Greenland, confirming Greenland's involvement and highlighting the fact that Hartley now knew about Alisha's affair with Johnson.

Mr Winn introduced the issue of the clothes, trainers and chloroform bottle found in Hartley's flat.

He called a witness from the Forensic Service who confirmed that Johnson's DNA, taken from hair and skin samples, had been found on Hartley's clothes and that the mud on his trainers matched that at the crime scene, Bermondsey Wall West on the Thames Embankment.

Mr Winn pressed home his point by presenting further evidence I hadn't heard.

"The police discovered Johnson's bloodstains and two fragments of his teeth on the concrete floor of a disused workshop underneath the arches close to Southwark Park. Footprints from a pair of Nike trainers were found there too… the same pair of Nike trainers found at the defendant's flat."

I almost got the shakes when Mr Winn asked the court official to pass over to the jury stills of CCTV evidence showing 'Hartley' driving his car from the railway arches to the Embankment close to the estimated time of Johnson's death.

He pointed out that, although the images were less than perfect, the driver of the car appeared to be wearing clothes similar to those the police discovered at Hartley's flat. Also, the number plate on the car was registered in Hartley's name.

"And, members of the jury, during the search of Hartley's flat, the police also discovered the key to the railway arch door in a sideboard drawer, which conveniently had the address written on the key fob." He held up and shook for effect a transparent evidence bag containing the exhibit.

I recalled Bruno reminding me to make sure I left it there.

"And now, I'm afraid there's a piece of vital evidence which I *can't* show you. I can't show you because it's been destroyed. *Someone* set fire to the defendant's car. The same car which the prosecution believe was used to transport Leroy Johnson to his death *and* used in the abduction of a key witness, Alisha Alleyne, whom you will hear from later. Convenient, don't you think?"

At 4.30pm, Judge Winter adjourned for the day.

It had been a good one.

★

The following day, the prosecution called their first witness, Hartley's ex-wife, Katherine Kelly. She'd reverted to her maiden name after her divorce. I had never given her existence a second thought.

Slightly overweight, aged about fifty with short mousey hair, she appeared a fading beauty. She wore a jacket and skirt last seen in ten-year-old fashion magazines.

She held her head low, avoiding any eye contact whatsoever with Hartley. He constantly glared at her with contempt. She spoke in a soft voice with a hint of an Irish accent.

Mr Winn, sensing her timidity, carefully and slowly cross-examined her.

He coaxed out of her what life had been like living with Hartley.

"We met in 1989. We were both married before. It was the second time for me and the third for him. At first, he was charming and romantic. He earned plenty of money and he spoiled me. He'd give me anything I wanted. But after a few years he grew bored with me. Never spent time at home; out having affairs all over the place." She glanced nervously at the jury.

Mr Winn encouraged her. "Please go on, Miss Kelly."

"Whenever I tackled him about it, he'd fly into a rage, like I'd thrown a switch. He's fine until he can't get his own way. Then he's violent and controlling. He got angry if I didn't do *exactly* as he wanted. I considered leaving him, but on each occasion, he talked me round. He's good with the blarney."

Mr Winn probed further. "Did his behaviour improve?"

"No. No. It got worse. We rowed every night. He said he wanted more excitement in his life and that I held him back. I didn't like to argue with him too much because if I did, he'd get more violent."

"Why didn't you leave him?"

"What could I do? I had no money. He controlled the finances. I had to accept that at least he provided me with financial security. I did leave him in the end. I'd been humiliated."

"Why, what happened?"

"I discovered one of the women he was having an affair with was Lynne Burrows. She worked in the same car dealership. I questioned him about it. Eventually, he admitted he'd been seeing her. Said he wanted to leave me and run off with her. Said she was expecting his child. Said, 'That's it, this marriage is over'."

"And when, *exactly* did you have this conversation?"

"I can't tell you the exact date, but around late January 1996."

"And how did you react to this?"

Katherine Kelly suddenly came to life. Her eyes blazed and she leaned forward, gripping the front of the witness box. Her Irish accent cut in strongly as her voice level increased.

"At first, it destroyed me. Then I decided to see what she looked like, what she had that I didn't. We'd been trying for a baby, but it didn't happen. He blamed me, of course. He had an obsession about becoming a father. He'd never had kids with his previous wives either." She glanced at the jury again.

Mr Winn prompted her, "And…"

"I found out where she lived and called on her out of the blue. I shocked her a bit, that's for sure. I told her to keep away from him. He's bad news, I said. She got herself in quite a state. Said she wanted nothing to do with him and to tell him she'd *never* go off with him. Said she had a new man in her life and was expecting *his* baby. It was all over between John and her. She pleaded with me to tell him to stop harassing her or she'd go to the police."

"Then what happened?"

"I went back, told him what she'd said. He went ballistic! He said, of course it was *his* baby. Told me not to be so stupid. Said he'd sort it out with her. His exact words were, 'If I can't have her and *my* baby, nobody else will!'"

The Queen's Counsel turned, faced the jury and said, "You're sure that's what he said, word for word?"

"Yes."

He turned back to face her again.

"Please continue."

"He wanted to be with *them*, not me. So I filed for a divorce, packed my bags and went to live with my sister in Belfast. I've been there ever since."

"Have you seen the defendant since then?"

"No."

"Thank you, Miss Kelly. That's all."

I recalled Lynne being decidedly edgy and fractious in the early months of her pregnancy. I put it down to her changing hormones, but now I realised she must have been under intolerable pressure.

Hartley going to jail in February saved her. She probably assumed Kathleen Kelly had persuaded Hartley that running away with her wouldn't work following her threat.

I never told Lynne anything about Hartley leaving the company, or discussed the embezzlement. This happened around the time Nick abducted Georgie and took him to Florida so she had enough on her plate. And at that time, I certainly wasn't her flavour of the month.

★

Anthony Jones QC led the defence team. He was built like a

heavyweight boxer and was at least fifteen years older than his adversary.

I thought the former Mrs Hartley would wilt under his aggressive cross-examination, but if anything, she became stronger. His last question summed up their verbal duel.

"Miss Kelly, by your own admission you say you were humiliated by the fact that your husband at the time had had an affair with Lynne Burrows and in his opinion had made her pregnant. So isn't it possible that your recollection of what he said is coloured by feelings of revenge on your part?"

Her eyes blazed again, indignant that Mr Jones had challenged her evidence.

"Absolutely not! I remember the conversation exactly. It turned out to be the turning point of my life."

"No more questions, your honour." Mr Jones had met his match.

The prosecution next called Alisha to the witness box. As well as being connected with the major players in the trial, DCI Flood had linked her abduction with the case against Hartley.

RP had warned us about the risk of Alisha being called as a witness. It meant the defence could challenge her over the precise nature of her relationship with Johnson. And with me, for that matter.

Prompted by Mr Winn, she explained, in great detail, the sequence of events regarding her abduction in Hartley's car.

When she finished, Mr Winn asked, "Do you have any idea who might have arranged this dreadful act?"

"I have an idea, yes."

"Please tell the court."

"The defendant, John Hartley. He got someone to do his dirty work."

"And why do you say that?"

"I think he found out about me seeing Leroy Johnson and thought he'd have told me about Hartley's involvement in the arson."

"And what did you do with this information?"

"Nothing. What could I do? I had no proof, only my suspicion. And anyway, it's difficult to get justice in the courts these days." Her eyes scanned the jury and settled on Judge Winter for a moment.

"Just answer counsel's questions, Ms Alleyne," the judge reprimanded.

Alisha had answered every one of Mr Winn's questions competently. I hoped she'd be as confident under cross-examination by Mr Jones.

Rising to his feet, he said, "I suggest, Ms Alleyne, the reason the defendant asked his friend to contact you is because the defendant suspected you were part of a plan to set up him up. That's true, isn't it?"

"He may have suspected me, but I didn't set anybody up."

"You didn't suggest to Leroy Johnson that it would be a good idea to get more money from the defendant?"

"No. I didn't know at that time the identity of the third party."

"Nor arrange a meeting?"

"No. I could hardly arrange a meeting with someone if I didn't know who it was."

Mr Jones checked his notes and continued.

"Going back to the abduction, there's no evidence to suggest Mr Hartley wanted to seriously harm you, is there? Maybe just to scare you a little."

Alisha, recognising bullshit when she saw it, all but accused the defence of spreading it.

"Have you ever been attacked from behind, had a bag

thrown over your face and been bundled into a car boot where you can hardly breathe? If he wanted to scare me, he did a great job. I wouldn't recommend it. I feared for my life. As far as I knew, whoever did it could have been a sadistic rapist. Hartley could have called me, couldn't he? Expressed his opinion."

Mr Jones consulted with one of his defence team before turning to face the witness box again and said, "That may not have worked. You'd have simply denied any involvement, wouldn't you?

"Now, let me propose something else to you. You were a very close friend of Lynne Hamilton, weren't you?"

"Yes."

"So close, you'd do anything to find out the identity of the person behind her murder. Isn't that so?"

"Yes."

"You might even go so far as to set someone up. The defendant, for example, if you believed him to be responsible. Is that correct?"

Before Alisha could reply, Mr Winn leapt to his feet again and objected.

"Your honour, where is this line of questioning going? This witness is not on trial."

Judge Winter upheld the objection. I squirmed in my seat.

We'd thought that framing Hartley for Johnson's murder greatly increased the chances of ensuring a guilty verdict for the man who'd catastrophically ruined my life. We regarded it as our trump card.

"Why didn't you go to the police with your suspicions?"

"I've just told the court. After what happened at Leroy Johnson's trial, I'd lost faith in the legal system. Everyone in the courtroom that day, including the judge, knew he was guilty." She glanced up at Judge Winter again. "I didn't think it worth pursuing."

"So let's be absolutely clear about this. You deny wanting to take matters into your own hands, meeting up with Johnson for the sole purpose of discovering the person behind the arson attack?"

"I'd never do that."

Mr Jones turned once again to the jury. "If the court accepts the mobile message evidence between the defendant and Colin Greenland, highlighting the defendant's blackmail by Leroy Johnson, then you have to accept the evidence contained in the same message that this witness appears to have become very close to Johnson, close enough to influence his actions."

He turned back to her.

"Now why would you want to have a relationship with, of all people, Leroy Johnson?"

Alisha cleverly avoided the trap.

"Pure coincidence. I happened to meet him at a dating agency. That's all. I met Colin Greenland there too. I've met many men at dating agencies. Sometimes it works out and sometimes it doesn't. It happens."

The late Leroy Johnson and the late Colin Greenland couldn't argue with what she said. I hoped she'd convinced the jury.

"I think this is an appropriate time to adjourn for today." Judge Winter rose and headed towards his chambers.

★

When we'd returned from Grenada, I'd told Alisha I wanted to hold off making any decisions about our future relationship.

I still hadn't sorted out my true feelings for her. I said that after the trial maybe everything would be clearer.

She'd shrugged her shoulders and said, "OK. It's no big deal. If that's want you want to do." I'd sensed her disappointment.

We still kept in touch during the trial and over dinner that night, in a restaurant tucked away behind Borough Market, we discussed the day's events.

"You were great in court today. You must have been nervous?"

"I was, but I kept thinking about what Lynne went through… it's so fucking unfair." She slumped back in her chair.

"I felt anxious when the defence barrister asked you why you didn't go to the police. Maybe we should have."

"You've a short memory, James. Look what happened last time."

CHAPTER TWENTY-TWO

September 2000

The next day, in front of another packed visitors' gallery, Mr Winn presented the case for Colin Greenland's murder in simple terms. He'd applied for and received the judge's agreement that the fact Hartley had spent time in prison could be admitted in court due to its relevance to the case.

Mr Winn produced written evidence from Her Majesty's Prison, Belmarsh confirming that Hartley and Greenland had shared a cell for several weeks whilst on remand.

Prison records also showed that Greenland visited Hartley in jail several times after Greenland's release.

Mr Winn continued, "It's the prosecution's case that the defendant's motive for wanting to dispose of Greenland was because he knew far too much about the arson attack. He believed that if Greenland thought he might become involved, he'd inform the police about their chats in Belmarsh; maybe do a deal with them to get a lighter sentence. Therefore, the defendant hired another hit man to deal with Greenland. His name is Desmond LaFayette."

This was news to me. Although RP had discovered that Greenland's killer had been charged and admitted his guilt within weeks of the murder, we had no idea that he'd implicated Hartley. At least this was one crime Flood couldn't lay at my door. I sensed that he'd be disappointed.

Mr Winn produced further prison documents supporting the fact that Hartley and Lafayette had also been in Belmarsh at the same time and knew each other.

"Desmond Lafayette has already been charged with Greenland's murder and found guilty. He's now awaiting sentencing."

Mr Winn called Lafayette as a witness for the prosecution by video-link from prison. Simon assumed the court made the call to avoid the considerable media scrum surrounding the Old Bailey every day. Or the CPS considered Lafayette may have been intimidated when facing Hartley in the dock.

A Jamaican, I guessed by his accent, Lafayette looked about thirty, with a set of huge bright, white teeth and a shaven head. He wore a white T-shirt and dark trousers.

Mr Winn asked Lafayette, "At your trial, you made a serious allegation that the defendant hired you to murder Mr Greenland and to abduct Alisha Alleyne. Do you still allege this?"

So that's who did it!

"Yeah, I do, man. It was business."

Mr Winn theatrically put on his glasses and read from his notes. "Also at your trial, the police disclosed that they'd discovered ten thousand pounds wrapped in brown paper and stuffed under a mattress in your flat. Bundles of £20 and £50 notes still had the bank wrappers on them, together with the defendant's fingerprints. You said that the money had come from the defendant. Do you still stand by that statement?"

"Yeah. 'Artley gave me the money. I didn't have no time to put it in a safe place."

"Let's be absolutely clear about this. The defendant paid you this sum to deal with Colin Greenland? Is that correct?"

"Yeah."

And he agreed to pay you more when you'd dealt with Alisha Alleyne?"

"Yeah."

Closing one of his files with a flourish, Mr Winn said, "That's all, your honour."

I shuddered at the consequences if Alisha hadn't escaped.

It was a paltry sum for a life, even for a lowlife like Greenland. Would Hartley have simply doubled the fee if Alisha had been murdered? I'd never know.

The irony of Hartley splashing out cash to Johnson and Lafayette from the proceeds of his embezzlement from my company added to my hatred of the man.

Mr Jones stopped scribbling a note and turned to the TV monitor.

"Have you ever dealt in drugs, Mr Lafayette?"

"Yeah. Sometimes."

"Have you ever dealt in drugs with the defendant?"

"Yeah."

"And have you ever fallen out with the defendant over a drug deal?"

"'E's tricky, man, 'ard to deal with. We fell out a few times."

It became clear from his tone there wasn't much love lost between him and Hartley.

"That's not what I asked. Have you ever fallen out with the defendant over a drug deal?" Mr Jones spoke the words slowly.

"Yeah."

"Is that why you implicated the defendant by suggesting his involvement with these serious charges?"

"No."

Under cross-examination, Lafayette's unswerving answers were categorically clear; he insisted he worked on Hartley's instructions and Hartley handed over the cash. Whichever way Mr Jones phrased the questions, Lafayette held his view.

Mr Jones addressed his final point to the jury. "It's the defence position that the payment made in cash by the defendant covered only the supply of drugs. When another drug deal went wrong, this witness decided to take revenge by making these fictitious claims."

Mr Jones thanked Lafayette and sat down. Judge Winter nodded at the court official, who turned off the video conference monitor.

Mr Winn got to his feet and said, "No more witnesses, your honour. That closes the case for the prosecution."

The defence would now present their evidence. They called Hartley to the witness stand.

He wasn't required to defend himself and Simon Brotherton told me that sometimes defence lawyers advise against it, on the grounds that the defendant would be vulnerable to cross-examination by the prosecution. This might not put them in a good light.

However, the defence team also knew the judge would inform the jury that if the defendant didn't give his side of the story, they could conclude that he had no answers to the charges.

I didn't think for one moment that Hartley wouldn't want to put his point of view, regardless of the legal advice. He always assumed he was smarter than anyone else and he'd relish demonstrating the fact.

He walked from the dock to the witness stand, maintaining his hangdog expression. He read out the oath in his deep voice, which reverberated across the courtroom.

Mr Jones waited for the court to settle. Adjusting his wig, he stood and clutched each side of his robe, his prominent thumbs pointing upwards, an open display of confidence.

"Let's start with the record of calls the prosecution state you made to Lynne Hamilton. Do you deny making them?"

"I can hardly deny it, can I? I wanted to have a normal family life, that's all. For us to be together. I'd missed the first two years of my daughter growing up; it got to me, here." He tapped his heart with his hand.

He gazed at the jury like a puppy at a dogs' home seeking a new owner. I suspect the defence team had coached him to employ this device whenever he made a statement aimed at eliciting sympathy.

"Why did you call so many times and leave so many messages?"

"I became desperate. I didn't know what else I could do. She'd rejected me. I wanted to win her back."

"And is that why you threatened her?"

"I didn't mean it to come across like that. Listening to the tapes now, I suppose I did come on a bit strong. But I'd never hurt her. And I'd certainly never harm my baby."

Again, he gazed at the jury with a doleful expression.

I wanted to throw up.

"The court has heard the audio tapes of your conversations with Colin Greenland and Leroy Johnson. Why do you think Johnson blackmailed you?"

"He's scum. He'd do anything for money; he's grasping and greedy. But he wouldn't have the brains to do it himself. Someone must have put him up to it."

Mr Jones looked down, inspecting the transcript of the mobile conversations and said, "So when you said to Colin Greenland, *Johnson's trying to blackmail me over that arson business'*, what did you mean?"

"Of course I knew about the arson attack. It involved *my* family. I knew the judge had acquitted Johnson. I followed the case in the papers. He thought if he could implicate me, he could make a few bob, I suppose."

"And what about the taped conversation between you and Greenland? That's when you discovered that Alisha Alleyne was seeing Johnson. What did you think of that?"

"I thought she might have put Johnson up to blackmailing me."

This wasn't looking good; too near to the truth.

"Did you employ Mr Lafayette to abduct her, put the frighteners on her?"

"Well, yes… and no. He went too far. I never told him to pack her in the boot. I just wanted him to get her to back off. I didn't think he'd harm her."

"Did you pay him for that?"

"No. He offered to do it as a friend."

"Why did he use your car?"

"He doesn't have one. He borrowed mine."

I couldn't believe how breathtakingly arrogant he could be. He believed in his invincibility.

Mr Jones turned over several sheets in his lever arch file and settling on one, said, "Let me turn now to the forensic evidence presented by the prosecution. This clearly shows that Johnson's DNA was present on your jacket and trousers. Your trainers too, had mud on them from the Johnson crime scene. Do you have an explanation?"

"The only thing I can think of is that I'm being set-up. Someone must have borrowed them, done the deed and returned them. All I know is, I spent the evening at home. I remember someone ringing my flat doorbell. I went to the door, opened it, and next thing I remember is feeling a strong-smelling rag covered with chloroform, or something else pungent, being held over my face. After that… nothing… zilch."

"So you have no recollection of that night?"

"No. I remember feeling rough when I woke up. That's all."

"And that wasn't you driving your car, the one the court saw from clips of the CCTV, from the railway arches to the Thames Embankment?"

"I was in no fit state to walk, let alone drive a car."

"And the key to the railway arches found in your drawer?"

"I don't know where the arches are. I've never been there. So I don't need a bloody key."

Judge Winter gave Hartley a reproachful glare.

Mr Jones continued. "Can you explain to the court why you went missing for three days and tried to leave the country?"

"I felt under pressure. I thought someone had set me up. I thought my life might be in danger. They'd already dealt with Greenland and Johnson. Maybe I was next."

"And what about your car? What do you think happened to it?"

"Joy riders must have stolen it and when they'd had their fun, they set light to it. It happens a lot."

Nodding, acknowledging his point, Mr Jones continued, "I see. All right, let's move on to Mr Greenland's demise. You've heard that the prosecution allege that you paid Desmond Lafayette to deal with Mr Greenland. What do you say to that?"

"That's rubbish! As far as Lafayette is concerned, I met him a few times after he got out of jail, to set up drug deals. That's why I paid him. You can do me for that if you want."

"It's a lot of money for drugs. You're certain the payment wasn't for something more sinister?"

"No. That's the going rate. Prices are going up all the time."

Mr Jones looked up at Judge Winter and said, "That concludes the case for the defence, your honour." He plonked himself down and turned to make a comment to a junior barrister behind him again.

The judge nodded and called a brief adjournment.

★

Suitably refreshed, everyone reassembled in their places an hour later. Judge Winter invited Mr Winn to begin his cross-examination.

"Thank you, your honour." He turned to face Hartley in the dock and said, "First, I want to go back to the record of mobile calls you made and messages you left for Lynne Hamilton in the month before the fatal arson attack."

Putting on his glasses once again, he flicked over a page of his notes, and reading from them, said, "You've already testified that you made the calls and left the messages. You said, *'I became desperate. I didn't know what else to do. She'd rejected me. I wanted to win her back.'* Is that correct?"

"If you say so."

"No, this isn't *me* saying so. It's a direct quote by you from the court's records. I suggest to you that calling her fifteen to twenty times *a day* for a month is far from normal behaviour. It suggests someone with an obsessive, manipulative personality who simply couldn't take no for an answer."

"That's your opinion."

"It's not *my* opinion that counts." Pointing to the jury he continued, "They'll decide if what I've said makes sense.

"Now, let's examine the messages in more detail. There's no doubt about their threatening tone, is there? Especially the final message. Let's hear it again."

The court official switched on the audio tape. For the second time, the jury heard, *'If you refuse to come away with me Lynne, believe me, you'll be sorry. No one else is going to bring up* my baby. You'll all suffer. I'm not kidding.'

"Do you agree this message represents a clear threat to Lynne Hamilton and her family?"

"I just wanted to frighten her, that's all. As I said before, I'd never harm my family."

Mr Winn poured water from a jug into his glass and took a sip. The courtroom remained eerily silent.

"Now let's look at the murder of Leroy Johnson. In the messages between you and Johnson and you and Greenland, it's clear Johnson blackmailed you by threatening to go the police and tell them about your *alleged* involvement in the arson attack. You said Johnson was trying it on, didn't you?"

"I've told the court. He's a lowlife, trying to make easy money."

"That may be the case. But why did Johnson single you out?"

"I don't know."

"I suggest he singled you out because you *were* responsible for the fatal arson attack. You paid Leroy Johnson to carry out the threat you made to Lynne Hamilton in your final message to her. However, it appears that you didn't pay him enough, did you?"

"That's rubbish!"

"And because you were losing control of the situation, you murdered Johnson. The evidence I presented to the court earlier proves it, doesn't it?"

"If you're referring to the clothes and trainers, I know nothing about them. I've told you, all I remember that night, is someone came into my flat. I have no recollection of anything else after that."

"So you can't explain how your jacket and trousers became covered in Leroy Johnson's blood and hair particles?"

Hartley raised his voice in exasperation.

"Someone must have taken them away and returned them. If I did wear them I'd hardly leave them stuffed behind my boiler would I?"

"Only if you didn't have time to dispose of them. The police obtained a search warrant for your flat shortly after the night of the murder. The clothes were still there, complete with a bottle of chloroform. And you had disappeared."

"I've told the court why already."

"And can you explain the footprints left by the Nike trainers, at the spot where you dumped Leroy Johnson's body into the River Thames; the ones the police also discovered at your flat? I assume they were *stolen* and returned too?"

"Yes. They must have been."

"And what about the discovery by the police of Johnson's bloodstains and fragments of his teeth on the floor of the disused workshop underneath the railway arches? Footprints from your Nike trainers were found there too. Can you explain that to the court?"

Hartley mumbled, "No."

"And what about the CCTV evidence showing you driving your car from the railway arches to the Embankment. Can you explain that to the court?"

"I told you. How many more times! I stayed in my flat the entire evening."

"And what about the key to the railway arch door that the police found in a sideboard drawer in your flat. Can you explain that to the court?"

Hartley, now thoroughly rattled, spat back, "I don't know anything about a railway arch. I don't recognise the key. And

I've already told the court, somebody had knocked me out when all this happened. I couldn't possibly have driven my car. I was out of it. The whole thing's a pack of lies! How many more times do I have to tell you? It's a set-up!"

Mr Winn had Hartley pinned on the ropes and laid into him for the knockout blow.

"How much do you weigh, Mr Hartley?"

Slightly bemused by the question, he mumbled, "Around fourteen stone."

"And you're powerfully built. We know that Leroy Johnson weighed around ten stone. I'd say it's perfectly plausible for you alone to dispose of the victim, especially after you'd applied the chloroform. Wouldn't you agree?"

Hartley's face, growing redder, looked fit to burst. His indignant glare at the prosecution team did his appearance no favours.

"No, I wouldn't!"

"Also, why, if you are innocent of all the charges brought against you, did you disappear from your flat for several days?"

"I've already told the court. I felt fearful for my life."

"I put it to you that you went on the run because *you* were responsible for these crimes and the net was closing in on you."

"That's rubbish!"

"Why did you set fire to your car?"

Hartley snapped back, "I didn't. Someone stole it!"

"That's not true, is it? You torched your car, didn't you? You wanted to destroy the evidence. I'm talking about the fact that the boot of your car, on separate occasions, held the bodies of Leroy Johnson and Alisha Alleyne."

Before Mr Jones could object, Hartley shouted back, "I've told you, the car had been stolen."

Mr Winn's model of calmness contrasted strongly with Hartley's increasing anger.

Mr Jones jumped to his feet. "Objection, your honour! There's absolutely no evidence to support the allegation that the defendant set fire to his car."

"Objection sustained. Please keep to the facts, Mr Winn."

"Why didn't you report your car stolen? There's nothing in the police files and nothing in your insurance records."

Hartley roared back, "I didn't have time to report it stolen."

"I suggest you didn't report it because you were on the run, weren't you? Trying to flee the country. The last thing you'd have wanted is to draw attention to yourself from the police."

"That's bloody ridiculous." Hartley's voice had reached such a volume, Judge Winter warned him about his language and told him to calm down.

Mr Winn said, "I have no more questions, your honour."

The judge adjourned for the day, allowing the barristers time to prepare their closing speeches. After that, the jury would consider their verdict.

Although impressed by the prosecution case, I didn't know what to think about our chances of getting away with what we'd done. I had doubts about why I'd ever got involved with RP's plan. Naively, I hadn't thought it through fully. The detectives were incredibly thorough in their investigation and the barristers' cross-examination skills placed great pressure on witnesses.

I shared my thoughts with Alisha that evening over dinner at her flat.

She said, "I had no idea it would end up in court like this. We've got to hope Mr Winn does his stuff tomorrow."

★

Mr Winn's closing speech rubbished his learned friend's attempt at putting up a plausible defence for all the charges against the defendant.

Summing up the prosecution case, brim-full of confidence, he derided the defence's claim that Leroy Johnson's blackmail attempt had been merely a try-on.

"The defendant, in the midst of a torrid sexual affair, besotted with Lynne Hamilton and desperately needing to be a father, couldn't face life without them. So he hired Leroy Johnson to burn down the cottage."

In a more sympathetic tone, he said, "You will almost certainly question whether any father would go so far as to murder his daughter. It's rare but, regrettably, familicide occurs in this country two or three times a year."

Mr Winn continued, "There is one common denominator. In many of these cases, the father suffers from an antisocial personality disorder of some kind.

"It's entirely plausible that this is the situation in this case. The major characteristics of such people are that, despite being superficially charming, they are manipulative, devoid of conscience and incapable of accepting rejection. The defendant, humiliated by the fact Lynne Hamilton chose to marry someone else, who would bring up his child, grew full of jealously, resentment and fury and took his revenge."

He dismissed Hartley's claim that he'd been set up for the Johnson murder. "It's ludicrous to suggest that someone could come up with such a perfect plan to frame him. It's laughable."

Not as laughable as you believe, I thought.

He said the circumstances of Greenland's murder were straightforward. He reminded the jury that Desmond Lafayette had already pleaded guilty and had indicted Hartley as the instigator. The wads of notes found in Lafayette's flat bearing Hartley's fingerprints were another clear sign of Hartley's guilt.

"And the prosecution simply doesn't buy the defence's claim that the cash paid to Desmond Lafayette had been for the supply of drugs. None were ever found in the defendant's possession or his flat."

He questioned again, why, if the defendant was innocent, did he disappear and try to leave the country and set fire to his car? He dismissed the joy-rider explanation, citing the lack of evidence provided by the defence.

His closing remark brought home to me the risk I'd taken in seeking justice outside the legal framework.

"Were it not for the clear-thinking of Alisha Alleyne following her abduction by the defendant's hit man, Lafayette, we may have been looking at another murder; such is the defendant's ruthlessness and determination not to be caught. In addition, he's trying to evade the consequences by suggesting someone set him up. There is simply only one verdict possible in this case. The defendant is guilty as charged on all counts."

Surely, we had Hartley now.

Forcing his large frame off the bench, Mr Jones stood to make his closing speech on behalf of the defence.

"The defendant accepts having an affair with Lynne Hamilton and contacting her in July and August 1998 on his release from prison, but emphatically denies planning with others to take revenge for what the prosecution alleges was the result of jealous rage.

"Being besotted with a stunningly beautiful woman with whom the defendant was having a sexual affair is not abnormal. It's certainly not a criminal offence. It's human nature to become obsessed in these circumstances, say things in the heat of the moment that later we regret. However, is it enough to suggest the defendant would want to murder the mother of his child, her son and his daughter? You will have to decide."

Regarding the mobile phone message evidence, he suggested that Johnson had been a chancer; just trying out his luck, attempting to blackmail Hartley for a quick return.

"And the messages between Hartley and Greenland simply referred to the blackmail attempt, that's all. It doesn't *prove* the defendant's involvement in the fatal arson attack."

Mr Jones slowly ran his eyes over each member of the jury, as if defying them to disagree.

"And as for the evidence we heard from the former Mrs Hartley, I'd ask you, members of the jury, to put it in perspective. Here is a woman, rejected by her husband, who had an affair resulting in his mistress falling pregnant with his child. I put it to you that her view of events could be prejudiced. What's the expression? 'Hell hath no fury like a woman, scorned'. Again, you will have to decide whether you believe her testimony or not."

Referring to the Leroy Johnson murder, he focussed heavily on the set-up theory. First, he referred to the chloroform.

"Doesn't it seem odd that the defendant has testified on oath that someone called at his flat and when he opened the door, this person held a rag covered in chloroform over his face? Isn't it too much of a coincidence that the pathologist's report, following the autopsy on Leroy Johnson, showed his face too, had been covered in red sores consistent with the application of chloroform, despite being submerged in the River Thames for two days? I suggest this shows someone else *must* have been involved in knocking out the defendant and using the same *modus operandi* for Leroy Johnson."

The courtroom grew thick with tension.

"That someone could easily have borrowed the defendant's car, jacket, trousers and trainers and returned them after Leroy Johnson had been dealt with. And it defies belief that Hartley's mobile, containing the messages referring to the blackmail attempt, just happened to be found in a cafe by a complete stranger and handed in to the local police station."

Mr Jones exaggerated his hand gestures, enjoying being centre stage.

"Is it feasible that the defendant could, on his own, have trussed up Leroy Johnson, attached a weight to him and flung him over a wall into the River Thames?

"And as for the key to the railway arch door being found in my client's sideboard drawer, this could easily have been planted, couldn't it?"

Mr Jones's oratory transfixed the jury. They hung on his every word.

"My learned friend for the prosecution has suggested this scenario is *laughable*. On the contrary, the defence maintains this to be a perfectly plausible set of circumstances."

I fidgeted in my seat. Mr Jones had accurately replayed the events on that damp, windy night.

"And regarding the Colin Greenland murder, the prosecution relies heavily on the evidence from someone who, it appears, had a score to settle with the defendant. You will have to decide if Mr Lafayette's version of events is true or not."

He took a deep mouthful of water, I suspected more for effect than need, and pressed on.

"Before retiring to consider your verdict, there are further points I'd like you to consider.

"If, as the prosecution allege, the defendant hired hit men

to murder Mrs Hamilton, her children and Mr Greenland, then why did he not employ the same *modus operandi* to murder Leroy Johnson? Why would he take the risk of dealing with him himself? It's not realistic. It doesn't make sense.

"And you've heard the testimony from Alisha Alleyne, Lynne Hamilton's best friend, explaining her dalliance with Leroy Johnson. She implies just a passing interest. Does she come across as someone so desperately lonely that she'd seek *him* out, of all people? No, I suggest it may well have been part of an elaborate plan to gain revenge for her friend's murder and to find out who else may have been responsible.

"Once the interested parties discovered who they *thought* was involved, the defence asks you to consider the possibility that it was *they* who planned to eliminate Johnson and Greenland and frame the defendant."

He eyed each member of the jury once more before facing the judge and saying, "That's all your honour."

Mr Jones flopped down on to the bench, looking pleased with himself.

My confidence in a successful prosecution nose-dived. Mr Winn hade presented the prosecution case well, but I wasn't convinced he'd done enough. No doubt, Alisha and I were the 'interested parties' Mr Jones had referred to.

I squirmed in my seat again at the thought.

Mr Jones had found us out.

But it was Judge Winter's final comments, after his summing up before asking the jury to retire, which unnerved me the most.

"You must now consider the evidence you've heard. You must decide whose testimony you believe. Please bear in mind, members of the jury, the prosecution must prove its case so that, having considered all the evidence relevant to the charges, you must *all* be sure the defendant is guilty. There must be no reasonable doubt in your minds. If you have *any* doubt whatsoever, then you must return a not guilty verdict on any of the three indictments against the defendant."

Judge Winter nodded at the court usher who asked the court to rise as the judge stood, and returned to his chambers.

I slumped back in my seat and closed my eyes.

That was it. Full time. Except we didn't know the result.

CHAPTER TWENTY-THREE

September 2000

Later that evening, I called Simon Brotherton. I explained in as much detail as I could remember the last few days' proceedings, particularly the barristers' comments and the judge's summing up. I wanted his opinion about the outcome.

He remained silent for a moment, considering what to say to me.

"Mm... James, I think you should be very clear about this. If the jury accepts Hartley had been set up, especially for the Johnson murder, the CPS will consider you and Alisha as number one suspects. I'd expect them to re-open the file immediately. You'd both be in the dock before you knew it."

"I thought you'd say that."

"We'd have a job on our hands to successfully defend you both. The prosecution could easily prove you and Alisha are in a relationship and therefore would examine her liaison with Johnson in much more detail."

I thought Alisha had explained her contact with Johnson well, playing down the intensity of their relationship. Fortunately, he couldn't testify otherwise.

Simon continued, "You told me Alisha explained to the court that Johnson had told her Hartley paid him to set fire to your cottage. So the big question in the jury's mind would be this; why didn't she pass this information onto the police?"

"She told the court. She'd lost faith in the legal system."

"It's a bit weak, isn't it? I hope the jury believed her. She's already perjured herself, which is a serious offence. Maybe you and RP made the plan *too* neat. Why don't you call him, see what he has to say?"

"I will."

I dialled RP's number immediately and didn't give him a chance to speak.

"Roger, this is looking fucking serious. The defence questioned everything; Hartley's MO for Johnson's murder being different from the other two, the chloroform 'coincidence' and Hartley's mobile mysteriously appearing at the police station. That's just for starters. They majored heavily on Alisha's affair with Johnson. You must admit it does appear like a set-up."

"Calm down, James. You're getting paranoid. OK… possibly the plan wasn't perfect. But look at it from the other side's point of view. Hartley posing as a victim of a set-up for the Johnson and Greenland murders doesn't add up."

"What do you mean?"

"Hartley's made several mistakes, which point to his guilt. First, he hires a hit man to abduct Alisha in his car. Then he tries to leave the country, but not before torching his car. Why did he do all that if he had nothing to hide? Obviously, to get rid of the forensic evidence."

"But Hartley's not dim. Maybe his car *had* been stolen by joy riders and set alight," I shouted down the phone.

"No, sorry James. I'm convinced the jury will believe that Hartley panicked. He realised he'd lost control of the situation. And we know he's uncomfortable with that."

"That may be true, but if they don't convict Hartley, Simon

told me Alisha and I are number one suspects. It's a bloody disaster!"

"I understand how you feel."

"No you bloody don't! It's all right for you. You always believe you're so fucking infallible. We're talking about *my* life. And Alisha's."

I slammed the phone down. I didn't want to hear any more of RP's assurances that everything would be all right. It wasn't.

I feared that if the police charged me for Johnson's murder, the CPS would want to resurrect Flood's assertion that I had something to do with my family's murder. He'd dig even deeper to prove that I knew about Lynne's affair with Hartley and Emily being his daughter.

Flood had once suggested that Greenland's murder also could be down to me. After all, he'd been the go-between, putting Johnson and Hartley together. It surprised me that he never suggested I could have employed Lafayette. He must have believed his story.

I called Alisha and explained the substance of my latest calls to Simon and RP.

"James, you *are* getting paranoid. I know it seems a mess, but there's nothing we can do to influence things, is there? We've got to hope that if there's any justice to be had, then we'll be OK. Do you want to come over to my place? You sound stressed."

"OK. Yes. I'll drive over now. Could be this'll be the last night we'll spend together."

"Don't be silly. We'll be fine."

We spent the evening going through every aspect of the case, yet again. After an hour intensely considering what we could or should have done better, we exhausted ourselves. I drove home, my mind frazzled. Although it had been good to share my fears with her.

★

The media's coverage of the case resembled bloodhounds sensing a kill. They'd covered the trial meticulously every day for four weeks.

Ubiquitous TV cameras whirred as I arrived at the court at 9.45am the next morning. I brushed past them with help from my minder.

It proved to be an anti-climax. Many of the courts were busy with other cases but Court 16 remained empty. The jury had spent the night at their homes the previous night, after failing to reach a verdict. They'd only just reconvened.

I wished like hell that I could spend time with them.

I'd explain what Hartley, Johnson and Greenland were really like; evil scum only interested in ploughing their own path through life, not giving a fuck about anyone else. Compare them to Lynne, Georgie and Emily, I'd say. They were angels. But they're dead and Hartley's still alive.

At midday, the jury still hadn't reached a verdict. I shielded my face and went across the road to a Greek cafe for a coffee. A notice on the door suggested that, for a small fee, they'd look after your mobile phone. They weren't allowed inside the court building even if they were switched off. I left mine at home each day of the trial.

I busied myself reading car magazines, studiously avoiding the newspapers.

I checked back with the court reception every hour in the afternoon until it became obvious the jury still couldn't agree.

Finally, at 3.45pm, they indicated they needed advice from the judge.

Despite the lateness of the day, the visitors' gallery quickly filled up, people appearing from nowhere. The foreman of the jury, a grey-haired, urbane, sixty-year-old man looking like a GP explained, apologetically, that despite discussing the case at length they were having difficulty in reaching a unanimous verdict.

The judge listened intently and told the foreman he'd accept a majority verdict of ten to two and asked the jury to go back to their room to reconsider. He also pointed out that it would be impractical to reconvene the court later that day but hoped the jury would be in a position to declare their verdict tomorrow morning.

I couldn't decide whether their difficulty in reaching a decision denoted good news or bad. I found it too difficult to call. I gave up trying.

When I got back home, although my stomach felt bloated, as if I'd eaten a bag of air, I felt I should eat something. I prepared one of my favourite pasta dishes, mushroom ravioli with a tomato and pesto sauce. After two mouthfuls, I pushed the plate away. I couldn't face it. I poured a good measure of brandy instead.

I updated Alisha, Simon and RP before watching TV to take my mind off things, but my head span like a top, going over and over the trial proceedings.

I concluded that our plan had failed to pass the legal process.

*

Arriving at the Old Bailey early the next morning and running the usual gauntlet of journalists, I learned that the court would be sitting at 11am. The jury had reached a majority verdict.

When I'd updated Simon, he suggested it might be a good idea if he attended the final day to support me, whichever way the verdict went. I gratefully accepted his offer.

At Johnson's trial, the air of expectancy in the packed court had been electric whilst we anxiously awaited the judge's decision on whether he'd allow the incriminating DNA evidence to be presented to the jury.

This time, the tension notched up a few degrees; not surprising given that my freedom was at stake… and possibly Alisha's. A stranger entering the court for the first time would grasp how momentous the next few minutes would be by the drawn, intense expressions on the faces of the barristers and the jury.

Simon sat next to me and when everyone had settled in their places, the judge asked the foreman if they had reached a majority verdict.

"Yes, your honour." He sounded more confident now.

The court official stood and asked, "On the count of conspiracy to murder Lynne Julia Hamilton, Georgie Iain Burrows and Emily Stephanie Hamilton, do you find the defendant guilty or not guilty?"

The consequences of either a one-word reply or a two-word reply could hardly have been greater… for Hartley or me.

"Guilty."

I closed my eyes, placed a finger and thumb on the bridge of my nose, and uttered under my breath, "Thank God!"

The extreme tenseness in my shoulders loosened significantly.

"On the count of the murder of Leroy Johnson, do you find the defendant guilty or not guilty?"

"Guilty."

Before I could react, the court clerk asked, "On the count of conspiracy to murder Colin Allan Greenland, do you find the defendant guilty or not guilty?"

"Guilty."

Simon's clenched fist tapped up and down on my thigh, signalling huge relief. Nothing compared to mine. It had taken over two years to get justice.

Voices from the visitors' gallery shouted out, "Rot in hell, Hartley!" and "You scum!" I couldn't have joined in if I wanted to. I felt numb. I stared down at Hartley. Shocked, his face contorted into a scowl. He said nothing. Just glared at the judge and the defence team.

Our plan had worked after all, albeit with major hiccups along the way. But I didn't feel triumphant. I'd have given anything to unwind the events of the last few years, have my family back again, not having to resort to taking matters into my own hands.

As the clamour from the gallery subsided, Judge Winter asked the barristers to make their closing statements before sentencing.

The court learnt from the prosecution about Hartley's previous criminal record. RP had already researched it and told me.

It still shocked me on hearing it read out.

He had several police cautions for beating up a previous wife. He'd spent a year in prison in 1988 for grievous bodily harm when he'd dragged her out into the street and slapped and kicked her in front of the neighbours.

He'd also been involved in a road rage incident, which led to him spending another six months in jail in 1991. The pattern became clear. He grew used to achieving his goals by using his intelligence, charm and charisma – ideal components for a con man. However, although he came across as a paragon of virtue, if he didn't get his own way, he lost it and reacted physically.

Mr Winn emphasised the seriousness of Hartley's latest crimes; his ruthless drive to cover his tracks resulting in the unnecessary deaths of two men, quite apart from conspiring to murder his ex-mistress and two completely innocent children, one, his own flesh and blood.

The defence made a plea for mitigation before sentencing. There wasn't a lot Anthony Jones QC could say.

"Crimes of passion are always difficult to judge. One never truly knows what goes on behind closed doors.

"It's entirely plausible that the defendant had been led on by Lynne Hamilton. After she met another man, she denied that the defendant could be the father of the baby and dropped him like a stone."

His contrite tone continued. "I suggest that under these circumstances, any man, especially one as obsessed as the defendant, would find this situation difficult to deal with."

When Mr Jones had finished, Judge Winter, who'd listened intently to both closing statements, addressed Hartley and said, "Please stand."

Hartley did so, shaking his head from side to side, still not believing the verdict.

"These crimes are amongst the worst I have had the misfortune to deal with. You callously conspired with Leroy Johnson to set fire to a house which you knew was inhabited by three people, one your own daughter, killed a man because he blackmailed you and conspired to have another man stabbed to death because he knew too much about your exploits, fearing he'd go to the police. You are manipulative, devious and ruthless, in short, an evil man. You have shown no remorse or accepted any blame whatsoever, and had no regard for the victims of your crimes."

Hartley couldn't contain himself. He yelled at the judge.

"Why should I? Someone set me up! This whole trial's a joke." Pointing at the jury, he ranted, "And they're no fucking better!"

Judge Winter glared at him severely.

"You will serve a minimum period of thirty years before you will be eligible for parole. If you die in jail, nobody will shed a tear for you. Take him down."

CHAPTER TWENTY-FOUR

September/October 2000

I didn't feel ecstatic. I didn't show any sign of victory in the courtroom. More a feeling of grim satisfaction, relieved that the plan had eventually worked. We'd ensured justice prevailed and we weren't implicated.

Before we left the Old Bailey, Simon said, "I think the press are expecting a statement from you, otherwise they'll be on your back for ages. I'll scribble something out if you like."

A few minutes later, he passed it over to me and asked if I agreed with it. I nodded.

A barrage of photographers and reporters thrust microphones in front of me, urging me to say something as I left the Old Bailey. I bottled it and asked Simon to read out the statement.

As the flashbulbs fizzed, he said:

"*My client, Mr Hamilton, is delighted that at last, justice has been served for his family. This is a very significant day for him. He has lived with the tragic circumstances of the murder of his wife, his stepson and a baby he believed to be his for over two years. He would like to thank the jury for their verdict, which will help him come to terms with his devastating loss. He also requests that the media now allow him to get on with his life and to respect his privacy. Thank you.*"

Reporters yelled out questions and the photographers'

flash bulbs continued to light up the overcast late morning. My minder ushered Simon and me to my waiting car and we sped off, leaving a phalanx of paparazzi in our wake.

I sat back in the car seat and let out a sigh. I called Alisha and told her the news.

I heard her gasp before she said, "That's great news! Thank God we got there at last." I heard her sob. She had a soft side after all.

I asked Simon about the possibility of Hartley appealing against either the verdicts or his sentence.

"He could appeal, yes, on a point of law or if there is fresh evidence. He'd have to get permission from a high court judge. Frankly, I think that's unlikely."

Over the following days, weeks and months, I realised just how close we'd come to being charged. I couldn't believe we'd taken such risks.

And I also couldn't believe how profoundly I'd reacted to Johnson's acquittal fifteen months earlier. It unearthed an overwhelming, deep-seated sense of unfairness within me I never realised I'd had.

I concluded that I'd never have gone ahead with murdering Johnson and framing Hartley without Roger Pendleton. He'd become a powerful influence. Full of anger, I felt vulnerable back then, determined to seek retribution.

RP had been as pissed off as Alisha and I with the unfairness and injustice. He'd always been on my side, albeit handsomely paid in the process. He became the 'fixer', with the resources to deal with the problem. And I took advantage.

It's something I'd have to live with.

However, on other days, it felt perfectly reasonable to me that those responsible for perpetrating such heinous crimes against my family, and never brought to justice, got their just deserts.

We'd righted a wrong.

I realised that if the jury had found Johnson guilty at his trial in Winchester Crown Court and he'd been sentenced to twenty-five years, we'd never have discovered Hartley's affair with Lynne and the subsequent trail of events. Perhaps it would have been better that way. But then Hartley would have got away scot-free. Justice would have only been partly served.

I imagined what thirty years in prison would do to Hartley, a killer with a reputation for losing his temper if he didn't get his own way. Spending the rest of his life in jail would be bad enough, but only the inmates would decide how tough it would be.

I reflected deeply about the motive of revenge. It drove people to do things they'd never normally consider. I proved to be a classic example.

Settling of scores is a powerful driver.

Revenge drove Hartley, too, which he took in a most horrific way.

I thought about Nick, due out on parole in less than two years' time. After festering in jail, much as Hartley had done, there was no doubt in my mind he'd be seeking revenge too.

I parked that thought at the back of my mind for now.

I realised all three of the men involved in relationships with Lynne were shaped by their attitude to revenge.

I made my peace with RP. Graciously, he told me he completely understood that I'd endured a great deal of pressure. Annoyingly, he sounded as infallible as ever.

Shortly after Hartley's trial, a judge sentenced Desmond Lafayette to fifteen years for his part in the murder of Colin Greenland. The police dropped the abduction charge against him, presumably in return for shopping Hartley.

Two days after the trial, Alisha and I visited Lynne's

mother, Margaret. We'd called her or popped in once or twice a month since Lynne's death, to see how she was coping. I could tell by the dead look in her eyes that she wasn't particularly interested in the outcome of Hartley's trial. She'd never recovered from the loss of her only daughter and grandchildren.

★

Something still bothered me about my current relationship with Alisha. I thought that, after the trial, I'd spend the rest of my life with her. She understood me, knew what I'd been through, and supported me when I needed it. She'd put herself at the mercy of Johnson in the cause of justice.

She once told me, "Every time I see him, I want to vomit. I've got to show him affection... all that touching and kissing... it's unbearable!" I worried she might be traumatised for years.

We'd been thrown together by grief and revenge. It didn't seem the ideal basis for a long-term relationship. I realised we *needed* each other at the time. But I never *loved* her. Not like Lynne and me.

It wasn't Alisha's fault, but every time we met after the trial, her presence reminded me of the terrible things we'd done. And I could never forgive her for lying to me about Lynne's quest to discover the truth about Emily's father. And at one point, thinking I might have been responsible for the arson attack.

I wanted to put it all behind me, find a way to live with myself. I needed time away from her. We both had issues we had to deal with.

I thought I might fly to the United States, hire a Mustang

Convertible and spend three months driving across the country from New York to California, something I'd always wanted to do.

After that, perhaps we could work something out.

I told her how I felt.

"If that's what you want to do, I can't stop you, can I?"

"Sorry Alisha. Look, I'm eternally grateful for what you did, really I am. It's just that I think we both need time and space …"

"I thought we had something special going on, that's all. Of course, I know I could never match up to Lynne, but who could?"

"I know. Let me get this whole thing out of my system for a few months. See how it goes, OK?"

"OK," Alisha said, close to tears.

My conscience stuck in my throat.

★

One evening, a few days after the trial, the headlights of a Ford Focus flashed into my living room as it drew up onto my drive. I wasn't expecting visitors. I went to the window.

My heart lurched when I saw DCI Flood get out and zap the remote locking.

I'd last seen him when he gave his evidence at the trial, but I hadn't spoken to him since my interrogation at the police station, where I'd spent three nights in custody. I fervently hoped I'd never set eyes on him again.

"Can I come in and have a chat?" he said as I opened the door.

"Yes, of course," I said. The pulse in my neck raced. I loathed my guilty conscience.

I offered to take his coat and suggested a cup of coffee. He declined on both counts, saying, "This won't take long. I'm fine."

He sat opposite me on my sofa and crossed his legs.

"Now that Hartley's trial is over, I thought I'd put you in the picture about what we believe really happened on the night of Leroy Johnson's murder. What I'm about to say is in complete confidence. You must not breathe a word of what I'm about to say. Is that understood?"

I feebly replied, "Yes, of course."

"First, I had my reservations about your involvement with the arson attack, but it's clear from the evidence we presented at the trial, the jury believed Hartley to be guilty. And I couldn't prove you knew about your wife's affair and Hartley being the child's father *before* the attack which would have motivated you."

At last, he got it.

"Second, with Desmond Lafayette's testimony, there's no doubt Hartley was responsible for Colin Greenland's murder."

I remained silent. I tried to anticipate with trepidation where these points were leading.

"Leroy Johnson's murder is the case I've been most concerned about. The jury believed Hartley did it but I always had my doubts. I *know* Hartley's defence of being set up is true. I'll tell you why."

I swallowed hard, trying to disguise my anxiety. I envisaged Flood putting handcuffs on me at any moment.

"John Hartley couldn't possibly have killed Leroy Johnson." He gave me that steely glare which had become so familiar to me.

"When we interviewed him, I couldn't understand why he'd been knocked out for the *entire* evening. The effects of the chloroform he said had been administered when he opened the door to his flat would only have lasted a few hours at the most."

He paused, expecting me to comment. My tongue stuck to the roof of my mouth. I wasn't capable of words.

"The forensic team ran a test to see if there were traces of something stronger that would substantiate his story. The urine, saliva and blood tests showed nothing, but they found traces of Rohypnol, the date rape drug, in a sample of his hair. In fact, it indicated a massive dose, enough to knock him out for anything up to eight hours.

"Most drugs can be traced this way. For some reason, they stay in your hair for anything up to three months, unlike bodily fluids, which show no traces after about forty-eight hours."

Our plan hadn't catered for this level of detailed forensic examination.

Flood paused again.

"There is only one explanation."

I thought if I said anything it would come out wrong. I willed myself to remain mute.

"Somebody must have injected Hartley with Rohypnol *after* he'd been knocked out by the chloroform."

Another short silence hung in the air.

Eventually, Flood said, "I'm sure you'll agree if this evidence had been presented at court, the argument put forward by the defence that John Hartley had been set up for the murder of Leroy Johnson by other 'interested parties', as the defence counsel called them, would have been considerably enhanced. In fact, I'm certain it would have led to a not guilty verdict."

I couldn't hold back any longer.

"Look, I don't understand why you're telling me all this. Why wasn't this evidence used at the trial if you're so confident about Hartley being set up?"

"Well, that's it, isn't it? We had the evidence, make no mistake about that. The forensic team were certain it would stand up to scrutiny from any expert witness the prosecution could provide."

"Why wasn't it used in court?"

"It became contaminated."

"What do you mean?"

"Well, let's just say it had been tampered with. I have a pal on the forensic team. *Unfortunately*, he used an evidence bag, which someone had used before for a different sample – strictly against the rules. We informed the CPS who advised us we couldn't use it."

The detective chief inspector sat back in the sofa.

"But you still haven't explained why you're telling me this now?"

"I see my job as getting justice. And professional pride, I suppose. I didn't want you to think we hadn't done our job properly. I investigated the crime and I solved it."

I had a grudging respect for his honesty. He was a winner, like RP.

"The judiciary despises vigilantes. They believe the rule of law is sacrosanct. However, that's not how I feel. The judges can't have any idea how they'd react if what happened to you, happened to them."

As he stood to leave, he shook my hand and said, "You aren't aware of it, but I do have an idea of what you've been through. I don't think the bad guys should be allowed to get away with murder, should they?"

"Of course not."

As he walked to the door, he said, "Ironic isn't it? You felt robbed of justice the first time round with the Johnson case. Now that's been cancelled out."

"There is a certain symmetry, I suppose, assuming your theory's correct."

He turned sharply to face me.

"I can assure you this is not theory, it's fact. Anyway, we can both say justice has been served, can't we?"

Reaching my front door, he turned to me again and said, "This conversation never happened, right? If you mention it, I'll deny all knowledge. Is that clear?"

"Yes, of course."

I closed the door behind him and stood with my back against it as I heard him drive off, relieved but still intrigued by what he'd said.

Flood's reference to having an idea of what I'd been through triggered my memory. I recalled the hand-written notes made by RP on the report he'd produced on Flood, regarding the tragic death of his wife in a revenge hit and run attack. The perpetrators remained at large.

I never mentioned the conversation with Flood to anyone.

Not even to Alisha or RP.

ACKNOWLEDGEMENTS

Writing *Blazing Obsession* required a great deal of help from the following people to whom I'll always be eternally grateful:

Adi Kingswell
Dave Locke
Terry Fitzjohn
Viv Wolley
Cathy Revis
Linda Hewett
Bill Mousley QC
Dee Waterman
Paul and Marion Stallard
Di Ingram
The editors at Cornerstones Literary Consultancy
Romsey Writers' Group, especially our tutor,
Brendan McCusker.

A special mention must also go to my ever-supportive wife, Lorraine. Without her belief in me, *Blazing Obsession* would still be on the drawing board.